NOTE TO MY ENGLISH READERS

There are expressions and dialogue presented within other than English.
For your convenience, translations are provided in a section at the end
of the work. Expressions are listed alphabetically within each language
while dialogue is given sequentially as it appears throughout the text.

PSALM 144

"Blessed be the Lord my strength which teacheth
my hands to war and my fingers to fight."

A Psalm of David

CLUB JED

2017 AD
Tel Aviv

Who wouldn't want to be G-d's favorite? And I'm not talking about the play. I mean, think about it. I was chosen above all others to inherit this earth: my blood, my kin, my kind. It's the perfect cover. A select group, an exclusive club if you will, like Club Med. Who would suspect?

I am neither the oldest of my kind nor the youngest. I was not present when first blood was given to my most ancient ancestors. I will be around however, for the End of Days. I will have the collective memories of my people tucked away inside my consciousness and would draw upon these to tell my story. Therefore, I cannot truly tell you when it began. You would have to ask Avram. If you see him, let me know.

I cannot recall when I first decided to set pen to paper. My colleagues advised strongly against the prospect of such a controversial, provocative work, let alone exposing us to the censure of so many different groups. Galen was most adamant in his reproach.

"Shira, you are writing about us? Is it a book about the Glory of G-d?"

"Why wouldn't it be?"

"Is it about Jews or vampires or time-travelling?"

"Yes."

1

"You cannot be serious. Your critics will think it extremely derivative. Indeed, look at the surfeit in the press regarding vampires/werewolves/apostate angels/paranormal/supernatural angst-ridden teens. Walk into any library and take a look at the shelves of YA Fiction. The genre is supersaturated. No one will pay the slightest attention to it amongst the glut."

"That is my intent, Galen. Humans will see this as just another in a long line of the 'flavor of the month' phenomenon. No one would ever imagine that this is a work of non-fiction. Besides, I am writing for grown-ups."

"Wait. Let me understand you. Your basic premise is to discover the nature and the will of G-d through the two protagonists who happen to be Jewish, time-travelling vampires?"

"Why not?"

"What about Hashem? Do you really think He will stand for this, let you get away with this?"

"Well, He does have a sense of humor."

Galen scoffs. "Take heed how you profane, Shira."

"C'mon, you know He has one. Just look at the platypus."

Completely deadpan and in staccato beats:

"Shira, you are going to burn-in-Hell."

"Ha-Ha."

THE ONE

"Shema Yisrael, Adonai Eloheynu, Adonai Echad." The Shema evokes in me an emotion stronger than any I have ever experienced. Even my vampiric nature pales in comparison to the visceral quality of that Call which pulls me back through time and space. Literally.

My gift, or rather Avram's gift to me if that's what you call it, is travelling. However, it is not the speed with which to move forward across a distance like others of my kind. That less than a blink of a human eye or beat of your heart and we are at your side and you are defenseless. Instead, it is the ability to move backward through time, any time in our history, all 5,000+ years of it.

When I hear the Shema it's like a Siren's call, but not the song that tempts me to my doom but rather sings me sweetly home. To my ears, the resonance of those voices lures me willingly, like honey to my tongue. At first, it is an almost euphoric sense of well-being, like being inside joy when those notes reverberate and course through my entire body. I become intimately connected by blood, by spirit, and by faith to all whom have ever voiced those words since the beginning of time. I am home. G-d whacks me on the forehead and says:

"I've been waiting for you! Oy! Finally! What took you so long, Shira?"

But the peaceful moment never lasts. I cannot keep my connection to the present for very long. Turning on the proverbial dime, I get a wrenching in the pit of my stomach. My hands clench the back of the chair in the row in front of me. There is this sense of disorientation, a loss of equilibrium. Faces blur; images recede. And then...whomp! I'm flat on my ass, *every single time*, plunked into I don't know where let alone when. Go ahead, ask your question. If you know it's going to happen, why are you there every Friday night? You my friend, obviously do not have a mother who would rather get some horribly devastating disease than be seen in synagogue without her daughter come sundown on Shabbat.

I have Avram to thank for my bruised tuchus not to mention my pride at landing in an undignified heap, usually in the middle of some busy intersection. Little did I comprehend that our first meeting all those years ago was merely a foretaste, a foreshadowing of events yet to come. I could never have imagined how two so utterly disparate people from vastly different eras could be cut from the same cloth. The entire fabric of my existence was soon to be turned inside out and irrevocably altered. My chronology, the course of events, and the sequence of history itself are now all inexplicably intertwined with that of the past generations of my forefathers.

TORAH, TORAH, TORAH

30 September, 2010 AD
Westport

My mother Miriam was in hover-mode, as usual. The monologue of her trying to fix me up with one of her innumerable acquaintances' relations (pick one): son, brother, uncle, third cousin's former roommate... "and such a nice boy, too" was an unending stream of clichés.

"Wear something pretty tonight, Shira." Rather cryptically she added, "You never know who will be at synagogue."

I roll my eyes and silently plead with my father Ezra to intercede on my behalf. He gives me that well-worn expression which conveys to me: let your mother fuss, it makes her happy, don't try to figure her out-who can? Give it up; I gave up long ago.

"Ma, please give me some credit. Of course, I'll dress up a little. It's Simchat Torah."

For the unacquainted, Simchat Torah, the Rejoicing in the Law, is dedicated to the greatest book of all, the Torah. This holiday follows Sukkot and celebrates the completion at the end of the Jewish year of the reading of the Five Books of Moses. We basically throw a party as we conclude with chanting the last line of Deuteronomy and then we read the first line of Genesis to start off the New Year. Then we start the Torah all over again and read it in its entirety throughout the course of the year. We sing songs and the scrolls are taken out of the Ark and carried around the synagogue in a procession called the Hakafot. Seven times it makes its way around the room. The Torah is then unwound completely, sometimes spanning the perimeter of the room more than once around showing the beautiful Hebrew text. Everyone is laughing and singing; the men are at the back throwing back shots. There will be a great feast in the Oneg room with all manner of sweets–I love those little jelly donuts! Essentially, it's like the best party you'll ever attend, with G-d as your host. Simchat Torah is when I feel most like a Jew, a kindred spirit among the congregation.

My parents have finished getting dressed and are now waiting for me in the kitchen. As I make my way down the stairs, I hear my mother kvetching. Again.

"Ezra. Honey. Look at your tie. Thirty years of marriage, you can't make it come out right? It looks like a bretzele."

"Yes, dear."

My dad is no dummy. He learned from his dad that the surest way to win the match is to not even enter the ring when it comes to women. I smile to myself as I enter the kitchen to find my mother still futzing with it. My dad shoots me a helpless grin and mouths the words "help me" over my mother's shoulder.

"Shira, give your old dad a hug. My, but you look lovely."

He tries unsuccessfully to extricate himself.

"Ezra, stop squirming! Mensch! I'm not finished with you yet."

"Mom, I'll do it."

I walk my dad over into the hallway. As I stand behind him, readjusting his tie in the mirror (the only way I'm able to do it) he pats my hand.

"Thanks, Shira-la. She's been clucking like an old hen all afternoon."

"I heard. I'm sure I'll have to go back upstairs and change at least twice before she deems me fit to be seen in public."

"She means well. But sometimes your mother is well, a little over the top."

"You'd think I'd be used to it by now, huh?"

"Well, she wouldn't be your mother if she didn't fuss a bissel, gell?"

"I know, I know."

We give each other the eye and without missing a beat, we say the oft-used phrase that has become our inside joke:

"It's better than a kick in the Hosen!"

That was my Zayde's favorite expression for always looking at the bright side of things. My dad and I always laugh when we remember how he could turn things around with his upbeat sense of humor. I make the final tug on his tie.

"There. I think you're presentable. Even she can't complain how it looks now."

We grin because we both know how ridiculous that sounds. Mom can complain about anything.

"Ezra! Stop noodling already, will you? We have to hurry; we don't want to be late."

Mom gives me the once-over as I re-enter the kitchen with Dad.

"Shira. Bubele. Are you sure you want to wear that?"

"Miriam, your daughter looks beautiful. Besides, if she takes the time to change her clothes, then we really will be behind schedule. We still have to pick up Ira and Jackie."

Bravo, Dad!

"Well, I suppose you'll have to do. But...well, can't you do something about your hair? It looks like a bird's nest."

Zap! I almost made it out the door without a jab.

"Ma, I'll fix it in the car. Na endlich, let's just go."

We finally actually make it to the garage. It's only a ten-minute drive to pick up my aunt and my uncle, but for me those minutes seem like hours as my mom keeps up a running laundry list the gist of which is completely lost on me.

Ira and Jackie are standing in their driveway; my aunt knows from experience never to keep her sister waiting. I smile at them both as I move back to the bench seat of our minivan to make room. Jackie pops her head in and smiles back at me.

"Have you gotten an earful, Shira-la?"

"You know it."

I love my aunt. She's always right on the money and has her elder sister completely pegged.

"What was it tonight? Shoes? Make-up?"

"Hair."

"Ah well, there's only so much you can do. Do you know how much some people pay for what you have naturally? Dinah charges over $200 for a spiral perm. Oy, such a price!"

"Sometimes I just wish I didn't always feel like I have my finger stuck in a light socket."

"You know, your Bubbe always told us that the Hand of Hashem is electrifying. It just means you've been blessed by His touch, Shira."

"Thanks, Aunt Jackie."

My aunt gives my mom a wink, they smile at each other, and then immediately launch into gossip about so-and-so's daughter. I totally tune them out as we drive off. Uncle Ira is up front with my dad and they are talking a blue streak as well about a topic that is infinitely more interesting and one the three of us are always discussing...the most recent game. Doesn't matter which one, which season. Basketball, football, baseball, hockey. Makes no difference. Once you get us going, there's no shutting us up. Come Sunday, ever since I can remember, the three of us were glued to the set watching any game we could find. That's when my mom and my aunt would tune us out. The yakking from all quarters is still going on as we turn down the quiet little street and make our way into the parking lot.

We arrive at synagogue way too soon. My mother is habitually early for everything; this gives her time to gossip with her cronies and to scope out potential son-in-laws. Her greatest shame so far, is that she has no grandchildren. I mean, it's not as if it's too late; I'm *only* twenty-nine. It's not like I'm dead or anything.

"Shira, make your mother happy already: go on and find yourself a nice doctor/lawyer/rabbi, settle down, start a family. Hashem forbid I go to my grave never having held my first grandchild!"

No pressure.

The room is filling up with people, children are laughing and running around, and there is the ever-present clacking of tongues (mostly my mother's). You know that old cliché about what you get when you put two Jews in a room? Three opinions. Imagine what a full synagogue will give you. Utter chaos. But that's what I love the most about my synagogue: the mêlée of my extended family coming together to worship, the music, the singing, the laughter and high spirits, the lit candles illuminating the way. The knowledge that we are connected to every Jew on the planet at that very moment, the sound of a hearty chorus of "Shabbat Shaloms" singing to me sweetly from all of my friends, and this holiday of unity are what will bring me back tomorrow and every week for Shabbat. Tonight, the mood is even more festive and as I mill about the room while waiting for services to start, I see Uncle Ira chatting up a storm with Rabbi. I don't need to guess the subject matter; Rabbi is a total hockey fan. I almost make it to the Bimah when I hear my name. My mother comes rushing towards me, all in a dither.

"Shira, you have to meet him."

Great. Another one. I grudgingly try to keep up as she pulls, no... yanks me across the room. I, none too graciously I might add, arrive face-to-face with *the* most luminous ice-blue eyes I have ever beheld. And that smile, welcoming but just a bit wry so that it crinkles around his eyes. He's beautiful and I am completely mortified at being dumped so unceremoniously at his feet. His presence is absolutely commanding: tall and muscular but just a little disconcerting. The kind of man you are not quite sure of; a little mystery surrounds him. I've never been uneasy around men but this one definitely makes my hackles go up. Even my mother (who eats most guys for breakfast) took a small step back as she gushed through the introductions, telling me his name is Avram and that he is visiting from Israel.

"Good evening, Shira. I have been waiting to meet you for so long."

Perfect icebreaker. And that voice. Rich and resonant, absolutely inviting. He grips my hand in both of his; it's a firm grasp to be sure, but there is something almost electric in his touch. He holds my hand just a moment beyond convention so that I am forced to look up. His eyes are smiling at me in a most provocative way and yet it's as if he is searching for something, a sign in my response. I actually blush (I haven't done that since my Bat Mitzvah) pull my hand away and mumble something completely incoherent about finding a seat.

My mother has her favorite spot in synagogue. She is not at all interested in sitting up in front as you might think, but rather more towards the back where she can command a better view of the goings-on during services. As we find our seats, she is naturally keeping an eagle-eye on Avram. It has not escaped her notice that he is sitting alone.

"Shira, go sit next to him. See...there is an empty chair on his right."

"Mom, we just met. Give the guy a little breathing room, at least."

She gives me that 'make your mother happy' look so I change gears.

"Besides Mom, I want to sit here with you and Dad tonight."

I must be brilliant this evening because this tactic actually works, although out of the corner of my eye I can see my dad smirking at me.

"Alright, Shira-la. Just promise me you will be polite and speak with him later."

"Sure, Mom. Anything you say."

Services are about to start and I catch my cousins and their children wending their way through the crowd. Jackie and Ira's son and daughter and their respective spouses are never on time but they each have several legitimate reasons, all of them under five years of age. We wave them over and as we get the last of the toddlers situated, I am hard-pressed not to try and at least sneak a peek every once in a while over Avram's way. Every time I do, I end up quickly with my nose in my Siddur because he seems to always be gazing in my direction.

The singing begins and the Torah is carried around the perimeter of the room. Rabbi comes up with some interesting calls this year for the Hakafot, inviting us to follow the Torah.

"Ok, Mac users come on up."

PC users boo.

"Now PC users, it's your turn."

Mac users hiss.

"This next one is for all you Dodgers fans."

Everybody cheers.

As the Torah passes by and is followed by those adherents to each invitation, we touch the cloth covering the scroll and bring our fingers to our lips. Rabbi's next call is rather unorthodox.

"Well, this one is at the insistence of my nieces. Those for Team Edward, come on up!"

I almost do a double take as Avram stands and hoists the Torah up with no effort that I can see and begins his circle around the room. I discover as I watch him, that mine are not the only eyes keeping tabs on his whereabouts. Every woman under sixty has her eyes glued to his location as he makes his procession. Some of these are grandmothers and even titter and blush like schoolgirls as he passes by and pauses in the aisle next to them. As he finishes his circuit, he stops to stand directly in front of me and I reach out to touch the cloth. When I bring my fingers to my lips, I realize he is staring at me intently with that gentle smile that lights up his whole face and I feel my cheeks go all rosy again.

"Ok. To be fair, those for Team Jacob, it's your turn."

I must say, Rabbi is certainly making a huge hit with the tweens tonight. A giggling gaggle of them practically leaps from their seats and surges towards us.

Avram is still standing in front of me and before I can protest, he nudges my shoulder and I find the Torah in my arms; I've no choice but to participate. It is heavy but no burden to bear. The act of carrying the word of G-d around the room always inspires me when I pause to let members of my synagogue reach out and touch the cloth. As I make my way around the room, I get this weird sensation on the back of my neck, as if someone is staring at me. Every time I turn around to look however, I find Avram engaged in conversation with a member of the congregation. I finish my turn and walk back to the Bimah, handing the scroll to the Rabbi.

As we ready ourselves for the unrolling of the Torah, I notice Avram speaking very graciously to an elderly lady at his side. She seems rather spry for her age and is quite animated as they carry on a lively conversation. I can see that she was very beautiful, still is in fact. On her face is the beauty that comes with age and experience: every line a story of her life. I've never seen her here at synagogue before. Maybe she is a new member or just visiting her relatives. She certainly must be an old friend of Avram's the way they are chatting. Every so often, he looks up and sends a warm, inviting smile my way which just makes me blush all over again.

At this point, all of the adults take their places throughout the synagogue in preparation for the unrolling of the scroll. One must be careful not to touch the front so as not to harm the script. That's why the adults hold it up above the children's sticky fingers but just at the top and bottom edge. As the Torah is being unwound, Avram makes his way through the cluster of children to come and stand next to me. This naturally does not go unnoticed by my mother. Out of the corner of my eye, I see her gently elbow my dad in the ribs to get his attention. He's still gabbing with Ira but he gives me a sweet, paternal smile.

As we sing, I try to sneak a glance at him. His profile is strong and his hair is so black that it almost has a blue sheen to it. I deduce that his profession must keep him indoors most of the time as he is very pale, not at all kissed by an Israeli sun. His lips are full and his voice a deep baritone, mesmerizing me with its richness as he sings along with the congregation. Our fingertips are very close on the scroll but he is totally absorbed in the music and staring straight ahead.

Then Rabbi, who knows the Torah inside out, upside down, backwards and forwards (who wouldn't after forty years of study?) shows us where our history lies upon the scroll.

"And there," Rabbi says, "where Ira and Jackie are standing, that is Exodus, when Moses led our people out of Egypt. Now, let me see, ah yes. Avram and Shira are standing directly behind the Ten Commandments."

"Of course," whispers Avram under his breath as he turns to look at me.

"Why of course?"

But his reply is drowned out by the din of laughter, the chatter of children, and the cantor's beautiful singing voice. The Torah is now being wound up, signaling that our celebration will soon be at an end. As it slowly comes our way and we prepare to let it go, Avram asks if he may see me again, perhaps tomorrow afternoon back here at synagogue before Shabbat?

Drat! I was just getting ready to bolt to the Oneg room. I give him an embarrassed smile but can only manage to stammer out some unintelligible nonsense. I had my refusal already rehearsed, about to make some valid excuse, but he stares at me with those great, liquid eyes. His voice, like velvet, is persuading me against my will and I find myself agreeing without even realizing I'm mutely nodding my head. Wait, did I just say yes? Agree to meet a man alone that I just met? He kisses the palm of my hand in farewell and blends into the crowd. I just stand there like an idiot, completely speechless for once. My mother is all over me in a New York second, pumping me for information.

We stand around schmoozing after services, eating of course (there is always food where Jews are involved). Then from across the room, I see the elderly woman Avram had been speaking to make her way over to me, accompanied by someone whom I rightly surmise to be a family member. Her walk is slow and aided by the gentleman but very direct and with purpose. She is staring intently at me as she speaks.

"You are Shira, I am thinking?"

Her voice is full of the old country, melodious in its thick accent.

"Yes, but how do you know my name?"

"It's me, Gertie. Don't you remember me?"

"Oh, do forgive me. Have we met before?"

"It was in Denmark. You helped me and my family."

"I'm sorry, but I think you have me confused with someone else."

I look to the gentleman for guidance and he nods to me as he turns to her.

"It's alright, Auntie Gert. You haven't met her before. Please excuse my aunt. She gets a little muddled sometimes."

"No worries, sometimes I feel the same way."

The nephew steers his aunt towards the table and I distinctly hear her remark as she turns again to look at me.

"But she looks just like the Shira I knew in Denmark."

The nephew replies that yes, yes but that was so long ago, it's not possible that it's the same person, Auntie.

We are making our goodbyes as we prepare to leave, thanking Rabbi for the wonderful services and generally trying to get out the door but being waylaid by last minute gossip. We finally make it to the car and I brace myself for what is to come: the interrogation. No surprises there. The grilling I receive during the drive back exhausts me. I must admit my mother was in fine form all during the car ride; I think she barely drew breath the entire time: what did he say, where are you meeting, what does he do for a living, what are you wearing tomorrow, yadda, yadda, yadda. We arrive home. How old do you think he is? I put my key into the lock. So...what are you wearing tomorrow? My dad is dead quiet the entire time; he knows better than to interrupt when my mother is going full-throttle. The barrage of questioning doesn't stop until I shut my bedroom door and collapse onto the bed. Just as I'm starting to drop off to sleep I think, crap! What *am* I going to wear tomorrow?

1 October, 2010 AD
Westport

I was looking forward to sleeping in a little the next morning but no such luck. At what seems like the crack of dawn, I am roused by my name.

"Shira-la. We've no time to waste."

I knew it.

Without fail, my mother has my wardrobe already completely planned out, right down to the last piece of ornamentation, not to mention the schedule for the entire day including a trip to the beauty parlor. In the past, this used to drive me absolutely insane, this broken record of hers. It was always the same refrain, repeated ad nauseum.

"Shira, this is my job and I take it very seriously. I take pride in my work. Someday, when *you* have children...."

Here we go.

"Mo-*ther*! I am perfectly capable of dressing myself."

Her snappy retort back then as I came down the stairs was totally predictable:

"You're wearing *that*?"

Now I am so totally used to this routine, I just smile and graciously accept her ministrations. She really does mean well, you know. However, I still am slightly miffed about the wake-up call.

"Ma, it's way too early. Can't we ever really take a Friday off and do nothing?"

She shoots me a look like I just told her that I'm marrying into a family of Goyim.

"Shira!"

"Okay, okay. I'm up."

We spend the day in a whirlwind of activity. My quick breakfast at home is even more quickly followed by a rapid succession of three or four shops to find just the perfect new pair of shoes to match what my mother has chosen for me to wear. Then it's a leisurely lunch at her favorite tearooms. Now *this* part I like because I'm able to take a breather. I get a break since the reason my mom loves these tearooms so much is the fact that she can table-hop and spend most of her time gossiping. After the world's second-best chicken salad sandwiches (Mom's are better) my mother rises.

"Oh, look. There's Irene just arriving. I've got to talk to her about what Mrs. Goldstein was wearing at synagogue last night."

"Sure, Mom."

This gives me a respite to sit back, enjoy my Irish tea and leisurely sample today's selection of petit fours. Oh, the petit fours here are absolutely to die for! As I watch my mother make her rounds about the room, I just have to smile to myself. There she is at Irene's table, talking about Mrs. Goldstein's fashion disaster. Table-hop. Another petit four for me. Now she's at Mrs. Rosenblum's table, probably discussing her eldest son, Joshua and why he still can't seem to find a real job. Table-hop. Oh, just one more chocolate one. As I savor every succulent bite, I get a vision of myself in about twenty or so years. There's no way I say to myself, no way am I ever going to turn into my mother and table-hop at a tearoom.

Next table, she bumps into Rabbi's wife, Rebekah. My last petit four (not) is halfway to my mouth when I catch both my mother and Rebekah looking straight at me from across the crowded room. Yegads. I can totally imagine the dialogue:

"So, you know my Shira is seeing that gentleman we met last night? Avram, you know, from Israel."

"Kine-ahora and G-d bless him I say. And such a handsome man, too. So polite and well-dressed. Where do you suppose he got that suit? What a Mensch his tailor must be."

That's my cue to stand up and try to wrangle my mother from the volley of questions Rebekah is rapid-firing her way. I shove the (sigh) last petit four into my mouth, pay our tab and commandeer my mom out the door as best I can.

Na endlich, we make it to the hairdresser. Another ripe opportunity for the ultimate Kaffee Klatsch, sans the coffee. My mother is in fine form as we enter the family beauty parlor.

"Dinah darling, you look fabulous...what *have* you done to your eyebrows?"

"Good afternoon, Miriam. Nice to see you again, Shira. What are we doing for you today?"

My mother launches into a detailed description of my upcoming encounter with the gentleman as if it were the date to end all dates. And you know what that means. No more dating because of course, after he sees how beautiful Dinah has made me, he's going to propose. Our worries are over!

"So Dinah, we are looking for something extra special today. This gentleman is worth impressing. His was a new face at synagogue last night but you know, come to think of it, he did look familiar."

"Ma, will you let up a little already! I just met this guy. Besides, you think everybody looks familiar."

Dinah twirls me in the chair to face the mirror.

"So, Shira-la. Who's this guy?"

"Nobody. Someone I met last night. We're just getting together before Shabbat, that's all."

"So, Bubele. What's his name?"

"Avram."

"Where's he from?"

"Israel."

"Where in Israel?"

"I don't know yet. I'll find out and get back to you."

"So, let's get you under the water here and find whatsit your mother's wanting for you this time."

"Super-do!"

My sarcastic tone is completely wasted on Dinah.

Several hours later and we barely make it home in time for me to change clothes. After an interminable amount of fussing over my hair (of course, it had to be humid today) she pronounces me fit for display. Thanks, Mom.

"Now honey, make sure that you text me as soon as you get there so I know you have arrived safely. Oh, and text me if you both decide to go someplace else. Don't forget to text me when you are on your way home as well."

Can you tell my mother is a texting fiend? My very traditional, very old-world, totally Jewish mother glommed onto cell phones and it was all over with my privacy. She does however, know full well that I am an absolute rube when it comes to technology. I don't know Palm Pilot from auto-pilot from Honda Pilot. It's not that I don't *want* to embrace the 21st century; it's just that I don't have the time to spare. But Mom loves her new toy and she conveniently forgets. Like clockwork.

"How about uh, I just call you? We'll see you at services anyway, Mom. I'm sure he will stay for Shabbat."

"Oh, I suppose that will have to do. Don't worry about me though, sitting here at home, waiting to hear from you. Hashem forbid you have a flat tire on the way there. How will I know?"

"Ma, I promise I'll call you."

The sun is just beginning its downward descent as I pull into the synagogue parking lot, not precisely on time. Unlike my mother, über-punctuality is not one of my strong suits. Avram is already there, leaning against a totally hot car. I know absolutely nothing about automobiles but even I can tell it's fast. Like some GQ model, he is impeccably dressed in a tailored dark grey suit-the cut of which tells me cost was no consideration. He leisurely leans forward off the car, walking with a lithe movement that reminds me of a cat. I park and try to gracefully make my way across the lot. It rained during the night and the ground is slick with water, engine oil, and gravel. Bad day to wear my new shoes I sadly discover. I try to catch myself but I am suddenly on the pavement, breaking my fall with the flat of my right hand. Before I realize it, he is at my side helping me up. I'm so caught up in my embarrassment that it takes me a few seconds to tell that my hand is bleeding. Avram guides me to his car.

"I have a first-aid kit, come sit down."

He opens the car door and gently lowers me into the driver's seat. My legs are outside the car as he leans down by the open door. Gracefully sitting on his haunches (no small feat in my opinion) he begins to minister to me, brushing the dirt from my hand. I turn away.

"What is the matter, Shira? Are you unwell?"

"Avram, I can't look. Would you just put something on it, please? I can't stand seeing blood."

My embarrassment rises to new heights as he chuckles at this confession. I need to distract myself from what he is doing, so I pretend to inspect the interior of his car and recognize that it has that 'just off the lot, I paid with an obscene amount of cash' smell. Immaculate, no trace of the owner's personality inside.

"This is going to sting."

I hear him rip open a packet, probably an antiseptic wipe. As I brace myself (when did I become such a wuss?) I become aware that I am starting to breathe hard. I am completely distracted from what he is doing to my injured palm with his *left* hand by the movement of his *right* hand at the hem of my skirt. I cannot believe this is happening. Slowly, but with intent, he is sliding the edge of my skirt upwards with only his fingertips, starting at just above the knee.

"Avram, what...?"

That's all I am able to say when I suddenly feel him tighten his grip on my palm; it's really stinging now. His right hand reaches higher, I don't understand what is going on and oh...he's not even touching me and I'm already there. I feel like I am being swallowed alive. My head is spinning; I feel myself falling, wanting to speak but the words will not come. They stick in my throat. My perception of the space around me is tilted, off-kilter like some B movie that abuses the Dutch angle. There's this humming, droning sound in my ears, a great buzzing like bees swarming and not just my hand is on fire. I'm lost in this moment as if time itself has stopped. I want to stay locked in this feeling but then the key suddenly turns, the door opens and I see dusky sunlight. But it is not without difficulty that I find my way back. The sun is very low in the sky by now and I have no idea how much time has passed between when I sat down in the car and when I look up. He is no longer near me but standing a few feet away. I'm still too fuzzy to read his expression correctly but his gaze is directed entirely at my face. I manage to squeak out:

"What just happened?"

I can't find my voice at first and I really need some water. Avram asks me the last time I had anything to eat.

"You must have become lightheaded from the sight of the blood. It seemed like you went away for a moment."

What a great second impression I am making.

"How do you feel now?"

"I'm not sure. Okay, I guess."

I take a look in the rearview mirror and am chagrined to see my lipstick smudged and my cheeks red, stained with tears as if I had been crying. I fumble in my purse for a tissue, dry my cheeks and reapply my lipstick.

"Avram, what time is it? Shouldn't we go in now?"

I stand up and get an instant head rush as I struggle to gain my footing. Why do I feel so wobbly? I notice that I no longer feel any pain in my hand. But it feels warm, almost hot like it's beginning to burn. I see that Avram has wrapped some gauze on it so I can't really tell how badly I scraped it. I want to take a peek but before I can lift the bandage, he calls my name and I look up. In a swift movement, almost before I even perceive he has moved, he is standing very close, uncomfortably close now. I take a step back and come in contact with the car.

"I needed to see you again, one more time before I return. Would that I could stay longer, but it is not permitted."

That plaintive quality to his voice is most endearing and elicits in me some guilt for not arriving on time.

"I'm sorry I was late, if I kept you waiting."

"I have had many years to learn to be patient, Shira. But soon, very soon my patience will be rewarded."

The parking lot is starting to fill up with cars as people arrive for Friday evening services. As soon as my head clears a little, Avram and I make our way into the synagogue. He is walking very close to me, rather protectively with his arm around my shoulder. This predictably does not go unnoticed by every single member of the congregation, including my mother. She is furiously waving her hand at me from across the room, motioning for the two of us to come sit next to her and my dad. As we make our way through the row of chairs, the music starts.

"Good Shabbos to you, sir."

Avram shakes my father's hand, says good evening and remarks how lovely my mother is looking tonight. As we take our seats, I notice the expression on her face which is very well-known to me. She is beaming; her smile is proud, almost gloating and wholly directed at all of the other women sitting around us as if to say:

"See, I told you my daughter could attract such a man."

FUNNY, YOU DON'T LOOK JEWISH

2017 AD
Tel Aviv

So...you are probably wondering at this point what I look like. I am neither your typical young Jewish woman nor do I appear to be a typical vampire. I am tall for my tribe. I do unfortunately, have a slight bit of a Jew-fro going on which is a constant source of consternation. Hashem curse humidity. Dark, wavy hair that tends to red and glints in the sun if ever I'm in it. Hashem bless aviators and sun block or I would fry. I avoided the sun anyway when I was human so my current pallor goes unnoticed. Sea-glass green eyes that change color depending upon my mood: ice-blue when I'm feeling peevish to midnight when I'm on the hunt. I had a severe weakness for rugelach when I was human so I'm not exactly a twig, but who wants to make love to an elbow? On the other hand, neither am I overly zaftig. Curvy in just the right places best describes me.

My colleagues and I are all living here in Tel Aviv. Why Tel Aviv, you ask? Why not? You really feel like you are home, like some sense memory. The noise, the sights, the smells, the very taste of the place all bring you back, even if you are newly made and have never set foot in Israel. But I *have* been here before so I do remember. Avram and I were both working in 1948, experiencing the crackle in the air of human emotion, the energy in the streets, the possibilities not yet envisioned, and rejoicing our success in our own very private way.

It just seemed like a good place to be with my colleagues since we are all working in 2017. It's a base of operations you might say, for the four of us. There is safety in numbers so Vietor, Zipporah, Galen, and I are roomies. Our work takes us all to other 'whens' and we have had brief encounters with each other along the timeline, carrying out our work in the past. The living arrangement however, just sort of happened haphazardly with no definitive advance plan.

Vietor hates the heat, though. I told him, blame your vodka-swilling, fish-eating ancestors for that one big guy, for making you believe anything above 65 degrees Fahrenheit is too hot. I mean, he can't really *feel* the heat; he just likes to whine about how miserable he used to be in high temperatures.

Zipporah (Zippy for short) was born, bred, died, and entered into immortality in the desert so she is completely in her element. She seldom complains about anything except that she doesn't have a *thing* to wear tonight, even though she is a total clotheshorse.

Galen misses Roman soil and grumbles right down his fine, patrician nose that he can't grow a blasted thing in this "damn, heathen, rocky landscape." See, he has this amazing herb garden out back which he tends like it's some lost child. He is very particular about it and none of us are allowed to go anywhere near it. Ever.

Me, I'm not so fussy. I've learned to adapt to almost any environment, having time-jumped into any number of different seasons in various years. Be flexible, that's my motto.

We are renting a fantastic villa in Tel Aviv. Two-story, three bedroom, very Mediterranean looking with a gorgeous veranda, beautifully landscaped grounds, and a terraced garden that Galen squealed over when we first took a walk-through. Even though a weekly gardening service is included in the rental price, he promptly quashed the idea and volunteered, saying he would be delighted to manage the estate. The property owners had me even at the access road with a bougainvillea-lined driveway and private entrances for each of the bedrooms. It's sequestered in this quiet little suburb, well out of the way of foot traffic yet close enough to the shops for convenience. We do have neighbors but the entire property is well-secluded by trees of many varieties: palm, mulberry, orange, lemon, pecan, juniper. In addition, we are surrounded by a very ancient olive grove with well-manicured ligustrum and pittosporum hedges, keeping us safe from prying eyes. We do value our privacy, after all.

The interior of the house is an architect's dream with tall ceilings, recessed lighting, and a spiral staircase leading up to the second floor. Zippy fell in love with the enormous, well-appointed kitchen at first glance and I loved the open, airy feeling of the whole place anyway. And then there are the bathrooms. Ah, the bathrooms are a religious experience. Victor interjected sporadically with questions regarding the alarm system but had been keeping mostly silent throughout the entire tour of the house. As we made our way out-of-doors to the backyard however, I saw a huge grin that slowly spread and took over his entire face when he saw the building at the back edge of the property line. I could tell that he was in seventh heaven just thinking about all of the cars he could build from scratch in the double garage he discovered there. We couldn't move in fast enough and have christened the place Villa Derekh Eretz.

So here we all are living together, an immortal quartet you might call us and you humans are bursting at the seams, dying to know. So...you are waiting for an engraved invitation? Go ahead, ask. Yeah, we can do it. And it far surpasses anything you can even remotely imagine or will ever experience.

Forget that hoary Isis/Osiris legend about her finding all but one body part when her old man was dismembered. Believe you me, male vampires are *fully* intact and not in the least standoffish. Think about it.

They have had hundreds of years to perfect their technique, combined with vampiric heightened awareness and sensitivity. Ergo, they bring you in quick succession to the moon and back without even trying. Suffice it to say, they really know what they are doing. So much so, that you don't really have to exert yourself very much. Here's the low-down:

Vietor-a 20th century man, my kind of guy. No nonsense. Get the job done. Don't spend too much time thinking about it; just do it. He takes his lovemaking cue from the Teddy Roosevelt rough-and-ready school but it's oh, so good when you want it so right *now*. Not when you want candy and flowers and an hour of foreplay first. That's Galen's area of expertise.

Galen-a romantic at heart but he basically lives in the ether, on a sort of rarified air. He's our little philosopher and always wants to understand why. But don't get him started on the merits/demerits of those Greeks. He's so serious. I asked him once:

"Galen, didn't you *ever* play with toys as a child? Personally, I remember never travelling anywhere without my play-dough."

"I would rather travel with Aristotle."

But Galen's your man if you are interested in being wined, dined, seduced, and made sweet, romantic love to. Just don't have anything on your agenda for the next six hours.

Zippy prefers sex with humans. Yuck! Don't ask me why. Well, actually I do have my suspicions that she gets some sort of sadistic glee from mind-fucking them as well. See, Zippy has this amazing voice. Rich and resonant. Beguiling and irresistible. No one can place her accent: it's a veritable mishmash of French/Moroccan/Algerian/Lebanese-ish. To say she is a complete enigma is an absolute understatement. But her victims are lured by this voice of hers and she absolutely loves to mess with their heads when they invariably ask her if she's from the Middle East.

"Mais oui," she drawls, "you could say that I come from the desert. Actually, I was born there. Twice."

Creepy, right? And yet strangely alluring as well. Zippy doesn't leave her victims too much time to puzzle that one out. We all know *when* she comes from but it's prudent to remain silent about her origins. Let's just say the genesis of her making makes for wild speculation in which it's better not to indulge.

Our vampiric escapades are a far cry from my love life as a human. In a nutshell, I had no love life as a human. I mean, I dated. Of *course* I dated. My mother was constantly fixing me up with future husbands, taking their measure based on their merits but mostly scoping them out to see what her future grandchildren would look like. For her it was a full-time job, even though my parents and I owned and operated our own café in Westport.

LAZARUS C✡FFEE

(WAKES EVEN THE DEAD)

1 MARCH, 2010 AD
WESTPORT

THE PENTADRIP

(FIRST FIVE COFFEES)

GENESIS JAVA–our special house drip
EXODUS ESPRESSO–resurrection in a cup
LEVITICUS LATTÉ–tall espresso w/steamed milk
NUMBERS NATURAL–our organic brew
DEUTERONOMY DRIP OF THE DAY–special daily blend

REVELATIONS IN A CUP

MOCHACCINO ON THE MOUNT–mocha espresso w/steamed milk
BURNING BUSH BREW–double espresso w/twist of lemon
CANTOR CAPPUCCINO–short espresso w/steamed milk
TETRARCH TEA–very black and very strong
SEPTUAGINT SIP–hot apple cider

KING OF THE JUICE

SERPENT SIP–cold-pressed apple cider
ORANGE OFFERING–freshly squeezed
GRATITUDE GRAPEFRUIT–ruby red
CONSECRATION CONCORD–grape

OLD RESTAURANT   NEW RESTAURANT

THE 10 SPECIALS
(SERVED W/A HOUSE SALAD OR SOUP OF THE DAY)

I LOX & BAGEL W/CREAM CHEESE

II BIBLE BORSCHT

III ADAM'S RIBS (BEEF)

IV CHICKEN AND DUMPLING SOUP

V LATKES W/SOUR CREAM, APPLESAUCE

VI BLT SANDWICH

VII PORK CHOPS/APPLESAUCE

VIII ADAM'S RIBS (PORK)

IX DON'T BE SHELLFISH DELIGHT

X MOLE CHICKEN

KiNG SOLOMON'S STEWS

BiBLE BORSCHT
CHiCKEN & DUMPLiNG SOUP
(just like Tante Miriam used to make)
MATZAH BALL SOUP
(you have to ask?)

VEGETARIAN PLAGUES

BLOOD ORANGE–fruit salad
TOAD iN THE HOLE–veggie sausage, garlic mashed potatoes
FRiED RiCE–w/mixed veggies
MAD COW–veggie burger
BOiLED BABY RED POTATOES–w/rosemary & vegetable sauté au gratin
HAiL, MARY FULL OF GRiTS–grilled polenta w/marinara & vegetable sauté
LOCUST–bean salad
MEAT iS MURDER–veggie meatloaf

GARDEN OF EARTHLY DELIGHTS

SERPENT'S DELIGHT
Waldorf-style apple salad on a Bedouin of crisp, mixed baby greens
PHARAOH'S DELIGHT
seasoned grains & legumes: amaranth, spelt, teff, lentils.
Onion/mushroom/garlic sauté
& freshly-sliced Temple Tomatoes
ANTIOCHUSLY GREEK SALAD
mixed baby greens, kalamata olives,
feta, red onions, cucumber, red pepper, parsley,
red wine vinaigrette
GARDEN OF EDEN
house salad

THE PEWS

(SIDE DISHES)

GEFILTE FISH
PILATE'S PICKLES
JERUSALEM ARTICHOKES
SAUERKRAUT
MACCABEE MACARONI & CHEESE
STUFFED CABBAGE
PHARISEE'S FRIED ONIONS
TORAH-TELLINI

DESERTS

(YES, WE KNOW...BUT MOSES DIDN'T WANDER IN A PIE FOR 40 YEARS)

PYRAMID SLUB–succulent strata of mixed fruit cobbler
with strawberries, raspberries, rhubarb
CALLING CAKE–sour cream & buttermilk
(when you really get the urge)
CONFESSION CAKE–decadent double dark chocolate
(very sinful-we won't tell)
EVE'S APPLE THINGY–fruit cobbler
(give in to temptation)
PASSION OF THE PUDDING
(need we say more?)
JERUSALEM GELATIN
Reed Sea strawberry, green with envy lime,
oranges & lemons say the bells of St. Clemens
DIGS AND FATES
fruit and cheese platter w/figs and dates
(come home to destiny)

Yes, that truly is our main menu. We were hard hit by the economy and our little Mom and Pop café was in sore need of an upgrade to attract a wider clientele. Sure, we had customers who had been loyally patronizing us for years, even decades. Our regulars came in for their daily nosh of a bagel and schmear and a cup o' java. Naturally, the homey atmosphere also made it a fine place to come in, meet your friends and kvetch about your ungrateful children. It just seemed to me that in order to hopefully induce a younger crowd to try us out, we needed something to draw their attention. Something provocative, eye-catching, and more daring than just Miriam's Café. So, I put my business skills to good use and came up with a new marketing plan. This included a total make-over starting with changing our name and revamping the menu. Et voila'... Lazarus Coffee.

My parents were at first a little reticent with my concept, particularly the new name. But hey, you lose a lot of laughs if you don't laugh at yourself. Oh, no they said, that will just make them angry. Hey, guess who our best customers are? It's our fellow Jews who are embarrassed. It's too Jewish they say; why do you have to be so Jewish? What up with that? I think being a Jew is the greatest thing since sliced matzah.

It's the secularists that usually are just speechless, stare uncomprehendingly at the menu board and completely do not get any of the historical references. No worries I say, I'm bilingual. I speak secular. Standing behind the counter, I patiently explain the menu items and try to show them the in-jokes.

"Oh, you mean like a Higher Power?"

"No, that's PG&E."

I'm sure Hashem *really* gets a kick out of being compared to a utilities company.

At this point, they generally just order a salad and stop asking questions. In fact, today I was trying to explain the significance of Purim to a Gentile (okay, a shiksa...I was trying to be polite) when she questioned me about the Hamantaschen in the pastry case. She accompanied her blank stare with:

"Uh, I'm not really up on my bible lore."

Lore? I'm sorry, that's Data's brother; this really happened.

My parents have had this restaurant since I was little and I basically have grown up in it. As far back as I can remember, I was doing something to help out. My preteen years were spent behind the counter taking orders, handling the cash register, and helping out with food prep. As I got older, I moved on to ordering supplies, stocking inventory, and dealing with vendors (one made the initial mistake of trying to overcharge me for artichokes–now he knows better). Once I graduated high school and began working towards a business degree, my time was spent less out front with the customers and more behind-the-scenes in the back office.

Back in college, my days were filled not only with papers, exams, and occasional frat parties but with the day-to-day grind of unofficially running a family business. I was in charge of everything from the books and payroll to hiring and firing employees. At that time, my friends razzed me more than once about the fact that I lived (and still do) at home with my parents. Jess and TJ, my two closest buddies who were dormmates at the time, kept trying to persuade me to be their third girl and go in on an apartment together.

"Shira, you are almost twenty-one. It's time to leave the nest, fly the coop, cut the apron strings."

"You forgot 'get outta Dodge,' Jess."

"Whatever."

TJ chimed in with, "Just think of all the guys we can have over if we get a place of our own!"

"Is that all you ever think of?" I asked.

"Why wouldn't I?"

Although my friends meant well, they had no sense of anything beyond next Friday's party. I explained to them that I have to think beyond this week, midterm exams, or next semester. It just seemed ridiculous and not very cost-effective to rent my own place. My parents are paying for my college education and I know eventually our roles will be reversed. In the future when they are ready to retire, I will be their sole means of support and the least I can do is make sure they will be comfortable. I mean, I take the 5th very seriously. And look at that, here I am still chugging away at the family café, essentially running the entire business aspect of it and still living with my parents. Not that I have anything about which to complain. I mean, of course I still complain. Whining is genetically pre-programmed at conception; I can't help it.

FOREVER 29

(and totally diggin' it)

2017 AD
Tel Aviv

Twenty-nine was intensely traumatic for me as a human. I don't know why but I just thought that well, I might as well be dead. Stupid, huh? Little did I imagine back then that that was an up-and-coming event. I will never turn thirty: forever twenty-nine, never past my prime, never lose my bloom. How could I have known that this transformation was to come? I wasn't even thinking about the future, any of the many possible futures that G-d had planned for me. I went along with the day-to-day just like every other human being on the planet thinking, oh well...no worries, there's always tomorrow. I have plenty of time, there's no rush, a 'what-me-worry?' kind of attitude. The truth is that I was just too busy to really take the time to ponder anything above the next invoice that was going into collections or why, oh why is my artichoke delivery late again? I have since learned that you can't make time, you can only spend it. Time. Oy, there's the rub. It is not immutable; it can be broken up into smaller pieces, cropped into incremental snapshots and changed. The mutability of time is the standard by which I will ultimately be judged. But we immortals constantly chafe at the dichotomy between what we can achieve and what is beyond our control: what is not within our power but in the Hands of Hashem. The world has become not as I knew it in my past, but rather altered in such a way that I can never return to it as it was.

Back then however, I had no indication that my world would do a topsy-turvy somersault in the blink of an eye because of Avram. I really was rather obtuse not to see it coming. I mean, this had been planned all along, since the very beginning. It was only later, much later that I began to put all of the puzzle pieces together and realized that I should have known or at least remembered him from all those years ago.

YOM HULEDET SAME'ACH

11 May, 1986 AD
Westport

It's my 5th birthday party and I'm pretty sure I'm not getting the pony. Relatives are swarming around me at the park where my parents have set up a picnic table with a pink tablecloth, pink plates, pink plastic cutlery, and the largest pink-frosted cake they could buy. Okay, so I was really into pink when I was five. That's not abnormal. It's probably also not abnormal to want a pony when you are five. Even though the sun is shining, the table is piled absurdly high with gifts of all shapes and sizes, and all of my friends from Hebrew school are here, all I can do is sniffle through my birthday song. Through my tears, I was hoping I just might catch my dad sneaking off behind some truck and coming out leading something by a halter on four legs. No luck. I'm just about ready to give in to full-blown sobs when I hear a soft voice at my ear.

"Hush, little Shira. Someday you and I will ride horses together. Will that make you happy?"

My eyes full of unstemmed tears, I see very blue eyes smiling down at me.

"I have something special for you. I have brought it all the way from Israel."

From behind his back he hands me a small box wrapped in sparkly pink tissue paper. I'm still holding back, ready to cry at any moment but

43

something about his voice and his smile makes me calm down. I thank him for his gift and run to hide behind my mother's skirt. I don't know who he is; I have never seen him at my parents' house or at Tot Shabbat before but he seems nice and is talking to my Aunt Jackie and Uncle Ira so I guess he must be a friend. My mother looks down at me and smiles.

"Go ahead, Shira. You may open your gift."

Like any five-year-old, I have no reservations about tearing the paper to shreds to get at my present. The gold star catches the sunlight as I pull it out by the chain. There are lots of "oohs" and "aahs" from my relatives who seem to be impressed at such an expensive, fine gift for a child. The man walks over to me and bends down.

"May I help you with your necklace?"

I nod my head as he unclasps the chain and fastens it around my neck. As he lets the star drop, I feel the weight of it on my chest. It's pretty heavy. I guess that means it cost a lot of money.

"Promise me you will always wear it, Shira. Do not forget me, little one."

I smile as I hold the chain out to look at my star.

My Star of David is what keeps me connected, not just to my people but to the one who gave it to me all those years ago. I would call him my soul mate but he lost his soul long ago. Well, lost is maybe not the most accurate word. It was taken from him but not by whom you might at first suspect.

I still wear that same star today. I have never taken it off.

THE LAWS OF ATTRACTION

2017 AD
Tel Aviv

If you want to know what really turns me on guys, it's housework. No, not me doing it, *you* doing it. The thought of you shirtless, in jeans and bare feet, pushing that vacuum back and forth is enough to send me over the edge. Watching you clean my house, working up a sweat, cranking out those pheromones is the ultimate stimulus for me. Like white on rice, I'd be all over you in a vampiric second–you'd have no time to even *think* it's hot. You might see a blur in your peripheral vision and then you're down, drained, dead.

Okay, so that's my *fantasy*. I couldn't really kill my housekeeper now, could I? Who would do the vacuuming next time? Not me. Most assuredly, my days of toilet-bowl scrubbing are wa-ay over. Certainly the cleaning service would tend to become a little suspicious after a few hunky domestic engineers turned up missing. I mean, we found a very discreet service but not *that* discreet. We have to make it look good though, like it's really lived in. You know, it's the little things that make you mortals so absolutely endearing and undeniably human: leaving food on the kitchen counter, trash in the cans, and laundry on the floor. Vampires are exceptionally fastidious and Galen goes absolutely thermal on cleaning day when he sees me 'human up' the place a bit. I have to literally drag him away from the mop and bucket and forcibly eject him from the house.

45

It is imperative that my colleagues and I make ourselves scarce on that day. You are far too enticing. Just the scent of all those sweaty bodies dusting the mantle...oy, you get real thirsty, real quick. All humans have their own scent. It's not the stinky side naturally, but rather their own particular smell that makes them who they are, distinct from all others like a fingerprint. Every human has one and some of us are almost powerless in our response.

It's especially problematic for Vietor. His victims always remind him of his mother. No, it's not what you are thinking. Men of my kind usually share with me that they seek out their female victims whose scent reminds them of their mothers. You know, that whole evocative sense memory thing with vanilla and cinnamon that makes them get all misty-eyed and wax nostalgic about their school days and coming home. They open the door and they are hit with the aroma of things freshly baked and there is Mommy standing at the kitchen sink with a heaping plate of cookies and a glass of milk, waiting for them. Maybe that's why when I was human, my mother always advised me to be baking something whenever a date was arriving at our home. Oedipal allusions aside, scent is powerful for us. It is primal and instinctive like a dog, whose head and body follow its nose following a scent wafting on the air currents, even though the food walked right past it. For me it's just as visceral, like something clicks in my brain and I get put on autopilot.

With all this temptation working around us, we definitely need to beat a hasty retreat. So we agree to exit en masse for the day. We all disperse, Zippy and I to the mall, Galen to the latest museum exhibit, and Vietor to the downtown garage.

The four of us generally agree on most issues regarding our day-to-day existence. We try not to sweat the small stuff but as we are all very unique individuals, sometimes conflicts arise and we have our little familial squabbles like any other group. Even with those who know, as Socrates (sorry Galen) put it so succinctly and with great eloquence all those years ago: "There is nothing new under the sun." Vampiric emotions can run high but our varied skills and talents are what drew and have kept us together. Leave us face it dearies, if you have been around for hundreds of years, your résumé is fairly well-padded out, more like an enormous portfolio that pretty much reads like a history book. I mean, we have to try to fit in somehow in the human world, so we all have some sort of cover.

Vietor shines as our mechanic: he has this uncanny ability with machines and can repair anything, even working in the past with limited technology and substandard tools and equipment. He's always been this way, even before he became a vampire. To be sure, he really saved our butts in Denmark. If he can repair a damaged cargo ship engine, he can do anything. Needless to say, we never have any car trouble. He's our millennial man though, up with all the latest technology and the proud owner of every single piece of technocrap available on the market. Lucky for me, he's taken me under his wing. I still can't figure out how to program my watcha-ma-callit but Vietor is right there to push one little key and it's running smoothly and I feel a complete dweeb. I no longer have to endure hearing "you don't call, you never write." My mother is pleased to finally receive periodic texts and an occasional webcam session from her doofus daughter.

The modern world holds no interest for Galen, however. A complete technophobe, he won't even learn to drive a car. Sometimes I feel like a Soccer Mom, toting him around everywhere. I don't know why he is so afraid to embrace the 21st century. Though he's extremely reticent to discuss his past, we get the impression those Greeks were somehow involved. We surmise medicine must also come into play and we fondly refer to him as our little mad scientist, always grinding herbs from his garden with his marble mortar and pestle. I feign interest to keep harmony within our group.

"What's that you have there, Galen?"

"This? Oh,...this is just foxglove I am preparing."

"What's foxglove?"

"Oh,...nothing. Poison. Currently used in its digitalis form for heart patients."

"Why are you messing around with poison, Galen?"

"Oh, you never know when it will come in handy."

Great. I have a de' Medici walking around my house.

The Old World and the new clash regularly. I'm talking about the occasional kerfuffle between Vietor and Galen, of course. Vietor is all action, all work and very little play most of the time. Galen is his polar opposite and is totally turned off by Vietor's machismo. There's something of the sadist in him that creeps out, sets his teeth on edge, and makes Vietor become completely unglued. Oil and water could not be more different. Water can caress you with its gentle flow but then turn on you with a raging torrent of tremendous force. Oil can be a balm, act to salve and soothe your wounds but can also burn. Galen loves to start fires by lobbing a verbal incendiary. He then follows it with an inflammatory remark which leaves Vietor to put out the conflagration, lick his wounds and wonder what the hell happened.

Mostly they argue about philosophy, the nature of man, and the will of G-d. Not exactly drawing room topics, so Zippy and I deftly remove ourselves from the firestorm and do what any stressed-out female does in that situation...go shopping.

Girls will be girls and I can't believe I got even girlier when I became an immortal. Zippy, as I've said before, is completely bonkers for clothes. Shoes. Accessories. Make-up. She's like a child who has been starved regularly, gets three squares a day now, but still stuffs her face at every opportunity as if the food is somehow going to run away off her plate if she doesn't. She could easily pass as a pantry hoarder who survived the Depression, currently enjoys no privation and yet still has forty-seven cans of tuna in the cupboard. Don't even ask how many little black dresses she has.

She and I have very different styles when it comes to what we choose off of the racks but variety is the spice. I prefer more conservative, upscale, tailored suits and dresses while Zippy is an utter throwback to the 60s. Every worn cliché and she's wearing it. To the hilt. Paisley, ick. Beads, gag. Nehru collars. Okay, those look cool.

The only cause of contention between the two of us is my wallet and the lack of what was in it in the morning by the end of the day. This woman does *not* know how to bargain shop to save her life. Mercifully, we are all employed with steady incomes here in Tel Aviv. Believe it or not, even vampires need day jobs-someone has to pay the rent. This means we never have to dip into our travelling funds adroitly sequestered (under pseudonyms) in various and sundry Swiss banks. Those monies are strictly for our work in the past-you can't go saving the world with empty pockets now, can you?

Naturally, Vietor works in the local garage and is the toast of the neighborhood, being the most mechanically-inclined one of the bunch. He is a major contributor to the family income as he is always picking up moonlighting jobs, keeping a steady flow of cash coming in for our work. That's all very well and good for our bank accounts but the added bonus for me is at the end of his workday. There's nothing sexier than when I sense him down the street and then hear him coming through the door. There he stands in the doorway in his disheveled overall, liberally daubed with axle grease, carrying his canvas bag and looking oh, so hot. Ah, a man and his power tools. It's a beautiful thing.

Galen puts his skills (the legal ones) to good use at the town pharmacy. He's totally in his element, mixing concoctions, discussing the relative merits of pharmaceuticals v. homeopathics and whether the efficacy of heliotrope is all it's cracked up to be.

Zippy sparkles at Tel Aviv's very chichi, most charming department store make-up counter. She is always bewitchingly made-up and loves every minute of it. It's a wonder she can bear to be in such close proximity to her clientele. I wouldn't last a minute if I were that up close and personal, applying the latest trend in foundation to a human's face and throat.

I've a good head for business and coffee houses are fairly profitable, so I put my café management skills to good use and have opened up a second Lazarus Coffee right here in Tel Aviv. My parent's dream of "next year in Jerusalem" is a reality. Needless to say, they are ecstatic that their daughter has made it. Start-up is a snap when you have cold, hard cash. I'm basically the silent partner in the venture as I have more important work that keeps me 'elsewhen' and otherwise occupied. Humans are in charge of the day-to-day running of the business and I just sign the checks and make sure deliveries arrive on time.

That's our family, so to speak. All the differences and bickerings aside, we solidly unite for dinner. But it's not some quickie in a back alley-we make an entire evening of it.

Our earnings as regular working stiffs help with our 'human-like' expenses. Zippy's closet rivals Imelda's. I'm more casual at home unless I'm going clubbing. Vietor unbelievably has a weakness for Armani-and he can so totally pull it off. Galen looks better in nothing at all but if pressed, will don the tunics and trousers he prefers. And barefoot. The man loathes footwear.

Zippy and I get all dolled up in little black cocktail dresses, garter belts, and stockings. You'd think working at a make-up counter she would have mastered the fine art of mascara application but I always have to lend her a hand at the last minute. I'm no more punctual in death than I was in life so the men are always waiting for us, ever so impatiently at the bottom of the stairs. We never fail to fail, in epic proportions, to make a grand entrance for our evening's festivities. We think we are all that and more but why do the men always outshine us? There leans Vietor against the banister, looking like a tall drink of water in the desert in his Armani pinstripe and I'm already melting. Galen, seeming every bit the old-world vampire, has outdone himself in a flowing white poet shirt and very snug Levi's. Zippy and I give each other the look and say screw it, let's just stay home and make a night of it. But no. Galen, being the oldest male vampire present, interjects with his well-earned authority and vetoes our request. Sexism exists even in death (sorry, ladies).

Vietor exits to fetch his latest automotive conquest, something really hot and very red but I forget the name; I still have no appreciation for fine automobiles. Four wheels and an engine, I'll drive a lawnmower, I'm not particular. My enjoyment is contained in the drive. Well, somebody else driving. I hate driving. I schlepped way too much as a human and I prefer to be the passenger in my immortal state. Plus, the anticipation of the evening during the drive adds fuel to the fire of our growing hunger. Vietor guns the engine as we take our seats. Zippy was too late to call it so I snagged shotgun and at this moment I always look forward to discovering how the night will unfold.

You know when you pull up to a red light and you only hear the hum of the other cars? But then, slowly coming into your consciousness is this throbbing backbeat, the bass of another car's radio. It pulls up next to you and it's way too high, extremely distorted. This thrumming reverberation courses throughout your body and the entire vehicle is hiccupping to that beat. That's how loud a human's heartbeat is to us, how we hear your life force throbbing within your body. It's the first thing we sense, even before we catch your scent. Sitting there in our car at that stoplight, we can hear every mortal's lub-dub for hundreds of feet.

The combination of those two sounds, this cacophony of pulsing, creates a manifold attraction for us. It is an overwhelming stimulus/response interplay. In other words, we are on fire before we even get to the club. We are drawn to them and they, the poor fools, cannot help but to move in our direction. Like a moth to the flame, we are the most primal object of their desire. There have been many, many occasions when we have been followed for quite a few miles by a car which has pulled up next to us at the intersection. Some poor schmo who was just going to the store for milk has no idea why he is changing gears to follow a little red sports car. Victor has to lose him in traffic though, or we'll never get to our destination. Shira has little patience for this interruption and just wants to dance.

So, I never got to go dancing much as a human. As a vampire, I am a dancing fool and I don't care. We make our entrance into our regular haunt, a discotheque called Ahava and tonight I hear the strains of my favorite band, Bubzagalor. I feel that techno beat of their first hit 'Soft White' and I'm the first one out there, whirling like a dervish. Galen, for all his ethereal qualities, is the sexiest, most seductive partner I've ever danced with and meets me on the floor. Victor refuses to dance. He says it's not dignified and stares at us glumly from the bar where all the human females are tripping over themselves to get close to him. He's really only here for the free buffet, anyway. Zippy is a total groupie and if it's live music night, she is right there pressed up against the stage, mooning over the lead guitarist. If she catches his eye, it's all over and he completely flubs his solo.

We attack the hottest, most upscale clubs to mix, mingle, and flirt with our prey to get our hunger up to a fever pitch. Foreplay. Then we retreat to the raunchiest bar we can find for consummation. The plan is fairly routine and generally follows the same scenario. After hundreds of years, luring humans can get dull, but for a newbie like me the thrill is still ever-present and palpable.

Zippy and I stumble in through the door of this little dive looking oh, so hot in our little black dresses. Pretending to be tipsy and disoriented, we make our way to the bar. All eyes are upon us as we grab a barstool. It's the perfect ruse and human males eat it up. It doesn't take long for two of them to sidle up, offer us drinks, steer us over to a booth and sound us out. Oh, we couldn't possibly we demurely protest, we have to get up early for work tomorrow; we are not those kind of girls, etc. We play it up, knowing full well that if they gave us any real trouble we could snap their necks in a flash. But...could you guys walk us to our car? No trouble. They grin wolfishly and rise to commandeer us out the back door into the alley, guiding us with intent exactly where we want to go anyway.

I love that first look on their faces when they become aware that they are no longer in charge of the situation as they see Vietor and Galen materializing into view from the shadows. Confusion followed by anger and finally fear. Then I mark my man and have him by the throat, pushing him, very much against his will, back against the brick wall. That first time I realized I could so completely overwhelm a man with my strength was unbelievably empowering. I was bigger, better, faster, more. I was utterly mesmerized by his futile struggling. So much so, that I completely forgot to drink. I just stood there, amazed that I held him in check with no effort whatsoever. He's cursing and struggling and I've got him by the neck like some hissing, spitting cat vainly attempting to escape my grip. I felt for the first time like a man who overpowers a woman with just his muscle. He is heady with the knowledge that he can do it at any time and she understands she is powerless to do anything about it. I felt like a god. I'm over that now; nothing distracts me.

As that first drop of searing hot blood hits my tongue, the fury takes over and I am totally focused. Believe it or not, it's better than the hottest sex you've ever had. Even vampiric lovemaking pales in comparison. I know it's a human cliché, but it feels like you are riding the gnarliest wave at Mavericks, cresting interminably and never crashing. Your victim is riding that same wave with you as well and you both are totally in sync. That's why he stops struggling when your teeth meet his flesh. He literally does not know what has hit him. Your bodies press closer; he wants to touch you but he can't move his hands, he's weakening with blood loss. He may moan a little which incites you further. It always does the trick for me; I can't help myself, I want it all. It is without a doubt, *the* most powerful and sustained release flowing through every inch of my body all at once and never ending until I force myself to pull off. I don't have that much control yet, being newly made. I would just keep on going, distracted by my victim who is coming closer to death with every passing moment. Your victim becomes simultaneously your savior and your executioner. Sweet killer, cruel lover. Oh, but that little death can be made to last. Zippy's favorite moment is la petite mort; she says there is nothing like it. Blood is at its sweetest as you climb higher, transcending space and time as you swallow their life. Believe me, it's the ultimate rush, the biggest high I have ever experienced and it is unbearably stimulating.

It's generally at this point that I hear a voice thunder in my ears but at first, it's as if from a very far distance, slowly penetrating its way into my consciousness. It reminds me of cannon fire reverberating through my eardrums, momentarily blocking all sound. I don't comprehend fully at first. Like a flea in my ear, the peskiness of which I can't quite rid myself, this intruder continues to vex me. But then I feel that firm grip on my shoulder that jerks me roughly out of my sweet lullaby of death. I draw back like a dog over his bone and then I become aware of Vietor's voice, coaxing me away from the depths, saving me from myself.

"That's enough, Shira."

I'm always, *always* the last one holding my victim. The others, older and more practiced at self-regulation and restraint have finished long ago. There they always are, waiting patiently for the novice (even after six years) observing me with amusement like I'm some brave toddler taking her first tentative steps, finally letting go of the coffee table. It is Vietor who, without fail, brings me back every time; he's my closest link to the 20th century.

I let my victim slide to the ground with a thud, wiping my mouth with the back of my hand. He and his buddy will wake up in the alley at dawn a little wobbly on their feet, slightly confused, and with the mother of all hangovers but none the worse for wear. Their wounds will heal. Remembering nothing of our real interlude rather, they will seem to vaguely believe that they had a wild time with two hot babes in the alley the night before.

We do not call our victims to us with our bite when we feed unless we seek them out to have alongside us in our travels. When this connection is made, they do not remain our victim but rather become our cohort: inexplicably drawn back to us wherever we go, lured by that same Siren call. They can't resist but must follow. There is no alternative. But this we keep in reserve. It is a great and terrible thing to make death.

Instead, when we drink it's a dry bite if you will, like a rattlesnake that strikes but does not release his venom. That's how we can feed and not kill. All of these things I learned along the way from when I was first bitten to where I am today, fully immortal. Without colleagues to act as mentors, one is merely a lone vampire, serving no purpose. Yes, we do retain some of those human, psychological quirks if you will, even as immortals, hence all our varied personalities. I guess it's muscle memory, ingrained in the flesh. It's true, nothing human can ever touch us. But like most of us, a sense of hubris that we once were human keeps us from completely renouncing some of our eccentricities. Even in death, one needs a semblance of life: humanity, home, and hearth.

We arrive back at the house, sated but always a little blue. We all have our own ways of coming to terms with blood. Galen wanders off to be in his garden; he says it is at its loveliest reflected in the moonlight. He's the moodiest one of us, forever wrestling with G-d. Vietor kicks into fix-it mode and promptly makes off for his man cave of power tools because of course, something immediately needs repair at three o'clock in the morning. The first thing Zippy and I want to do is wash that human smell off of our bodies. Girlie, to the last.

Sounds like one big happy family, right?

A GRAIN OF SALT

18 May, 2002 AD
Westport

"Miriam, we've already had our family celebration. Let your daughter go out and have some fun with her friends. Nu, at least she'll be *legally* consuming alcohol tonight, gell?"

"Dad!"

I shriek from the upstairs bathroom. How mortifying. I always thought I was so clever at hiding my illegal collegiate activities from my parents. Guess not. So much for all those years of underage drinking, sneaking out of my bedroom window on a Saturday night and attempting (apparently unsuccessfully) to sneak back in oh, so quietly after a late night out. How do your parents always know? What...do they have some vast MI-5 network engaged in espionage activities that they periodically pump for information on you? Can you even trust your friends not to spy and betray you? Are they secretly being paid under the table by your mom to observe and report back with your latest high school and college hi-jinks? Wait, what if they really did? Okay, I'm totally getting paranoid now. Anyway, at least I'm finally able to participate in that age-old, hallowed American custom of the legal set, that of drinking like a real grown-up. Well, no more sneaking and at least I can toss my fake ID now.

It's my 21st birthday, I'm going clubbing with my girlfriends, and my hair is totally not cooperating right now; it's as if it has a mind of its own tonight. Damn this humidity, I feel like a fuzz ball. I certainly have the 'Madwoman of Chaillot' look down pat. But I found the hottest little number at the mall today and the three of us are going to dance our asses off. We are taking a cab so that we can totally get ripped tonight. Jess and TJ pick me up about 9pm, to the totally predictable tune of my mother's parting shot out the window as the cab drives off:

"You forgot your sweater!"

We arrive at Westport's trendy new club, Choreo. It's a totally '80s night so I am in seventh heaven. There's a very long line snaking its way down the block but the bouncer is TJ's second cousin so we are able to cut to the front. We get a lot of cat calls and wolf whistles for that from some frat boys we recognize from our rival school in Northport.

"Northport sucks!"

TJ may not have a lot of class but she certainly is succinct in her disdain for our sister city across the river.

Once inside, we all make a beeline for the bar. My friends detest the fact that I can drink them and everyone else under the table. In fact, I hold the record for nickels in all the frat houses on both sides of the big water. That's like quarters with beer but we use gin instead. You know that game. You try to bounce a coin into the shot glass. If it lands inside, you get to make someone else drink the contents. If it misses the glass, you have to down it. My record for gin shots was eleven. Even Tank, Northport's college football quarterback and built like his moniker, was unable to make it even to ten.

Must be that Jewish blood; I've always had a strong constitution when it comes to hard liquor. However, I'm a real pantywaist when it comes to beer or wine: one glass and I'm the one under the table. But I can easily down seven shots of Patrón with no ill effects the next morning.

"That's fucked up, Shira."

Jess always tells it like it is. That's why we're friends. TJ just goes out to scope out the guys and is in college solely to find a husband.

"That's fucked up, TJ," we both say to her.

"Fuck you. Let's dance."

The DJ starts spinning 'Hungry Like the Wolf' and the three of us make our way out onto the dance floor. We assume our usual positions: in a circle, dancing around our purses and jackets which are piled in an untidy heap at our feet. At first I just stand there, wishing the DJ had played something else. I was never a huge Duran Duran fan; they are a little before my time but the beat is good and I feel the tequila starting to warm me as it's coursing through my body. The floor is absolutely packed like sardines and it's dark, stuffy, and then the strobe light starts up. That's my favorite way to dance. I begin to move, finding my rhythm. I am completely in my element with the music and the beat and the flashing lights, letting them consume me, not self-conscious at all. In my opinion, real dancing is not for sissies. I quit caring about what other people thought of me by the time I was seven. I'm as free as I'll ever be when I dance.

I close my eyes as the backbeat penetrates my body. As I start to sway and turn, I sense someone close to me and I come to a dead halt. I open my eyes and I'm suddenly face-to-face with a man who has the most startling blue eyes I have ever seen. From out of nowhere he has slid up directly in front of me. I stop dancing as I realize he is staring straight into my eyes. In my slightly inebriated haze I feel him, without a word, slide his left hand around the curve of my waist and pull me close. His touch is like that slow, painful recognition penetrating my awareness, like when you are trying to pet the pony and you come in contact with the hot wire. It's a numbing vibration, that buzzing that you can't quite locate at first but you know eventually is going to knock you on your ass.

He then takes my hands and puts them behind his neck. I try to lean back to break contact but he pulls me closer. I'm completely open to him, at my most vulnerable. We are slowly moving left and right, even though the music is fast, loud, and obnoxious. I'm so close to him now that my eyes blur; it's hard to focus on his face. He leans forward. He's very near, breathing in my scent like he's drinking me in, he can't get enough of me. Brushing his cheek against mine, moving his body in rhythm with me, I perceive that I no longer hear the music. It's as if we are enclosed in some soundproof glass cage to which everyone around us is completely oblivious. Everybody keeps dancing as if the music is still alive to them. But there is a complete hush all around me and this stranger who has wrapped me up in his cocoon of silence. There is something however, that I do begin to hear, to start to recognize. It's only the backbeat though, thumping in my entire body. The rhythm of those beats seems to drown out everything around me, as if all I can hear and feel is the push of each one falling and rising, a decrescendo and then the suspense of anticipating the next crescendo.

Slowly, as we move together, it dawns on me that it's no longer the bass of the music that I'm hearing. It is so still that I sense what I am actually hearing and feeling is my own heart beating against my ribcage. The strobe light, which has been flashing the entire time during our dance, begins to slow to match the rhythm of those same beats, as if time itself is procrastinating, shirking its responsibility, loitering in its duty. I look into his eyes. They are no longer blue but seem very black now set against the flickering of the strobe. The expression on his face both unnerves and enthralls me. There is longing to be sure, but there is a sadness as well, a bittersweet commentary that elicits a physical response in me for which I am unprepared. I want to speak, to ask him his name but then his features relax as he looks into my eyes.

The music at once comes crashing down all around us, like cymbals at the end of the performance. It's roaring in my ears as he leans close, curling his fingers around the chain of my necklace. I hear him distinctly as he whispers in my ear with a voice like honey:

"Soon little one, very soon."

With a sudden thrust, the press of bodies crowds in upon us as the music revs up to an even faster beat. We are separated by a swift surge of dancers careening and crushing us. I stumble backwards into my friends who are bumping and grinding those frat boys behind me. Traitors, one and all. I look up and the man has merged with the crowd so quickly, so seamlessly, it's as if he melted into them, as if no one needed to make way. I lose sight of him.

"Do you know who that is?"

I yell in TJ's ear. Neither of my friends has the slightest idea who I am talking about. They are so engrossed in leading these Northport guys on that they didn't even notice I was slow dancing with a complete stranger. I'm not even certain it was real myself. I just stand there, stock-still with dancers gyrating all around me, waiting. He might come back.

I simultaneously feel the first pangs of a dehydration headache, need a glass of water and/or another drink, and have to pee. I lopsidedly weave my way to the bathroom, trying to spot his face amidst the sea of bodies out there. As I make it to the first available stall, I press my hands and forehead against the cool tile of the wall trying to steady myself. I hope I remember what he looks like when I wake up tomorrow.

19 May, 2002 AD
Westport

Something completely unpleasant and wholly annoying is invading my consciousness the next morning.

"So, did you have a good time last night?"

"Oy! Mom, let me sleep in."

I'm in a complete fog. Why do I feel like I have a hangover? That is so not Shira.

"Did you dance with some nice boys?"

"Ma, I'm just trying to remember if I even had a good time or not. Could you please just bring me some coffee?"

Mom sighs and reluctantly gets up off of the bed. Heading downstairs, her voice trails off as she mutters just loud enough so, of course I hear:

"Is it so wrong I should want to know if my daughter had a good time last night? Ezra! Sleeping Beauty wants you should make her some coffee."

My dad actually brings up the cup and takes one look at my appearance, probably not so good as I surmise from his expression. He grins impishly and asks me at what point do I think I'll be ready to join the land of the living?

"Ha-Ha, very funny Dad."

After a few sips, I feel like I am gradually becoming at least partially human again. I don't even recollect how I actually got home last night. Most of the evening is just one big blur. I remember getting ready to go out, arriving at the club, and starting to dance. After that it's just blank. But wait. Some memory *is* creeping into my head as the caffeine slowly permeates my system. Some guy. Some really *hot* guy. Older, I'm guessing around forty but really good on the dance floor, almost feline in his grace. Not effeminate at all but so completely masculine that you instantly felt powerfully feminine; the feeling was intoxicating, like a drug. You innately knew that he wanted you, that you were foremost in his mind. To be wanted so by someone triggered something deep within you; his desire for you made him intensely attractive. Did he really dance with me, hold me close, whisper in my ear? Or was it just some alcohol-infused euphoric vision of wishful thinking? Okay, Shira. That is just way too deep, way too early in the morning, and well before my third cup of Joe.

SWING YOUR VAMPIRE...

2017 AD
Tel Aviv

It's tough to fit into a new neighborhood, even if you are a human. It is especially tricky when you don't even have a pulse. One cannot avoid the Welcome Wagon Lady forever, so my colleagues and I do our darndest to create a cover, make ourselves fit in, and be accessible to our community. Keeping up with the Cohens we call it.

We try to be as inconspicuous as possible, to appear just as human as you guys. Being out and about at night is no problem but we have to try to blend in as much as we are able in daylight. How do we pass you may ask? Hashem bless Ben Nye's matte foundation palette. And with Zippy's expertise in the make-up department, particularly with a vampire's best cosmetic friend, the airbrush, we can do it. She has us all coming out looking like the cover of some glossy magazine: sun-kissed, bronzed, and beautifully mortal in appearance. You could say we are a throwback to our ancestors who were desperate to assimilate from the old country to the new. But since some of us are from the New World anyway, I'm not sure if that metaphor is wholly analogous.

Coming across as human is crucial for our day jobs in the public sector, obviously. It is doubly so in the private sector when we are at home. As my mother so repetitively said during my life and still does even in my death: "what will the neighbors think?"

By the way, we have great neighbors here in our own little slice of suburban heaven in Tel Aviv. Slice? It's the whole damn pie. We are surrounded by a lot of love, let me tell you. Throughout the course of our entirely chaotic move-in day, the whole neighborhood flocked to our door to meet and greet and ply us with endless quantities of food. Baskets of it. Doesn't sound Jewish at all, does it?

Naturally, we reciprocated by throwing the biggest block party the community had ever seen and everyone was invited. Our property has this great pavilion out back, big enough for a large barbecue pit (we roasted a whole pig-just kidding). Vietor set up a killer sound system that night and was in his element as DJ mixing music. Dancing and party games rounded out the evening.

Unbelievably, Vietor and Galen cooperated for once. Privately they loathe each other; professionally they give each other the respect they deserve. They know that what they bring to the table for their work is of the utmost importance and channel their respective energies accordingly. Today, they rose above their petty differences and outdid themselves with the decorations. Lights were festooned within the wooden trellis over the dining area, sparkling throughout the bougainvillea. Potted plants (Wandering Jews, thank you very much) lined the flagstone walkways and freshly-cut flowers adorned every table thanks to Galen. At almost the last minute, he remembered his deadly garden and whisked away to the potting shed the most heinous of his flora.

Zippy has this rare and totally unnecessary talent for cuisine. She never gets to put her skills to good use in the kitchen since we always eat out, so she was totally jazzed and completely insistent on preparing all of the food. She spent hours at the open-air farmer's market on the Thursday and Saturday preceding the party, selecting just the right ingredients for her creations. I offered to help her out in the kitchen; I do have some experience with food prep, after all. I even thought of having the café cater the entire gig but she was adamant. She toiled all morning long at the center island in the kitchen, endlessly chopping, expertly sautéing, and artfully arranging. The buffet table displayed a masterpiece of gastronomic delights, laden with incredibly exotic dishes. Most of them I had never heard of and were from her immense repository of truly authentic Middle Eastern recipes with a decidedly French flair that date back to well, nobody really knows when. Her intensive labors paid off with the warm response we received from our guests.

I don't know what came over me but all of the sudden I kicked into cruise director mode and organized crafts, musical games and prizes for the neighbor kids. Maybe I was just feeling a little wistful, remembering my childhood and my little cousins, who aren't so little anymore. We are just putting on the finishing touches by lighting the candles when our guests begin to appear.

The four of us greet the first arrivals at the door, welcoming them into our home. I know it sounds wildly aberrant and completely counter-intuitive that vampires would open their home to humans. But we would be even more conspicuous if we were reclusive and standoffish. Humans are just too curious for their own good; they can never leave well enough alone and the last thing we need or are in the mood for are nosy neighbors poking...well, their noses into our personal affairs. Yes, secrecy regarding our work is vital. But eventually the present will become the past and one never knows what year we will be in or where we will be located when we have to travel back to 2017. That is an eventuality, make no mistake. Humans are forever screwing up and needing our assistance, so we must establish our identities here to be prepared for the future.

Initially on move-in day, we had our cover story fully prepared in advance and introduced ourselves as two married couples sharing a house to help defray living expenses. The economy is tough everywhere so this ruse was completely believable to our neighbors. Besides, this is the land of the kibbutz; communal living has a history here.

The neighborhood has turned out in full force: couples, families, and the odd singleton here and there. They are all streaming in, greeting each other, catching up on gossip, clustering around the bar. Small children are running around in the garden, full of laughter and gaiety. The craft table is a big hit and the kids are cutting and pasting to their hearts' content. Zippy is in her glory with all of the praise she is receiving over the buffet table and I see Galen beaming as a guest asks him about his herb garden. The scenario reminds me a little of my synagogue in Westport: people coming together to rejoice in an evening's festivities and enjoying a break from their daily lives. This gathering gives the four of us a chance to relax as well.

The party is revving up when I see Vietor embrace a very beautiful woman over by the bougainvillea, where he has been keeping the music flowing. She is unbelievably exotic, almost Mediterranean in her looks with deep olive skin, almond eyes and a knockout figure. They are standing very close to each other when I see her lean in almost intimately and whisper in his ear. Vietor throws his head back and laughs uproariously. This does not appear to be their first encounter and I find I'm unable to look away from the two of them. I can't believe I'm actually feeling jealousy. I thought I was so over that petty human emotion. I guess immortality does not preclude the green-eyed monster from perching like an imp upon your shoulder and whispering in your ear from time to time. He takes her glass and makes his way to our bar where I am blending margaritas.

"So, Vietor. Who was that woman you were talking to at the music table?"

"One of our neighbors. Her name is Sophia. Why?"

"She certainly was friendly, almost familiar with you. It seemed like the two of you knew each other. Had you previously met?"

"As a matter of fact, we bumped into each other last week when she brought her car into the garage for a tune-up. An Aston Martin and in excellent condition. You should see it, Shira. It is a fine piece of machinery and she keeps it in top form. We struck up a conversation and she invited me out for a drink. We've been spending some time together since then."

Don't ask him, I say to myself. Don't do it, just let it go. But of course, before I can hold my tongue I blurt out:

"What do you mean, you've been spending some time together?"

Stop. Stop-right-now.

"Are you sleeping with her?"

Drat! Too late.

Victor grins at me wolfishly and cups my chin in his hand.

"Are you jealous, Shira?"

"No...not at all."

I try to stammer through a denial but I just end up sounding like a busted teenager caught in a ridiculous lie, attempting to recover some minimal shred of dignity. Epic fail.

"What you do privately is your own business, I don't care."

"Of course you don't, Shira-la."

He is totally smirking at me now in an infuriatingly patronizing way.

"No, I mean it. We are all grown-ups here. She is certainly lovely. I just thought she didn't seem like your type. Is she Jewish? She doesn't look Jewish. What is she, Greek or something?"

"Uff da! I don't understand why *you* are complaining. You got a little Greek last night."

"Vietor!"

I'm mortified and I'm sure my cheeks are blazing as I recall our pre-dawn interlude.

"Do you have to advertise it to the entire neighborhood?"

"But I think Shira, you enjoyed yourself...hmmm? Just a little?"

He takes the margarita I have made and strolls back towards the bougainvillea. Just before Sophia sees him he turns and shoots me a wink over his shoulder. Oy! Sometimes he can be so maddening, I just want to scream. In another century, the term 'rake' would not have been far wrong in describing his opinions regarding women.

I realize I need to cool off and head to the kitchen. I love Vietor but I often see red because he knows just what buttons to push with me. His archaic attitudes about women color my reactions and like a dolt, I fall for his machismo every time. Of course, I probably set myself up for that one anyway by asking about Sophia. There are no absolutes that say we can't have romantic liaisons with humans but it is generally frowned upon and regularly discouraged. However, sometimes it's a necessary part of our work in the past. Occasionally, the only way to effect change is to develop a personal, intimate relationship with a human. I've certainly had my fair share of job-related romance but common sense dictates discretion.

Casual affairs can be tricky and are potentially fraught with danger, ripe for paradox not only for us but for the human participant as well. If you take one of these entanglements to its ultimate conclusion, you have created an event for this person that becomes part of his or her history. The present we create eventually becomes the past and we never know if our current trysts will have deleterious effects for the future.

I make it to the kitchen, still hot under the collar to find Zippy, cool as a cucumber but working like a dervish at the center island. Man, can that woman chop vegetables fast. Her speed and dexterity with a blade are unsurpassed. Tray after tray is streaming out of the kitchen, whisked away by some of the guests who have volunteered to help serve. As the last one takes a platter of stuffed mushrooms out, Zippy looks up and gives me a big grin; she is absolutely in her zone and loving every minute of it.

"Hey, Zip. Can I give you a hand with anything?"

"That would be great. The mushrooms are going fast. Could you do another tray?"

"Sure thing."

It's been a long time since I've actually handled food (not since I worked with my parents at the café in Westport) and I'm a little uncoordinated. I'm all thumbs at first with the piping bag but after a few stray blobs, I soon find my groove. Handling the food, preparing another tray, and being in the kitchen all start me thinking about Mom and Dad. It's been years since I've visited them and well, webcam just doesn't seem to cut it anymore. I mean, I'm grateful to Vietor for helping me get set up with all that but...dang, now I'm thinking about him again.

"Cherie, what is the matter?"

CHRISTINE BROWN

"What do you mean?"

"Shira, mon petite. When you walked in here you looked like you were ready to murder someone."

"Oh, it's nothing. Actually, being around all this food, I was just thinking about my folks."

"Well, why do you not go and visit them?"

"Zippy, you know we are not supposed to go back."

"Come on, Shira. When have you ever played by the rules?"

"I know, I know. Nobody ever told me I needed to grow a pair. Chutzpah I'm not lacking. But speaking of rules, umm...do you know anything about this Sophia that Vietor is seeing?"

"Sapristi! I thought something was up. Now I know why you came in here with daggers in your eyes."

"Daggers?"

"I recognize that look, Shira. It is reserved exclusively for our little Norwegian rascal. You should not let him rile you so. He does it on purpose you know, that louche, just to get your dander up."

"I know, I'm an idiot and I fall for it every time. I guess I've always been attracted to bad boys and Vietor is the ultimate bad boy. But, who is she?"

"Sure, I know her. Sophia works in jewelry at the department store. She really is very beautiful, n'est-ce pas?"

72

"Yes, she's quite lovely. But that's not really what I mean. Did you know that he is uh, intimate with her?"

"Pour quoi pas? We are all well aware of Vietor's proclivities as a bedpresser. You know his mantra: la nuit, tous les chats sont gris."

"Well, don't you think it's risky?"

"Vietor is a big boy, he can handle himself."

"I get it. It's not that."

"Hey, girlfriend...are you jealous?"

"He asked me the same question. Is it that obvious?"

"Shira, ever since I have known you, you have worn your heart on your sleeve. We can always tell how you are feeling. Your emotions are right there at the surface. That is why none of us ever mention Avram when you are around. We know how distraught you get if his name ever comes up."

I'm too shocked at this to even speak. I haven't said his name out loud for oh, such a long time. My face must show my distress because before I can protest, she cuts in.

"Pardon, s'il vous plaît! I should not have said that. I do not mean to spoil your evening. But you should not worry so. I know how deeply Avram loves you. He will find his way back. You just need to be patient and give him time."

Zippy is always perfectly frank and unnervingly direct but this is totally not what I wanted to talk about. I can't even look at her.

"Shira, I can see that you are hurting. But separation is a normal part of our existence. You accept that the work we do is paramount to any other consideration. That is the design of it. It is not for us to question why it is so. It is enough to know that G-d is directing the course of events and placing us where we need to be. He will bring you back together when the time is right."

"I understand why. It's just hard to go on every day not knowing."

"You will learn to be patient. It is just because you are so very young. When you get to be an old-timer like me...."

"Oh, Zippy. You could never be old."

We are interrupted by a woman coming back into the kitchen with an empty platter.

"Zipporah, the pâté de foie gras has flown off the tray. It's a huge hit. You simply must tell me how you prepared it. My husband insists."

"Certainement! It would be my pleasure. I will have to try to remember how I made it; you know I never write anything down. I have been making it for so long, I basically just wing it."

"Where did you get your recipe?"

"This is from my mother's collection and you know what those old-fashioned cooks are like: a pinch of this, a dab of that, if it feels right... bake it."

"Oh, that sounds just like my mother's way of cooking, too!"

"Well, let us see if I can jog my memory. I believe we could make a start with some of the ingredients I have on hand. Grab a pencil and we shall see what I can recall."

"Oh, that would be wonderful. I would love to."

The women are too busy with the recipe, mixing and measuring and keeping up a constant stream of neighborhood gossip to notice my exit. I really should get back to the party, anyway. As I stroll through the house making my way to the garden, I reflect on what Zippy has said. All of it was true, every word. I know that in my head. But it's my heart that gives me the trouble. Oh, my Avram! You were my first true love, the only person I would have given my life for (such as it is). When will you return to me?

Honestly, Shira. Snap out of it! Be strong. What does Avram call you? A woman of valor. That kind of woman doesn't waste her time moping and mooning about for things that cannot be. Cannot be? I don't know that for sure. I *will* see him again.

The backyard is filled to capacity and the party is in full swing when I notice Galen chatting amiably with a man I have not yet met. I smile as I see him escort the man over in my direction. Galen is a gentleman (when he wants to be) in the truest sense of the word: gallant, chivalrous, and will always open the door for a lady, an utter throwback to the Old World.

"Sweetheart, may I present Malachi. Malachi, this is my wife, Shira."

"Good evening. I am very pleased to meet you, Shira. Thank you so much for inviting us to your lovely home."

"It's our pleasure, we are happy you could come."

"Well, we are certainly glad to welcome you to our neighborhood. I've just been admiring Galen's handiwork in your garden."

"Yes, he definitely has the magic touch when it comes to living things."

The three of us continue to toss about the usual subjects you discuss at parties with someone you have just met: the back and forth of children, jobs, and interests. Then Malachi throws something my way that I am not expecting.

"I wonder Shira, if you might be interested in an upcoming community event that we have planned? Your husband here has been saying that you are a good dancer."

I turn to Galen and play my part.

"Oh, honey. Have you been puffing me up?"

"Not at all, my dear. Malachi has been telling me about a local club that has dance workshops and I happened to mention that you love to dance. He has invited us to come down and give it a try. What do you think?"

"Oh, we'd be delighted."

Now, don't laugh. Square dancing is HUGE in Tel Aviv. I know, I know. You are totally smirking right now. You probably have this very warped, clichéd, stereotypical image in your mind of what you perceive square dancing is all about: country music, petticoats, bolo ties, senior citizens. Totally uncool. You are wrong. Dead wrong. Well, granted there is some of that to be sure. But dig a little deeper for your own edification and you will find that there is an absolute youthquake happening in modern square dancing. All ages, from young children to teenagers to thirty and forty somethings and beyond are rocking out to some kick-ass music: rock, disco, pop, techno/electronica/trance/house, even hip-hop! We have this ultracool caller here in Tel Aviv who plays a great mix of current hits. He found out that I have an especial affinity for techno so if he knows I'm coming, my playlist is cued up and greets me at the door. Square dance callers have all the latest technocrap at their disposal for dances. The days of vinyl are long gone. Three guesses (and the first two don't count) who was right up front at the caller's table the first time we went to a workshop class? Vietor! After chatting with our caller and discussing the latest version of some computer music program (I forget the name) he has hinted that he may even want to learn to call! Although Vietor is a total horndog when it comes to women, he is rather introverted when it comes to expressing himself in front of the public eye. I am discovering an entirely new artistic side to him that I never realized. Goes to show you that you cannot judge even a vampire by his cover.

See, if vampires square dance, it *must* be cool.

WHO ARE YOU AND WHAT HAVE YOU DONE WITH MY DAUGHTER?

2017 AD
Tel Aviv

So, I didn't have much experience, let alone success with men when I had a heartbeat. Now that I'm dead inside, I have to beat them off with a stick. How's that for irony?

The first time my vampiric aura induced a guy to walk across the room to seek me out I did one of those classic looking-over-my-shoulder moves. Because of course, he's walking towards the babe standing behind me. He couldn't possibly have made the effort to cross the entire room at this party to come and stand in front of me. Me, the former marching band geek who read the dictionary for fun. My high school friends always teased me about that one. Without missing a beat, I was dead serious in my reply:

"What do you mean? Doesn't everyone? Who doesn't wake up every morning trying to see how much information they can stuff between their ears before sundown? I know I do."

Yeah, back then the guys *really* wanted to ask me out after that confession.

In retrospect, I was rather dense. But that observation is made with ultimate vampiric clarity (hindsight is always 20/20, but in my case the numbers don't apply). Hence, I shouldn't judge my past human self too harshly.

Now, it was a different story. Overnight (and I know now the exact date because that was the night I met Avram in the synagogue parking lot) I discovered I was suddenly appealing to guys who previously never looked twice at me. And not just for my brain; not that any guys I met were ever interested very much anyway in what was between my ears. It was as if I had suddenly become this pheromone-driven magnet; all at once they were flocking, flirting, and attempting to do the other 'F' word as well. At the time, I was completely oblivious as to why this was occurring. There was absolutely no connection whatsoever in my brain between what was by now happening to me almost on a daily basis and my encounter, albeit brief, with Avram. Now, I can see it all clearly. My transformation had neatly begun as if I were on the receiving end of some supercharged, paranormal make-over. It was just little things at first, so minor that I was unaware of them. Looking back, it was only later, much later that everything started to click.

My parents were way more astute than I was regarding these changes (although they didn't understand the real reason; they still have no idea what I have become). My mother concluded that I *finally*(!) decided to 'turn it on' because I was (one or all of the following):

A-on the wrong side of twenty,

B-recognizing that I should forego my stubborn insistence on waiting for 'Mr. Right' which segued into...

C-resigning myself to the fact that settling for less-than-perfect, second-best, it's possible that a better offer is not coming your way so you better get a move on, consider yourself lucky, the-clock-is-ticking kind of guy, any guy wasn't such a catastrophe.

I sensed that my mother was eerily intuitive about the entire situation, way more perceptive than I could ever have imagined or given her credit for. She had to do double-duty as watchdog, particularly when I was at work behind the counter at our café.

2 October, 2010 AD
Westport

Saturday morning after Shabbat services when Avram had left so abruptly, my first thought as I am waking up is: why is there an armored tank careening all around the inside of my head? My second thought is: why the hell is it so bright in here? I've never had a hangover in my life (thanks to that little worm inside the bottle) and yet I feel like I've been on the receiving end of an 18-wheeler. I didn't even have anything to drink last night. Unless you count the thimbleful of Shabbat wine in the Oneg room (and that *never* counts as imbibing).

As I bring my right hand to my forehead to shield my eyes from the sunlight streaming in through the curtains, I come across the bandage. And how it got there. Just another shining example of Shira's lack of grace in public. Oh, and now I'm really flashing on the embarrassment factor. Great. Avram must be thinking I'm a total klutz. No wonder he skipped out early last night. Well, I'm sure he is long gone, on his way back to Israel, never to be heard from again. My mother will be disappointed but at least she won't be haranguing me about him. It's a shame because he did seem like a 'nice boy.' More than that however, I found him extraordinarily attractive and I don't just mean physically. There was something about his manner, his elegant grace, and the way in which he carried himself that invited you in and made you feel completely welcome. You really wanted to be near him; you almost couldn't help yourself, as if no other option presented itself to you in your mind. I found myself dwelling on his features, lingering on the movements of his hands, bathing in the richness of his voice as he spoke to me. I admired his gentlemanly behavior and his gentleness with me when I took a spill in the parking lot. He was the complete antithesis of every other man I had ever met or dated.

Oh, well. I'm going to be way too busy to spend much time musing about Avram today. We have a produce shipment coming in early and I have a backlog of paperwork to do in the office. But for some strange reason, I'm having a little trouble getting motivated this morning. I've never been lazy in my life and yet here I am still lounging in bed, daydreaming. I better get going or Mom will be yelling up the stairs for me to get my tuchus in gear. With a start, I realize that I can hear my parents moving around in the kitchen downstairs. How long have I been lying here? As I push myself up with my hands to a sitting position, I give a yelp. I must be getting an infection because my palm is really starting to burn now. I didn't have the stomach to look at it yesterday so I groggily pull the bandage off now and brave a look. Okay, it's not so bad. Just really red. But why does it still sting so? Well, sting is not the right word. It's almost like it's vibrating, pulsing right under the skin.

"Shira!"

Right on time.

"Coming, Mom!"

For once, I don't trip over my bedroom slippers or run into the door jamb as I head for the bathroom. I'm usually pretty blurry in the morning until I put in my contacts. I really don't want to see my reflection in the mirror but I can't resist taking a peek. Well, that's not so terrible. Apparently I don't look as awful as I feel. My hair is actually cooperating this morning and that is very unusual. Must be that new frizzy hair pomade but I don't think I have been using it long enough yet for it to have made much difference. To my chagrin though, this morning I can see every crow's foot that has begun to appear in the last few years around my eyes. Quite clearly. Oy, I hate getting old.

I know what I need. A nice, long hot shower. Maybe that will clear the residual car wreck that still seems to be cluttering up and clanking around my brain. As I stand there under the water, I let the scalding temperatures work their magic. The heat is taking the tension from my neck which makes me relax my shoulders. My head just doesn't seem to want to clear though, as the steam rises up, filling the bathroom. I press my forehead to the tiles and just stand there, letting the water wash over me. Without meaning to, my thoughts stray to last night and Avram. It all seems fuzzy and unfocused. I remember meeting him there, falling in the parking lot, and going into the synagogue. After that, the remainder of the evening all has a rather dreamlike quality to it. I must have been leaning there in the shower for longer than I thought because slowly I began to notice a change in the water temperature. It was downright warm, not volcanic like I like it. Well, I guess I've used up enough hot water for one morning. Wake up, Shira and get going! I towel dry off and try to keep myself on track.

My contacts are totally not cooperating this morning. Why is it I have no trouble getting the right one in? No trouble whatsoever. It slides in perfectly every time. Pop! It's done. But that left one. Oy! That left one is an absolute nightmare. It always takes three times. That is, if I'm lucky it only takes three times. Normally, I always end up with one very red left eye. This must not be my morning because they both are giving me difficulty. I decide to forego them and wear my glasses. What the heck? I'm more blurry with them on then off. Maybe I need an appointment for a newer prescription. One more thing to add to my ever growing 'To Do' list. Whatever, I'll just squint all day. Hopefully, I can remain in the office this afternoon and do paperwork and not have to deal with customers. I find my parents in the kitchen in their usual positions. Mom is at the stove cooking up the breakfast of champions and my dad is completely invisible.

"Good morning, Mom."

"Good morning, Shira."

"Hey, Pop."

"Mmph."

My dad has his nose plastered in the sports section of the paper. He is totally not a morning person until about noon, whereas my mom is bright-eyed and bushy-tailed from about 4am onwards. She just can't wait to wake up even before the crack of dawn. Saturday mornings we let the A.M. crew handle the crowds at the café because we actually aren't supposed to be working at all today. It's generally not until late afternoon that we make our way there to take over. No such luck this morning. The three of us are leisurely sipping our second cup when we receive a frantic call from Nikki, one of our baristas. I pick up the phone and get an earful.

"Oh, Shira! Thank goodness you're home. This place is crazy with out-of-towners for some convention and we are packed to the gills. We really need some extra hands."

"Okay, Nikki. Don't panic. We'll be there as soon as we can."

So much for a morning off. My mother is completely unruffled because she is always go-go-go while my dad grumbles during the entire drive to work. Of course, when we get there, there is a lull and Nikki is completely embarrassed at having called us.

"It's okay, Nikki. I've got office work to do anyway that I've been putting off and you know how much my mother loves being here. Do you think you could get a coffee and Danish for my dad, though? You know he doesn't like missing his Saturday mornings."

"For sure, Shira. No problem."

About midday, just as I was steeling myself to brave the pile of neglected papers over which I had been lollygagging, I hear my name being yelled from the front of the café. Oh well, now I have a good excuse for not getting to the paperwork. Again. I make my way from the back office up to the front and before I see the crowd, I hear them. All of them. I'm flabbergasted to see that the line of customers is streaming out the door and seems to be wrapped down the length of the shops next to us. Even though we have a full complement of staff today, both Mom and Dad look harried. I relieve my mom from the cash register so she can give Nikki a hand at the espresso machine. I whisper to her over my shoulder as I ring up the customer she had been helping.

"What's going on? Are we having a white sale?"

She is too busy with coffee orders to reply so I take the next customer, a young man.

"Hi, what can I get for you?"

No response. He just stands there rooted to the spot, staring at me and holding up the line. Hungry, impatient people are starting to fidget behind him. I am thinking maybe he is just confused by the menu so I make some suggestions.

"Are you in the mood for a salad?"

Nothing.

"What about a deli sandwich?"

Nada.

"Well, it's good soup weather. How about some matzah ball?"

Zip.

I'm not sure what to do next but the patron behind him comes to my aid.

"Dude, flirt on your own time. I only get an hour for lunch!"

Most of the patrons snicker and this seems to snap him out of whatever fog he is in and he moves out of the line, still grinning at me stupidly. The impatient customer makes his way up to the register.

"Whatever have you done to that poor guy?"

"I have no idea."

I honestly didn't. The only guy who ever hung on my every word at the café was Micah, this guy I knew from my college days. I didn't even know who this guy was. He was now standing over by the drinks case and still looking at me like he'd never seen a girl before. It was actually kind of creepy at first, but after he finally made it out the door without ordering anything at all, it happened again later that afternoon. We were slowing after lunch as we always did, customers becoming infrequent, allowing us a little breathing space. During the pause, I decided to take stock of our pastry case to see what I needed to pull from the back. I was squatting behind the sliding door, pencil and pad in hand when I had this funny sensation, like the shivers you get when someone rakes their nails across a chalkboard. It was like all the hair on the back of my neck shot up. I lifted my eyes from my notepad and saw someone on the other side of the case also squatting down, looking past the trays of rugelach directly at me. Utterly transfixed. I bolted up. So did he. I walked over to the register. He followed me.

"Good afternoon, sir. What may I get you?"

This one was older and a little more coherent than the young, flirty dude from before but no less creepy.

"What's your name?"

I was wearing my name badge but his eyes had never left my face.

"Shira. Are you interested in something from the pastry case?"

"No, I don't think so. I don't even know what I'm doing in here. I was walking by outside and I saw your face through the café window. And now I'm in here and...uh...you are really beautiful."

"Oh...thank you, but I'm very busy right now. Are you sure you don't want anything? Maybe a coffee?"

"Sure, okay I guess. Whatever you think."

At this point, I realize that asking him what *style* of coffee he would like would take an interminable amount of time and probably further confuse him so I just proceeded with a latté so I could get back to my work. As I steam the milk, I can still feel his eyes upon me. Every time I try to take a surreptitious peek, I find his gaze glued to my backside. I quickly finish up the coffee.

"Here you go, sir. That will be $3.08."

He hands me a five without taking his eyes off of my face. As I put the change into his outstretched palm, he suddenly grips my hand and does not let go. I feel the warm, hard metal of the band upon his finger. I look right into his eyes.

"Sir, you need to let go of my hand...now."

"Oh, sorry."

He seems disoriented, like he doesn't really know what to do next but he finally takes his coffee and goes to sit at the counter by the window. He sat with his back to me the entire time he remained in the café, but I could always tell when he turned to stare at me even if I was not looking in his direction. It was that feeling that you were being watched but you didn't know exactly how you knew. Every time I caught him looking at me he turned crimson and whipped his head back towards the window. I don't even think he took one sip of his latté, he was so distracted. He eventually got up, tossed his paper cup in the trash bin and made for the exit. He was just about to push the door open when he turned around one last time, as if making up his mind to come back to the counter. He never made it. Our late afternoon dinner crowd was descending upon us and the jostle of people surging in through the doors seemed to snap him out of his fixation and he left the café, albeit rather unwillingly. I had kept my eye trained upon him during his stay and was now relieved he was gone. We've had our fair share of creep-a-zoids in here and this guy was no exception. But he seemed slightly more flustered and he was most definitely married so I felt a little sorry for him and a tad confused myself. What up with the men today? Is there a full moon or something?

The rest of the day was fairly routine: busy during the evening rush with another respite just before closing. Unfortunately, there were more transfixed males dancing attendance which was totally unnerving. Quite a few guys seemed to stop all of the sudden and look through the window as they made their way past the café. Some of these men even had a girlfriend/wife/gaggle of children with them. Halting abruptly, generally mid-stride, causing their partner to bump into them, they would just stare for a few seconds. Inevitably they would be jerked back by the arm by said girlfriend/wife/gaggle, usually with an angry word at him and a glare through the window in my direction.

I kept noticing that the majority of customers who came in were men. That usually only happens on special occasions, like Valentine's Day. That's when the entire line of shops in our little strip mall is brimming with last-minute, invariably male patrons who want to get their shopping done all in one fell swoop and could you hurry, please? I'm late. First they hit the flower stand, then the chocolate shop, then the drugstore for a card, and then our little place for a coffee recharge and any impulse-buy sweets for their sweet. We definitely see our fair share on that day of forgetful husbands and boyfriends who have procrastinated until the last minute.

But today was unlike any other holiday rush I had ever seen. Like lemmings to the sea, they just kept pouring past the shop. Some of them actually made it in, clogged up the line, and stammered through their order if they even actually ordered something.

It was a distinctly odd day, to be sure. The whole café seemed to be buzzing like a very busy hornet's nest. Not all riled up like it had just been on the receiving end of a stone chucked by some incautious youth but rather deeply humming with purpose. Everybody either in line or seated with their food was in a perpetual state of chatter and I thought to myself, are they all speaking really loudly or am I just psychic or something? I seemed to hear every word. That elderly married couple sipping their tea at Table 4 were discussing an upcoming surgery and it didn't sound pleasant. Most of the pairs of women at the double tables along the back wall were enjoying their lox and bagel with schmear and were as usual, just kvetching about their ungrateful sons and daughters. Those two teenage boys over by Table 7, with their heads bent together, kept stopping every few seconds to glance up at me. I'm not paranoid or anything but I thought for sure I caught my name more than once. Every time I did, I'd snap my head up. I thought someone was calling me. When I caught them staring, they went a deep shade of scarlet, flushing beet red from their necks all the way to the roots of their hair. Then their eyes flew to their sneakers. By the end of the day, I knew everybody's business. Even the really personal stuff that I actually didn't want to know, like they were all sharing the most intimate details of their life with me, pretty much a complete stranger.

I was relieved when my shift was over and my parents and I removed our bedraggled selves from the café. On the drive home, it seemed the cacophony followed me. At each stoplight, it was as if every driver on the road around us was listening to talk radio. Full blast. By the time we made it to our neighborhood market and pulled into the parking lot, my ears were stuffed full of all the noise around me, packed inside my head like a late night at the loudest rock concert you've ever attended. It was unbelievably distracting.

"Hey, why are we stopping?"

"Well, ladies. Howsabout we have a treat, a little celebration tonight? I'm feeling generous after our very trying but very profitable day. What say you two to some porterhouse?"

"Let's have a feast!"

"Miriam, you took the words right out of my mouth. Let's make a night of it. What do you say, Shira?"

"Huh? Oh yeah, okay. That sounds great. I'll make my potato casserole."

We enter the store and split up, each with a list in our heads. The fluorescent lights in the market seem to me like they are on overload this evening because I squint and actually hold my hand up to shield my eyes. I fish in my purse for my sunglasses, fumble and end up dropping them on the floor at my feet with a clunk. Great, I think. There goes another pair. As I bend down to retrieve them, I catch something in my peripheral vision. It's hair, red hair, shockingly red hair and very close. So close we nigh crack our skulls together not only on the descent but the ascent as well. My eyes are drawn to a glint of gold reflecting off of the fluorescent lights: dangling from a chain around his neck is a large gold crucifix, swaying with the movement. The shock of red hair is connected to a head, then a face, and then the rest of him comes into view way too close for comfort. At least he is smiling. I wasn't quick enough to get the glasses myself. His hand was lightning fast and he snatched them first.

"I believe these are yours?"

Of-course-they're-mine-you-idiot. We almost just gave each other a concussion. Then I stop. I stop because I hear it. That lilt. That unmistakable, mellifluous lilt that screams Ireland. That explains the red hair. That also explains why I am mesmerized by his voice. What is it about men with those English/Irish/Scottish/Welsh accents that makes women go mad and all weak in the knees? He has a glint like the sparkle of his cross in his eyes, his very green eyes as he hands the sunglasses back to me. I notice right away as his fingertips brush my hand that they are colder than mine. I find that strange because I've just come in from the outdoors.

"Oh, thanks. How embarrassing. I don't usually wear shades indoors. Is it just me or is it really bright in here this evening?"

"Do not be embarrassed. It takes time getting used to the change."

"Change?"

"You know. Coming from the dark and into the light."

"Ye-es. Well, thank you. I've got to get back to my shopping."

"May I accompany you?"

"Oh, that's very kind. But I'm here with my parents and I should be getting back to them."

Who *is* this guy?

"Your parents? Ah, I understand. How charming. Well, perhaps we will meet again soon, Miss...?"

"Shira. I apologize, but I really must go."

I'm scanning the store over his shoulder trying to see if my parents are anywhere near.

"It is a pleasure to make your acquaintance, Miss Shira. Allow me to introduce myself. I am called Seamus. You are in no doubt by now I believe, where I come from and who I am?"

"Well, it sounds like you're Irish but I'm no expert on counties. I'm sorry, I can't tell much more than that."

"I see. How strange. But it cannot be that you are unaware. No, that is not possible."

"Please excuse me, Seamus. I see my dad over in the produce section. He's probably forgotten to get the...asparagus. It was nice meeting you. I really have to go."

He extends his hand so I am forced to extend mine. His grip is very strong but I can't get over how cold it still is. He doesn't let go right away but looks me straight in the eyes.

"Farewell, Shira. Until we meet again."

I'm too unnerved to say anything so I just smile and dash off. Okay, that was just more weirdness coming my way. I actually fibbed and didn't see my dad by the asparagus. He was starting to really creep me out and I just felt like I didn't want to keep standing there, conversing with a total stranger (even though he was very attractive) trying to find out what he was talking about. What *was* he talking about? Change, darkness, light, awareness? This encounter was definitely one for the 'Mom was right again, don't talk to strangers' list. No, I definitely do not want to meet this guy again, especially here in the market (that's embarrassing enough as it is) even if I was melting at the sound of his voice and being stared at by his beautiful Irish eyes smiling down at me. Focus, Shira. Focus. What's next on the list?

I'm perusing the cheese display, looking for my dad's favorite Parmesan when I feel like I am being watched. No, not just the feeling like someone is burning a hole in my back with their eyes, but I actually hear breathing. Quite close. This time, it's me who is quicker.

"Look, Seamus...oh. Dad, I'm glad it's you."

"Who else would it be? Hurry up, your mother is already at the checkout."

We make our way over to where my mom is waiting for us in line.

"Mensch, now I remember why I never take the two of you shopping. I've been waiting here for twenty minutes."

"Ma, we haven't been in the *store* for twenty minutes. Cut us some slack."

My dad just smiles as he sets the food on the conveyor belt. As I stand there while our purchases are being rung up, it happens again. I feel like someone is staring at me. I look over my shoulder a few times but all I see are harried mothers chasing small children and trying to keep them from grabbing the candy placed on the shelves at toddler-level. I don't see anyone except regular customers doing their evening shopping. But I can *feel something*. Someone. Watching me. Observing my every move. I don't know why I feel this way but I'm sure of it. My unexplained sense of paranoia is interrupted by my mother's voice.

"No, honey. That's not right. That didn't scan correctly. The asparagus is $2.89 per pound, not $2.99 per pound. I saw the sign myself in the produce section. I'm thinking you should do a price check, yes?"

I turn back in time to see the checker just smile, ring up a void and manually re-enter the correct dollar amount. She knows better than to argue with my mother. We are regulars here. This is our neighborhood market and all of the checkers and management staff know full well that my mother is never wrong on pricing on anything in the store. They quit price checking ages ago.

We eventually make our way out of the store, each of us carrying several bags. And I thought we were just coming in for three items. What was I thinking? My parents are ahead of me, chatting on about preparations for the meal and I am just trying to get out of the building without dropping my packages when I hear my name.

Whispered.

Softly.

Caressing me with its alluring tone, like a lover's persuasion in the dark. Pulling me back into the store.

I stop short. A full stop that causes the lumpy, plastic bag of unwieldy produce to swing forward with momentum, slip from my fingers and go flying. Ejecting the contents with a cascading splat onto the floor just inside the doorway.

"Oh, crud."

The automatic doors begin to slide shut but suddenly jerk back as I bend down. I hear my name again: that seductive call spoken so gently as if the whisperer had his cheek pressed to mine, his lips resting at my ear. But there is no one near me at all as I gather up the vegetables strewn all over the black mat of the market entryway. I stand up and take a swift scan of the parking lot and see that my parents are already at our car. They are under the open hatch of our van and almost finished loading the groceries into the back. I'm still standing there as I give a holler.

"Hey, wait up!"

I step forward and walk quickly over to them, put my packages inside and slam the hatch. As I head around to the passenger side, my mother speaks just before she opens her door.

"Shira, who was that man?"

"What man? Where?"

She cannot be talking about that weird guy I met in the store. That strange man named Seamus, can she? I'm pretty sure my mom did *not* witness my brush with him.

"That man in back of you at the entrance to the store just now."

"What?"

"He was standing directly behind you, just inches away. You didn't see him? He was so close to you he could have easily whispered in your ear. You didn't know him? He was a total stranger? Honestly, Shira! You really need to pay more attention to your surroundings."

I whirl around to face the storefront but all I see are the unfamiliar faces of shoppers surging in and out through the automatic doors. Not a single thatch of red hair at all to be seen anywhere.

We make it home and our supper that night was a grand treat of a meal after our strangely hectic day. My dad busied himself at the barbecue in the backyard with the steaks while my mom and I worked together in the kitchen. I put the casserole in the oven first thing and now I'm chopping vegetables for the salad while my mom is liberally drizzling olive oil over the asparagus. In between sips of wine, I go over in my mind the little interludes I had had today, trying to figure out each one. I wasn't having any luck and I had kept silent about it all the way home but the weirdness of the afternoon was well, just too weird not to say anything.

"Mom."

"Yes, Shira-la."

"Did you notice anything strange today at the café? I mean, what up with the customers? Not only were we swamped but some of them were freaky. That is, more so than usual."

I don't think I can even mention the supermarket without her getting all maternal on me so I hold that segment back. She turns to me mid-grate, a large chunk of fresh Parmesan in her hand; crumbs of cheese are flying, falling as she waves it around.

"Praise Hashem we have such a day! I don't know why today was such a busy one, but I'm not going to question today's register tape."

"Ma, you're getting schmutz all over the floor."

As I bend down with a wet paper towel to clean up, I think that she is just not getting what I am saying.

"I know it's great for us business-wise. But that's not what I mean. Umm...for instance, did you notice anything unusual about the guys, our male patrons? It seemed to me that most of our customers today were men. Some of them were downright creepy."

"What do you mean, creepy? Were any of them impertinent to you?"

I could tell my mom was shifting into stranger-danger mode so I was quick to allay her rising apprehension.

"No, not at all, Mom. It wasn't that. It's just, well...almost to a man the guys were uh, they seemed overly interested. Like they were kind of flirting. One was even married and coming on to me, although he appeared rather perplexed about the whole idea. It gave me the shpilkes."

"Oh, you must be imagining it."

"No, seriously Mom. Guys were all over the place today. Swarming, you know? Like we were handing out free beer and peanuts. I don't get it."

"Shira-la, did you ever stop to consider that maybe it was something you did?"

"Mom! I've never flirted with any of our male patrons! You know I've always considered that most unprofessional."

"I know dear, but maybe you weren't aware of it yourself. Your dad and I see how delightful you can be in social situations, but you know how men are. Maybe they would see your charm and ease of manner as more inviting than it actually was. Perhaps they just took it the wrong way."

"But I haven't changed how I interact with any of our patrons at all, particularly the men."

"No, honey. I think you are mistaken. I think you *have* changed and I believe it has something to do with Avram."

"What are you talking about? He just left me without a word last night. How could he possibly have anything to do with what happened at the café today?"

"Shira, even your father could see that he liked you very much and you know how obtuse he can be when it comes to his daughter and the subject of men. Everyone at synagogue noticed it as well. Avram was attentive to you and very courteous to the both of us. Maybe he was just the spark you needed."

"Spark? Mom, don't go getting all matchmaker on me now and think there is a correlation between our busy day and me being on the prowl for a husband. Please don't turn this bizarre day into some sort of subconscious ploy on my part. That is the *last* thing on my mind right now and...."

I got no further.

"Shira, it should be the *first* thing on your agenda right now. All of your cousins are married and have children with more on the way. You don't want to end up like Mrs. Goldman's daughter, do you?"

Here we go again with the Mrs. Goldman's daughter speech. Mom always brought this one up when she was lamenting her lack of grandchildren. See, Mrs. Goldman's daughter Leah waited too long. Leah wanted a career outside the home (gasp!) and her mother almost had a coronary when she told her. Mrs. Goldman begged. She pleaded. She cajoled. She bribed. Nothing worked, nothing doing. Leah wanted to get her education and climb the ladder of success. There's plenty of time for that, Mom. I want to see the world first, she said. I've got to hand it to her; she actually did see some of the world first as a very successful motivational speaker. Her self-help books are best-sellers and she is certainly kept occupied with travelling all over the country on book tours and giving lectures and seminars that are very well attended. Trouble is, she was so busy being busy for so many years that before she knew it, she was thirty-nine. Although she was a success in her career outside the home, when she eventually did come home it was to an empty house.

But Leah was resourceful. She tackled this little snafu like any other business proposition. Predictably, she did the mad, desperate dash for domesticity. Her plan of attack was as follows: whirlwind romance and speedy courtship (Avi is a great guy) and then even speedier nuptials and making for a baby right out of the gate. No luck. And they tried everything. Drugs, in vitro, surrogacy, all to no avail. I'd heard this story so many times, I was tired of it.

"Mom, I know all about Leah Goldman. We all feel bad for her. But that's not going to happen to me. Someday I will get married and you will be a Bubbe, I promise. I don't know when but I'm sure it will happen. I just don't understand why there is such a rush for all of that."

"How can you be sure? It seems like you are not even trying to find a husband."

"Well, it's not like they are beating down my door with a stick or anything, Mom."

Come to think of it, after today's shenanigans I wasn't so sure anymore. My dad comes to the rescue just as my mother draws breath.

"Steaks are done."

He walks in carrying a great platter of steaming meat and comes to a full stop.

"What's all the katzenjammer? You two going at it again?"

"Ezra, your daughter and I are not 'going at it again.' We are just having a discussion."

"Miriam, you and Shira never just have discussions. It always turns into world war three and I try to duck and cover but I always end up getting sucked right into the middle of the maelstrom."

My mom and I just stand there looking at each other stubbornly, not saying anything.

"Okay ladies, what is it this time?"

"Well, I...."

That's as far as I got.

"Your daughter seems to believe that she has all the time in the world to get married and start a family and I was just thinking...."

That's as far as *she* got.

"Miriam. I know that this is a hot-button issue for the both of you. How about we call a truce for now and just enjoy our celebration dinner? These steaks aren't getting any warmer, you know."

Ah, blessed are the peacemakers. Thank you, Dad.

DANIELLE IN THE LION'S DEN

(Part One)

2017 AD
Tel Aviv

Or, it's really problematic being a conservative Jew, particularly if you are also an immortal. It's like a double whammy of 'anti-ness.' Some groups don't like you because you are a Jew. Other factions resent the notion, are emotionally supercharged, and on fire that you are conservative. Actually, the only people who *really* don't take a shine to us vampires (and we don't care anyway) are our victims.

Humans have this completely illogical idea that vampires are so romantic. They put us up on some kind of ethereal pedestal: we are completely misunderstood, we really aren't evil, we only kill to survive, and we just want to be loved. The media has perpetrated and perpetuated this mythology that the idea of immortality is irresistibly desirable. Who wouldn't want to be a vampire, to live forever and to never age? I know it all sounds just so fabulous but there is a downside to everything, even immortality. You never age but everyone else does. I will have to deal with the eventual loss of all the people I hold dear. Not just my parents, every child knows that is a given. At some point in the future, I will grieve for the loss of my mother and my father. But what about my extended family? Knowing that all of the amazing people I have ever known in my eternal lifetime will wither away and perish is devastating to contemplate. I will never experience any human frailty ever again but I will have to witness the pain and anguish of everyone I have ever loved. That's not romantic. It's horrifying.

What mortals really should be thinking about is how much they should fear us. We are alluring for one reason and one reason only. Truly, you humans shouldn't be trying to get closer to us. Rather, you should run. Now. And as fast as you can. Not that it will do you any good. Well, actually the only ones who have anything to fear from us are the bad guys. And you know who you are. And so does everybody else. Some people just refuse to admit that evil really does exist in the world. Ding! Did you miss the memo? From G-d? Everything has its opposite. That's the way Hashem intended it: day and night, sun and moon, man and woman, good and evil, the sacred and the profane. You cannot have one without the other. Where there is light, there will also be darkness.

I have to confess to you that I do indeed have a dark side: I actually enjoy killing bad guys; it's the ultimate adrenaline rush. Is that so wrong? I refuse to give succor to my enemies. Why does society constantly tell me I need to make nice-nice with the bad guys? It's not like they are an endangered species. The population is plenty full of criminals. Hey, no worries. I don't mind pulling a few weeds to make this a greener planet. From my perspective, I am giving a great gift to society by eliminating them from the gene pool. Just look at it as one more service I provide. If I can assist just a little in keeping the already overflowing prisons slightly less crowded, like winnowing the chaff from the wheat, I am happy to oblige. It's really not that taxing anyway. I never have to sing for my supper. All I have to do is walk into a room and my dinner comes to me. Very little actual physical work on my part is required. But believe me, it's a full-time job. And you know what? I never have to worry about job security. I will never face downsizing, be made redundant, lose my benefits or ever have to try to collect unemployment. Why? Because evil will always exist. Consider what a shortage of news there would be if everyone obeyed the Ten Commandments. I'd probably starve. Naw, that'll never happen. Yes, I admit we are evil. But G-d is putting evil to good use by having us fight evil. Does it follow that it is evil to destroy evil? That's the $64,000 question.

1 November, 2008 AD
Westport

"Mom, will you please stop trying to milk a cash cow?"

We are butting heads again. Nothing new. Well, the venue my mother wants me to attend is new but the Spiel is not. She's been haranguing me for weeks but I've been politely refusing to engage.

"Shira, you know that all the small businesses in the area are getting together to have this function tonight. Obviously, it would be a great way to collaborate with other professionals, promote the community, and get people to shop locally. Besides, I hear it's being held in the banquet room of the Holiday Inn this year. Pretty impressive, wouldn't you say?"

My mother is detailing our communities' first annual merchant association get-together like it's this phenomenal event, fraught with unbelievable retail opportunities and marketing tools that will pluck your establishment from the depths of obscurity to the dizzying heights of instant success. The only snag is that she just read the glossy, full-color brochure and doesn't understand what it actually is: between the lines and in the fine print she would uncover that it's a singles matchmaking event sponsored by all of the synagogues in the tri-county area in the guise of a business seminar. Oy! Not another mixer!

I decide to give the brochure a glance. Okay, there are some interesting lectures you can attend if you have no economic savvy whatsoever. The buffet menu looks kosher and there are opportunities to engage with the locals if you care to schmooze. But I bet the real reason most people go is for the free bar, the dancing, and the fact that the entire hall will be filled with young, upwardly mobile, Jewish and very unattached males and females.

"Mom, it's probably just another mixer posing as a community business event."

"Well, what if it is? What's so wrong with meeting some nice, eligible men who actually have *good* jobs?"

"But it has the vibe of a debutante ball with all of the available young women on display on the auction block."

"So, are you telling me you are ashamed of your family's business?"

"Of course not, Mom. I'm very proud of our café. I just don't see the need to parade myself in front of everybody. Besides, most of these 'nice men' end up drinking way too much and making fools of themselves. They get a little drunk and start spouting politics and you know where that leads."

Then it starts. First comes the look. Whenever she stares at me with those piercing eyes of hers, I feel as if I'm five years old all over again. It's that same look I remember from my childhood that made it completely impossible (and mostly unthinkable) to get away with a fib. You might make a halfhearted attempt but one smoldering eye and you were stammering away, eyes glued to the floor, shuffling your feet, obviously caught.

"Well, Shira. It's too late anyway."

"Mom...what do you mean it's too late?"

"I've already signed you up."

With that parting zinger, she gives another one of her triumphant grins and whirls out of the room.

Oy a broch! Why does she always do this to me? Just when I was getting ready to tell her I was planning to go anyway, she has to go and have the last word! In truth, I had been thinking recently about our café. We've been puttering along, business as usual for many years. But just puttering along doesn't mean much in today's economy. We really need a boost, something eye-catching that would draw all ages to our little café. Coffee shops are a dime-a-dozen these days so you really need a gimmick, something to create a local buzz that would set you apart from everyone else. But I was fresh out of ideas. Maybe this merchant association shindig wasn't such a bad idea. I actually was getting inspired just thinking about it and all of the new ideas I might explore tonight. Of course, I couldn't tell my mother she was right; I couldn't let her think she had won. I'll have to think of something...and fast.

My rescue came later that same afternoon from my dad, who volunteered to be my escort and protect me from those big, bad liberals. Little did we realize at the time that we were strolling right into the proverbial lion's den.

YOU CAN'T PICK YOUR RELATIVES

(so choose your friends wisely)

8 September, 2010 AD
Westport

My Uncle Murray thinks he's this total badhkin-the greatest comic since Jackie Mason of the Borscht Belt. He's got this one joke, just one and he never fails to tell it at every family gathering like it's the first time he thought of it. Naturally, out of respect for our elders, we pretend we've never heard anything so hilarious in our entire lives and time our laughter exactly at the punch line. Granted, it gets a real guffaw the first few times you hear it. But like most jokes, it loses its hilarity after a few dozen High Holy Days.

See, Uncle Murray could never understand the Gentiles and their variety of faiths. It's all Goyim to me, he would say. He likens the other religions of the world to a tree, he says, with all these branches, see? There's a branch here, a twig over there. And that leaf. Oy! That leaf wa-ay over there, you don't know *what* they are, but they're still tax-exempt. (Insert courtesy laugh here).

It's okay if you don't get it. I still think it's funny.

I DREAM OF JINO

2017 AD
Tel Aviv

With the light brown hair. No, not really. Rather, he dreams of me.
What's a Jino, you ask? In an acronymistic nutshell: Jew in Name Only.
Attend to the following and learn.

Question: How can I spot a Jino?

Answer: A Jino is proud to be ashamed to be Jewish.

Question: What can I do to avoid a Jino?

Answer: Be a good Jew and they will never come near you. In other
words, attend synagogue, read the Torah, practice Tzedekah, observe
High Holy Days, follow the Ten Commandments, support Israel's
legitimate claim to its Biblical boundaries. Full stop.

No worries, I speak secular. Jinos can claim Jewish genetic heritage:
they've got the blood but not the balls to be a Jew. Believe me it's hard
work, especially today. Well, especially whenever. It's never been easy.
So many groups throughout history have not taken a shine to us. If you
do the math (and who doesn't love math?) and read uncensored history
books, you will discover that Judaism is the longest 'living' religion on
the planet. The same prayers I say today, my ancestors have been saying
for thousands of years. Hmmm...I wonder what the royalties on the
Shema would be? But that begs the question, how would one collect?

Survey says: we are here to stay, we're not going anywhere, get over it.

For whatever reason, Jinos reject all things Jewish and have become so secularized, they don't even believe in G-d anymore. They have the luxury that they *feel* they don't *have* to be Jewish. That's the job of all those Jews way over in Israel. Far, far away. Let them do all of the heavy lifting maintaining the faith and keeping it alive; I can't be bothered. I don't want to work that hard. Why should I think about being in the line of fire? The constant threat of annihilation from all quarters doesn't touch *me*. Jinos are not even into 'Jewish Lite.' Lite meaning just going through the motions of Judaism and not throwing yourself wholeheartedly into it. Every day, every thought, every action, every moment steeped fully in your faith. Personally, I take my religion like I take my coffee: strong, rich, intense, and full of flavor, not watered down with milk and artificial sweetener. Trust me, the following is a segue. Benjamin Franklin said (and I've seen it on a T-shirt, so it must be true):

"Beer is proof that G-d loves us and wants us to be happy."

Well, I can go one better: Chocolate is proof that G-d loves us and wants us to be happy. I can prove it as well. The melting point of chocolate is 98 degrees Fahrenheit. The normal human body temperature is 98.6 degrees Fahrenheit. That's why chocolate melts in your mouth. These are facts. The fact that a square of chocolate dissolves oh, so deliciously on your tongue could not be an accident. It's not random or happenstance. This means there is an order to the universe. Ergo, Intelligent Design. I rest my case.

But Jinos have a ready-made, feel-good substitution for Intelligent Design, the tenets of which I am a little fuzzy on but it has something to do with the planet and some Moshiach who arrived on the scene about ten years ago. Faulty satellite sensors aside, that's just wrong, on so many levels. Jinos condemn their heritage and I don't get it; I want to sing it from the rooftops, daily! They absolutely reject the values and give me an unnecessary amount of crap on a regular basis for my beliefs. And what up with those self-hating Jews? How could you possibly hate who you are? I do not understand. Never will. Listen up, humans. I got people waiting in line to abuse me; I don't need to take a number as well.

Additionally, Jinos make it virtually impossible for an immortal to get a proper meal. Soft on crime, criminals have rights too, blah, blah, blah. Yeah, the right to be my dinner. I mean, I have needs too. How is it that as a human, I couldn't afford to go to law school, but my tax dollars funded the behind bars law degrees of more than one bad guy?

I'm not making this up, I have direct experience.

So, when I was human, there was this *guy*...total Jino.

THE DEFATTED CALF

1 August, 2010 AD
Westport

All through my college years, Micah hung about my heels like some sad puppy dog. No matter how dismissive I was, he never backed off, just kept coming back for more, thinking maybe next time she will say yes.

I first saw him when I was a sophomore and he was an incoming freshman. He had this Struwwelpeter shock of curly brown hair and was a few inches shorter than I and built like a wrestler. He came up to the table I was at in the student union and asked if I knew where the bookstore was. My friends Jess and TJ were there with me and were hard-pressed not to giggle at him. He was a total frosh, wearing a sweatshirt with the school logo and mascot and that fresh-scrubbed eager face of one who doesn't quite yet know how college will knock you for a loop in a very short time. The three of us girls, being sophomores and obviously so much more advanced than he was since we had already been there an entire year already, looked down our noses at him. We were politely amused by his naiveté. Without asking, he invited himself to sit with us and began his one-way conversation (all about himself) for which he later became famous. He talked about his classes, his schedule, where he lived (with his parents) and what he wanted to major in, which was liberal studies. Shocker.

We could tell right away that he was a jock-wannabe. He regaled us with his weight training regimen, all of the various protein powders and supplements he took, his insistence on a vegan diet and he just couldn't figure out why his mom was perturbed by that. At this point Jess and TJ, avid carnivores, excused themselves from the table and beat a hasty retreat. I made the mistake of telling him that I had to be off as well to go to work.

"Oh, you have a job? Really? Where do you work?"

Oops.

"Um, at my family's café."

So, of course it would be rude not to tell him now where it was and the name. Although we never had any classes together during the three years we were at college together, he followed me around campus like some needy spaniel. How did he get my class schedule every semester? He was always finding excuses to bump into me on the quad and ask me out.

"Hey, Shira. Guess what totally awesome thing I just snagged?"

"What would that be, Micah?"

"Tickets to the graphic novel convention here in town next Saturday. I've got two in my hot little hand right now. We are going to have a blast!"

"Oh, umm...look, Micah. I don't think I can make it. I work every weekend. Besides, I'm not really into comic books."

The look he gave me, you would have thought I called his mother a whore.

"Shira! Don't call them comic books! They are graphic novels. They really are truly so much more than just comics."

"Okay, okay. I'm just not into graphic novels then. Besides, don't you need to ask your mom first if you can borrow her car? You still live with your parents, don't you?"

"What's the big deal? So do you."

"That's different. We have a family business. We work together."

No matter what I transmitted, he was just not receiving.

After I graduated, he became a permanent fixture at the then called Miriam's Café. Somehow he had this sixth sense about when I would be working and was always trying to chat me up from across the counter, inviting me to go to the gym with him.

"C'mon, it will be fun. You work out regularly, don't you? We should do the water aerobics class. It's really great for toning your lower body. You know, there is nothing more beautiful on a woman than a perfectly formed gastrocnemius."

"I beg your pardon?"

I'm trying and utterly failing I'm afraid, not to blush.

"That's your calf muscle, Shira."

"Oh, of course."

"Then we can hit the tanning booths and bronze up. I always feel like a new man after the booths."

"But I heard that those are really bad for you. Bad for your skin."

It's then that I notice how tan he always was, almost orange and not just during the summer. Obviously, melanoma means nothing to this man; the browner he is, the better he feels. I politely pass on the invitation and ask him what he would like to order. He never seemed chagrined at my constant refusals to go out with him. It was as if he was completely oblivious. I mean, he just wasn't my type. This was a guy who still lived with his parents, in their basement no less, was out of work and relied on them for everything. The icing on the slacker cake was that he spent the better part of each and every day immersed in computer war games.

This young man had certainly been dogged in his pursuit; he unbelievably carried the torch for me for ten years (talk about tenacious) and I felt a little sorry for him. So, in a ridiculous moment of weakness, I finally relented and agreed to a date with Micah. My mother was not so thrilled. She always thought that he was a nice boy, never in trouble, always respectful to her, but there was something missing. He wasn't quite what she was hoping for, for her daughter. Oh, wait. That's right, he's a Jino. Ma *never* saw him at synagogue and that was a *huge* strike against him. She also knew very little about his parents and that is absolutely crucial to a Jewish mother:

"...does he come from a good Jewish family?"

"...what do his parents do for a living?"

"...why do I never see them at synagogue?"

"...what, are they Communist or something??"

Surprisingly, on the afternoon of the date my mother did not hover. I think she felt that since this wasn't a date with potential, she had better things to do. Apparently, I had enough skill to make myself look presentable for first dates that will definitely not lead to second ones.

Not surprisingly, he was late. So there I am, standing in the café near the front door tapping my foot under the shadow of my mother's disapproving eye. I was uncomfortable enough as it was with Ma keeping tabs on me but it was more than that. For some reason, I had this creepy feeling that all of the patron's eyes were blazing in my direction. I must be imagining it I thought, but it seemed as if every single customer that afternoon was someone I knew. They were all vaguely familiar. Wait, it's not my imagination...the café is packed full of my mother's cronies from synagogue! Urgh! Thanks, Mom! Not only will I be hearing about this for years to come and the date hasn't even started yet, but even now I can hear the whisperings of dozens of little old Jewish mothers right now:

"...and does Miriam know who this Goy is?"

"...no, no, no, he's not a Goy. But Miriam says she never sees him in synagogue."

"...ach, du Schande! Well, what is he then? I don't know him from Abraham."

"...he is someone from Shira's college, I am thinking."

"...so, is he at least Ba'al Teshuvah? He can't be Frum."

"...this I am not knowing. You want I should go over there and ask him? Look. He is just coming in. Late. To have such a son...oy. I'm gonna pray for his parents."

At this point, I am actually grateful that Micah has arrived to rescue me from the onslaught of disappointment emanating from these mothers. I'm not even listening to his excuses for why he was late as I wave a quick goodbye to my mother who is standing behind the counter.

But it wasn't quick enough to avoid the admonishing glances from a sea of cronies seated at their tables, sipping from their tall glasses of hot tea.

Whew! I am glad that's over. Wait, my date hasn't even started yet. As we walk out to the parking lot, I hurriedly turn my phone over to silent. I learned this maneuver long ago: never leave your cell even on vibrate on a date or you'll be listening to it hum in your pocket the entire night.

I knew this was going to be a trial of an evening when the first thing he said to me after we got into his mom's car was could he borrow twenty bucks for gas.

"Sure, Micah. No problem."

"I'm really embarrassed, Shira. I promise I'll pay you back."

"No worries, I understand."

Boy, did I ever.

"So, um...where would you like to go?"

"Wherever you like, Micah."

Let's just get this over with. Fast.

After a short stop at the gas station, we end up at a coffee house (how original) that was jam-packed with people and so loud with chatter, Micah fit right in. He told me to grab a table that was just opening up and he'd get us something. I tried to yell through the din at his retreating figure with what I would like, but he disappeared into the crowd that was milling around at the counter. The line is really long and they must be short-staffed tonight because it's moving at a snail's pace. I decide I better just make a quick check of my cell. I'm sure there can't be too many missed calls as I haven't been gone more than twenty minutes.

"You have seven voice messages."

Of course, all from Mom. No, wait. There's actually one *not* from my mother.

New message: "Hi, honey. Just making sure you arrived safely. Call me back." Delete.

New message: "Hey, it's Mom. You didn't text me back." Delete.

New message: "Where are you?" Delete.

New message: "Okay, now I'm getting worried." Delete.

New message: "Do I have to call 9-1-1 to get you to call me back?" Delete.

New message: "Shira, it's your Aunt Jackie. Do me a favor and call your mother...she is driving me crazy!" Save. Future ammunition.

New message: "It's your mom, again. Could you swing by the café on your way home? Your dad is craving some pomegranate juice. Oh, and not that it's important or anything, but I'm sitting here waiting for your call." Delete.

Typical. I text her that everything's okay, we are just at a coffee house. She zaps back with:

"What kind of schmendrik brings U 2 a coffee house?!?"

She's right. If Micah were a little more in tune with something other than himself, maybe he would have put a little more effort into planning a date that would be of interest to his date. Look, I make coffee all day, he knows that. Who wants to spend an evening away from work in a place that you spend all day in? By the end of the day, I'm sick of the smell of coffee, the noise of the place, and the frenetic quality that can sometimes max you out. I mean, I love my job and it's really fun working with my parents, but sometimes I just need a break. I guess tonight won't be one of those nights. I gather Micah didn't hear my request through the noise because he returned with two house coffees and nothing else. I guess I'll get my dinner back at the café; my mom can grill me something while she grills me.

He sat down and I wondered how on earth I was going to strike up a conversation with him; I knew we didn't have much in common. He was only one year younger than I but the way he interacted in the real world reminded me of a two-year-old in the throes of a temper tantrum. I mean, I guess we could talk about the Vikings or even the Dodgers, but I didn't think he was much into sports. I had nothing to fear because after his first sip of coffee, he immediately launched into a running diatribe of astronomical proportions. I guess I must be old-fashioned because I believe that there are still a few subjects that one does not raise in polite conversation, especially on a first date. Religion, obviously. Politics, no duh. Sex, totally taboo. War, the death penalty, gun control, abortion. You name it, he brought it up. Repeatedly. Circuitously. Ad nauseum. The default mode that most people have in social settings is usually slightly reserved until you sound someone out, figure out where they are coming from, and then decide where and how far you can go with them. Micah seemed to have his internal editor permanently set in the 'off' position. I don't know why he's never at synagogue. His fervor would fit right in with those who insert politics into the conversations heard during services. Now, I don't particularly care to mix politics and religion. One or the other is fine by me but no double-dipping, please. I go to synagogue to worship G-d and commune with my fellow worshippers, not to discuss who's going to be our next president. Hey, I know it happens; I just wish it didn't. My Gentile friends feel the same way. They get peeved when politics are preached from the pulpit and my opinion concurs: it's just as bad lambasting from the Bimah. But Micah would love it and see it as a challenge and an opportunity to take center stage.

I sadly understood that I couldn't even talk to him; he hadn't changed much since our college days. His knee-jerk reaction was just as involuntary as ever. You know how in a conversation, there is a give and take. You speak for a while and then you pause to let the other person have a go. Like we learn in Kindergarten: you take a turn, then it's my turn, then it's your turn again, etc. This guy must have been absent that day. I could not, for the life of me, get a word in edgewise. I must admit, I did admire the fact that he had totally mastered the fine art of the filibuster. But that is really no fun to be around. He might draw breath for a nano-second before building up steam for his next outburst...ah-ha you think... here is my chance. Slam! I maybe got three words out before he was steamrollering right over me again. Even when I did try to respond with an actual fact from a good, reliable source, he was not interested. Or, if he did pause to listen to the words coming out of my mouth, he really didn't want to hear them anyway. He's the product of this great and terrible machine I thought, spoon-fed since infancy and from all quarters. It's still propaganda if you are told to hug every tree and not at least put some of them to their good use. Just because you agree with the principle doesn't mean it's not propaganda.

"Shira, you just don't know the real truth, you are not listening to the right people for your information, blah, blah, blah."

Like I'm some sort of congenital idiot, swallowing the wrong doctrine because it's not his doctrine. Like I'm evil for having an opinion of my own. Why should I have to apologize for living? I'm not the one floating down a river in Egypt. Why is it if he agrees with it, it's a fact, but if you disagree with it, your facts are just opinions, you are so opinionated? I had to keep reminding myself he was a lifer; he had never left academia, never removed himself from his comfort zone. He was still a student, hanging on to his college days, trying to relive his youth, getting endless degrees in programs of little use and even lesser value in the workforce. Perfectly content to just float along with his fellow passengers aboard an exclusive vessel aptly named 'The H.M.S. Intelligentsia', AKA the "I'm smarter than you are and let me tell you why" ship. Standing on the deck of this massive, floating, heavily laden ocean liner, he and his comrades were cruising along the calm, undisturbed waters of denial, completely oblivious to the fact that they had been sucking down their fruit-punch ideologies since babyhood. It is a place where the same, tired, dried-up old rhetoric flows only like so much dreck. A zone where he never had to tax himself with an independent thought, nothing contrary was ever presented to him, every passenger aboard thought like he did and spoke the same language. I mean, what's the point or challenge of a good, honest, fair, impartial debate if you are just preaching to the choir? They are just going to agree with you on every issue, every time. Sing the same lyrics to the same melody. Is that reality? Personally, I think it's a waste of oxygen.

Does the boat ever dock? Will it make port and tie up its mooring lines upon the opposite bank? Would he dare disembark and walk upon the unknown shore, curl his toes in the sand, having risen like Viola from the foam to discover a new country? I think not. He will remain perfectly satisfied with his addiction to the monotonous buffet: chewing up, spitting out, regurgitating the same slogans ad infinitum, never really digesting but spewing forth dried up clichés in unwieldy chunks.

We left the coffee house after about forty minutes. The noise had begun to give me a wicked headache which actually worked to my advantage of trying to end the evening early. As we walked back to where he had parked, I began to notice the people coming towards us. From my perspective it looked like they could not get away fast enough.

They would see us coming down the sidewalk: the woman trying to shrink into the pavement, the man, not only flapping his gums but his arms as well, becoming shrill, hyperventilating while trying to prove his point, his words supercharged, not with facts, but rather with emotion. It was as if an increase in volume, volubility, and vitriol elevated the veracity of his argument. If pedestrians weren't fast enough to sidestep us or cross over to the other side of the street, he just barreled right through them gesticulating wildly. Basically, it was like being an invited guest (more like captive prisoner) for the entire evening on his favorite talk radio show:

"Hi, My Name is Micah, and It's All About ME."

Everyone was staring. And I mean everyone. Well, not those two. That man standing by his open car door didn't even look up from the woman whose face he was all into, arguing about a parking space on the street.

"Look, if you just pull back a little ma'am, then I can reverse a bit and get my front bumper out of the red zone."

"Look, buddy. If I pull back any farther, then I'm too close to the car behind me and I'm pinned in between the both of you."

"Look, lady...I just need six more inches."

"That's what they all say."

Wow. That went over really well with the guy. The look he gave her could have melted titanium. I tried to stifle a snicker but failed. Micah just kept blathering on, oblivious to his surroundings and the fact that my interest had been waning for quite some time. It was incredibly fatiguing. What bothers me now in retrospect was that I was actually looking forward to getting out of the café office, having a nice dinner, and reconnecting, catching up on old times. What a huge disappointment! The evening for me essentially sucked; it was a complete disaster. I felt like I had been through the wringer, chewed up, and spat out on the ground.

Even more than that, I was saddened by his utter lack of respect for me as his longtime friend. But what I found most disturbing, in an even more basic sense however, was his complete lack of consideration for me as a woman. That's not sexist; I would totally respect a man who was talking to me. He had absolutely no sense of decorum. Now, I am not a prude and I don't know about you, but my mama raised me right. She taught me to never interrupt someone who was speaking unless my pants were on fire. Well, his pants were certainly on fire about something, but after almost an hour, I had completely tuned him out and stopped listening.

Now I know why he's unmarried, has few friends, and still lives in his parents' basement. It's just too physically and emotionally exhausting to be near him for more than about five minutes. He's like some emotional vampire who sucks the life out of you, draining your energy and the will to fight back. As he continued to blather on, I wonder why he is still unloading on me. He must notice that I am no longer even politely listening. He's not cognizant of anything other than the sound of his own voice. I have to shout to be heard.

"Micah...MICAH!"

"Oh. Yes, Shira?"

"Listen, I don't mean to spoil your evening, but I think I feel a migraine coming on. Must have been all the noise in the coffee shop. You don't mind if we end a little early, do you? I have an opening shift tomorrow at work."

"Oh. Sure, Shira. I understand."

I could tell he was disappointed but I didn't think I could politely suffer through any more discomfort a moment longer. We stood there for a minute, in an uncomfortable silence, as if he didn't really know how to proceed.

"Uh, Micah...could you take me back home now? My mom texted that she needs me to get something for my dad."

"No problem."

We drive back in silence but I can tell that he was itching to ask me something, probably for another date. I need to quash that and fast. As we pulled up to the café, I realized I just had to say it.

"Micah, I hope you won't take this the wrong way but, uh, I'm just really busy at the café now and I really don't have a lot of time for extra activities, you know, like a social life...like dating."

"Okay."

I don't think I'm getting through to him.

"You know, it's not you, you are a great guy but...it's me."

Oh, crap! I can't believe I'm actually using that line, those exact words that are so clichéd and everyone hates to hear because they sound so false. I shouldn't be so cruel, it's not like it's his fault or anything. He can't help being who he is.

Hey, I know what he needs...oy, do I sound like my matchmaking mother, or what? What he really needs is someone who thinks like he does or at least, if she doesn't, she should have the patience of a saint to be able to put up with his self-absorbed, egocentric oratory. I should ask Mom for help on this one. Maybe she knows of someone who needs a cause or is on a rescue mission. Somebody to take him outside himself, get him interested in other, more important issues. Hook him on a new hobby, show him that happiness is possible and you can find peace of mind. That there really is a way to actually save something that is infinitely more important than a tree or a cow. I mean, I love my dog but she's not getting a driver's license. Micah needs a nice Jewish girl (not me...Hashem forbid) to let him know that there is a better community of people out there who are actually waiting for him, to welcome him back into the fold.

Well, for him it would really be like coming home for the first time.

IN VINO VERITAS, IN AQUA SANITAS, IN SANGUIS VITA

2017 AD
Tel Aviv

No, I am not in my cups. Do not mistake the aforementioned Jino with a Vino: a vampire in name only. Vinos look like a vampire, act like a vampire, have mad skills like a vampire, but do not keep kashrut (what we immortals refer to as vashrut). There is nothing kosher about them. In other words, they do not *eat* like a vampire.

News flash: we're carnivores.

Hey, we're vampires; we don't have to be politically correct. Yeah, we are strong. Yeah, we can run fast. But so can your average, run-of-the-mill, fresh-off-the-factory-floor vampire. *We're* not so much impressed by *those* gifts. Those gifts are a given. *Our* gifts are divinely bestowed. Na-na-na-na-na. We were intelligently designed by our Creator and we have a *real* job. Since we are all about our history, we are the sum total of our history. Ergo, our gift is *making* history. Via time-travelling. But even we are not infallible. It's always a crapshoot, a spin of the wheel, fortune's hand. Success is elusive; you try and grab it but sometimes you fail. One might say in this we are both blessed and cursed.

HEY, WE'RE THE GOOD GUYS

2017 AD
Tel Aviv

Got a cellular phone? Thank a Jew. Can you read this even through your astigmatism? Thank a Jew. Low on funds for a 15th century jaunt across the big water to discover a New World? Thank a Jew. You get the picture.

I don't understand why we are so much maligned. Every day we get an awful lot of bad press because you Gentiles have such short memories. Jeez Louise, show a little gratitude, for Pete's sake.

Do you own any single piece of technocrap whatsoever that houses a microchip/operating system/microprocessor? Thank a Jew. Done research for school/work/leisure using a popular search engine? Thank a Jew. Into sci-fi and escape with videotape/lasers/virtual reality? Thank a Jew. Garnered that plum job offer you've been dying for via voicemail? Thank a Jew. Communicate with your kids in college 2,000 miles away with instant messaging? Thank a Jew. Kept in touch with your gazillion friends on the planet via a social network? Thank a Jew. Does the electricity you need for all that technocrap come from the Mojave sun? Thank a Jew.

Survive a hospital stay because your meds were administered accurately by a computerized system that effectively eliminated human error? Thank a Jew. Swallowed a camera pill which uncovered that yes indeed, you are not a hypochondriac, you really *do* have an ulcer? Thank a Jew. Received a radiation free, fully computerized breast cancer diagnostic? Thank a Jew. Hashem forbid you ever need a defibrillator, but a thank a Jew anyway. Still alive and kicking because you have a neat little pacemaker resting alongside your ticker? Thank a Jew. Know your blood type? Thank a Jew. Expertly treated for TB? Thank a Jew. Does your surgeon know how to safely remove your diseased appendix? Thank a Jew. Didn't get knocked up because you were using contraceptives? Thank a Jew. Acne cleared up? Thank a Jew.

Are your jeans blue? Thank a Jew. Got your girlie on and are wearing lipstick? Thank a Jew. Write your love-notes with a ballpoint pen? Thank a Jew. Ever take a photograph of your honey with a camera that spat out the picture instantly? Thank a Jew. Too lazy to get up and change the channel of your TV? Thank a Jew. Been mesmerized in a movie theater? Watched the Oscars? Specifically thank a European Jew.

Like to laugh? Remember listening to music on vinyl? Appreciate art? Thank loads of Jews because the list of entertainers who have made our sometimes boring lives more aesthetically pleasing, enjoyable, and just plain fun is way too long to mention here. If you want, you can use that aforementioned popular search engine to find a long list of Jewish accomplishments and contributions in every field imaginable in the United States and Israel and not just in the arts. The major fields of science, mathematics, philosophy, literature, psychology, law, and politics have all been influenced. C'mon, don't make me do all the work. You can at least put forth a little effort for your own education.

Indebted to the fact that you live in the greatest Judeo-Christian society that ever will be which practices English law? Look it up if you don't know what English law is. Life easier because you have a bank account? Thank a Jew. My all-time favorite...like to shop at department stores? Thank a whole bunch of 'em.

Love American chocolate? Thank a Jew. Gone fishin' with a pocket-sized pole? Thank a Jew. Does your sweet tooth appreciate the fact that you know what $C_6H_{12}O_6$ is? Thank a Jew. Never got polio *and* don't like needles? Thank two Jews.

Stop complaining. Sheesh, and I thought we had cornered the market on whining. Start acknowledging all the wonderful, life-extending, time-saving, enhancing and enlightening inventions and discoveries made by the Jews on the planet that you happen to share with them. Put on your big girl panties and just deal with it. What do I have to do, manufacture a bumper sticker: 'Have you hugged a Jew today?' Or maybe I should compose some beatific little ditty:

> Thank, thank a Jew,
> You know you ought to.
> For all that we do.
> Indeed, thank a Jew.
> Whoa-oh. Thank a Jew.
> Yeah! Thank a Jew.

...brought to you by Jews. We're everywhere; get used to it.

FALL INTO THE REVERSE GAP

1 September, 2010 AD
Westport

So...my parents watch CNN, I watch Fox News. Enough said. Talk about a generation gap. Needless to say, there is a wide chasm between their ideologies and mine. I'm conservative, they are liberal. Now, don't get me wrong, I completely understand why. I get the historical significance of why my parents vote the way they do. Jews embraced the freedoms and ideals afforded them in this new country that were denied to them in the old. My parents are liberal because their parents were liberal, their parents were liberal...and so on, and so on, just like that '70s shampoo commercial. I follow the politics and the history. But the concept of schlepping in your family's political footsteps just because that's the way we've always done it really doesn't work for me today. If it doesn't jibe with your sense of how the world operates, kowtowing to familial pressure is just wrong on so many levels. At least I've kept my sense of humor about our differences. If you can't laugh at yourself, at whom are you going to laugh? I'd laugh at my politicians, but they don't make me want to laugh, they make me want to cry (or throw something). I know, I know. Change is good. Dollars are better.

For example, my mother was completely crushed and morally chagrined when I (oy!) became a member of the NRA. Now, I'm no wallflower and I've never been clingy. Hide behind? There ain't no behind. G-d's got my back and you'll be staring down the twin barrels of what I'm holding up front. It's you that had better hide. I stand firm. I am a firm proponent of the three F's: family, faith, and firearms. I regularly keep my trigger finger in readiness at our local shooting range. My mother has an absolute conniption every time I suit up for target practice. We are all sitting at the kitchen table one morning after breakfast when she starts up. Again.

"Such a daughter!" she wails. "What will the neighbors think?"

"Ma, I think they will be eternally grateful when I pop some intruder breaking into their house. Besides, the police will thank me."

"Why?"

"Paperwork for a dead perp is easier to process."

"Ezra...speak to your daughter, knock some sense into her. To think I have this meshuggene child who runs around playing shooting games. Oy veh's mir."

Ma leaves the room abruptly and races upstairs. No doubt she is dialing my Aunt Jackie this very moment to kvetch about my strange behavior. My dad, peacemaker that he has always been between us, is used to me being fiercely independent and understands me very well, sometimes better than I understand myself. He still gives me the Spiel as I check my weapon of choice, a Glock.

"Now, Shira. I know you feel strongly about this. Personally, I don't mind if it may someday prevent a break-in here or at the restaurant. Your mother however, needs a little reassurance. Let me go talk to her. Just be careful, gell?"

I assure him that I will be very careful and that I'm getting together with some of my friends from synagogue. See Mom? I'm not the only one.

I meet my girlfriends at the range. Naturally, I got Jess and TJ hooked on firearms long ago. Jess is a Glock-woman like me but TJ prefers the big guns. Her weapon of choice is a .44 Magnum revolver with an 8-inch barrel, á la Dirty Harry. I still remember the first time the three of us walked into the place. We must have sat in my car in the parking lot for a good twenty minutes before we struck up enough courage to actually enter the facility. It took a lot of convincing on my part that it was the right idea. I don't know what we were so apprehensive about anyway. But TJ wasn't at all sure her mom would approve.

"Shira, are you sure this is a good idea?"

"It will be okay, guys. We need to learn how to defend ourselves."

Jess chimes in.

"Couldn't we just take a self-defense class or something? They offer those at the community center, right?"

I've heard this one before, so I'm prepared.

"Self-defense classes are great Jess, if somebody grabs you. But what good are those moves if your attacker draws a weapon? No matter how quickly you react, you are not faster than a bullet."

Jess considers this for a moment but makes one last-ditch effort.

"Our moms are going to freak! Besides, we don't know anything about guns. I've never even handled one."

"Look guys, that's the whole point. I've never handled one either. I'm just as much of a greenhorn as you are, but I'll be right there with you the whole time. I know we can do this if we stick together. What do you say?"

"Umm...."

"Well...."

"Ladies, are we brave enough to dance with the big boys and their big guns?"

This always does the trick with Jess and TJ. I call it my 'Annie Get your Gun' strategy. Neither of them can stand to sit out on any sort of competition, especially when guys are involved. Their theme song regarding members of the opposite sex is 'Anything you can do, I can do better.' My words work like a charm, every time.

"Alright ladies, let's do it."

It seems laughable, now that we have a few years of practice under our belts but that first day was pretty nerve-wracking. The instructors were fairly patient with us but were probably unnerved the first time TJ screamed when her gun went off. It took forever and a lot of coaxing to get Jess to even touch her weapon. She just stood and stared at it for the longest time; you would have thought we were asking her to pick up a cobra.

So there we were, goggles and headphones on, assuming the position, each in our own individual cinder block stall, shrieking ridiculously every time the gun went bang and completely missing the paper target. Then we just started laughing. We sure were making a lot of noise when TJ let out a whoop that she had hit the outermost ring. After that, it was an all-out war between the three of us. Jess and I didn't make too bad a showing for our first attempt either. At least we all had made some contact with the paper. These days we have a running competition to see who can hit the most number of bull's-eyes in the shortest time.

After that first session, we needed to wind down at our favorite ice cream parlor. Over triple-fudge sundaes, we all looked at each other and grinned. For a few minutes, all we could do was dig in. At first, we didn't know what to say but then Jess broke the silence.

"Oh, man. That was awesome! What did you think TJ?"

"Wicked sweet! I had no idea how powerful I would feel. Was it the same way for you, Shira?"

"It was unbelievable! Holding that piece of metal in my hands made me feel so strong. Now I know why guys like them so much. I can't believe we were so chicken at first."

Both my friends laugh but then Jess frowns.

"How are we ever going to tell our parents? My dad will never let me go back once he finds out. He is so totally against guns."

I tell her she's not alone.

"My folks are too. Our politics are so different. You should have seen their faces when the ballot packet came to our house after I turned eighteen. They both cringed when they saw Republican on the voter registration card."

TJ makes a face at this.

"My dad went through the roof when he saw mine. We had this big argument about how I betrayed both his family and my mom's."

"Say, TJ. I've been meaning to ask you. How come your dad hasn't converted yet?"

"Your guess is as good as mine, Shira. I just think he doesn't want to give up Kwanzaa."

"He doesn't have to give it up. You could do both, you know."

"I don't think that would go over too well with my mom. She's very particular about how we celebrate Hanukkah."

"What if you mix it up a little, like Kwanzukkah?"

"Ha! That's funny. I don't know how they'll take it. They never agree between themselves let alone anything to do with me. We argue about everything. We are so different."

It's true, I thought to myself. All of my friends from synagogue have said the same things to me about their relationships with their parents. There's this huge culture clash going on between the old guard and the young turks. Young adults everywhere are defecting in droves from the traditions of their parents' political beliefs. But it's an absolute reversal of what happened between the youth and their parents almost fifty years ago. In the 60s, young people rejected everything for which their elders stood. Politics, way of life, and most assuredly morals were tossed out the window. It's all the fault of all those hippies: free love, if it feels good do it, if it makes you feel bad, deny it–talk about cognitive dissonance. My job is much harder today because they screwed it up for the rest of us G-d loving, gun-toting, patriotic Americans who LOVE their country and will fight to defend it from anyone, without or within. Hashem bless the fighters everywhere who are kickin' ass to save mine.

C'mon, man. Can't you at least be grateful and loyal to the government that actually let your people in? If you don't like the country you live in, there's the door and don't let it hit you in the tuchus on the way out. Hey, I'll even help you pack.

BECAUSE JEWS ARE SEXY, TOO

2017 AD
Tel Aviv

Galen was on my case again about my work. The two of us had just
returned from some other 'when' (actually right here in Tel Aviv but
the 19th century-not permitted to be more specific at this time and Mr.
Clemens promised to keep it on the down-low). We generally need
some wind-down time after a mission and the jump itself is pretty hairy.
It takes a lot out of you physically as well as emotionally. Galen always
retreats to his garden not only to commune with his belladonna but to
also inspect what Vietor has murdered in his absence. I don't know
why he always asks him to care for his plants while he's away. Galen
understands well enough not to mess with the man cave. Vietor raises
the roof if anyone so much as touches his power tools. But Galen
certainly knows from experience that Vietor is an absolute schlub
when it comes to living things. I believe it's a little passive/aggressive
psychodrama that he secretly likes to play out and he enjoys setting
himself up to become indignant upon his return. Vietor just stands there
in the garden, shoots me a withering glance, Galen a truculent one, and
braces himself against the storm. He knows it's useless to protest or try
to defend himself from the onslaught. It's best to not even enter the
fray; Galen is a master swordsman in the art of the verbal skirmish and
once his rapier-like wit is engaged, he can slay his opponent with one
well-timed jab. His tirades are legendary and his crackling raillery is full
of sardonic insults that go right over Vietor's head (and everyone else's).
But sure enough, you will be giving yourself a Treppverter face palm
later on. Sometimes you finally get it that afternoon. But for most of

us it usually takes longer, like the next day while you are at a crowded intersection or in the reference section of the library. Whap! I was just insulted. Yesterday. You blush, your forehead now also red and really stinging as you realize that everyone has stopped what they are doing and staring at you like you forgot to take your meds this morning. After some odd looks, every human around you takes a few steps backwards, pulling their toddlers behind them as they beat a hasty retreat to the nearest exit. Even by his absence, Galen has a tendency to impact your day.

We all tend to dissolve into the shadows when he is on the warpath. After a mission, I like to completely wrap myself up in my private work and relax. No such luck on this occasion. Galen seeks me out in my office to complain that not one but two of his deadly nightshade plants have withered away at the hand of Vietor. I am trying to concentrate and am only half listening.

"Look Galen, I just want to write right now."

He is completely oblivious to the fact that I don't even look up from my work as I answer him.

"But, Shira. The man vexes me so, he is absolutely impossible. I do not know whether he is subliterate or preverbal but I cannot get him to explain to me what happened to my plants."

Pushing myself back in my chair away from the desk, I know that unless I calm him down, I'm never going to make a start. It doesn't matter to him that I'm in flow right now.

"Galen, you know we all have our strong suits. Vietor's strengths lie in his mechanical ability and technological expertise. I praise Hashem we don't have to rely on you for repairs."

"But Shira...."

As he continues to vent spleen, he casts his eye upon the mêlée of papers scattered haphazardly (well, I know where everything is) on my desk. Before I can stop him, he picks up a page from the top of an untidy stack and begins to silently read, a deep frown forming on his face.

"You are not still working on an exposé of us are you?"

"You have to ask?"

"Shira, why do you always answer a question with a question?"

"How can I help it?"

"Shira!"

"Why wouldn't I? I told you I was."

"But why us? Why now, why this story?"

At this point, Zippy makes her way into my office, completely disheveled and really looking like something even a cat wouldn't drag indoors. She's more than likely been out screwing humans again. She deposits herself in a heap upon the large Persian carpet near my desk and completely ignores us.

"Look, Galen. Don't you think it's a palpable presence by its glaring sin?"

"What sin?"

"The sin of omission."

"What omission?"

"Jewish vampires."

"Shira, who but us will read it?"

"My point exactly. Aren't you aware that there is a ready-made fan base of almost 14 million out there who are starved for vampire literature that speaks to them? It can't be completely outside the realm of possibility that I may have struck a rich vein, can it?"

Galen is unconvinced and never easy to persuade. I look down at Zippy, hoping she may concur with my argument and give me some moral support. She is still stretched out on the floor lying on her stomach, propped up on her elbows, swinging her feet in the air just like a teenager and wholly engrossed in the latest Paris Elle.

"Zippy, don't you think we are grossly underrepresented in the vampire literature out there today?"

Silence.

"Zippy."

Nothing.

"Zippy, are you ready to receive?"

"Comment? Hey, I just had the wildest time with this guy from Jerusalem. Mille tonnerres, was he ever hot! He had this weird way of...uh, never mind. I am going to go take a rinse-off. Would you care to join me?"

She rises from the floor, yawns and stretches luxuriously like some pampered cat and pads off for the master bath. Hopeless. Zippy is an utter hedonist and doesn't care two figs for any hot-button issues that don't involve the fashion world. Her most recent cause célèbre was whether or not orange was the new pink. I turn back to Galen who has continued to read my papers. He is obviously discomfited. Taking a deep breath, I try to be obliging and allay his concerns.

"Galen, I know you. I see that you are always wrestling with G-d. Well, you are not the only one. I want to question, investigate, and discover the nature and the will of Hashem just as much as you do. This work helps me do that. You know as well as I do that modern vampire literature has become so completely secularized. I think it's about time someone put G-d back into the eternal conflict between good and evil. He's been missing for so long from that genre which is chock-a-block full of evil characters, full of sin, full of all the malevolence in the world. You can't have one without the other. Hashem must be present to explain our story or we wouldn't have a story."

"Shira, be serious. No one today even believes that evil exists. Humans in this century are way too compassionate. Too compassionate for their own good. Consider the proponents of the current ideology that even bad guys have freedom of speech."

"I know they do, but a strong moral compass cannot coexist alongside a tolerance of evil. They must remain mutually exclusive. Let me ask you something. If you were human again, with whom would you rather have dinner, Satan or a vampire?"

Galen grins and his eyes flash. He loves these types of philosophical mind games. I can almost hear the cogs and wheels clicking as he ponders my question.

"That is a most intriguing dilemma. I would need time to formulate my argument."

"Don't spend too much time debating it. The answer should come easily. I know what I would do. If I were human again, without hesitation I would sup with Satan."

"Why would you choose him?"

"Because I can defeat him. I can defeat any circumstance or trial that Satan may use in his effort to defeat me. The strength of the conviction of my faith will vanquish him. There's nothing a human can do to overcome a vampire. You know that, Galen."

"What you are planning on exposing is wholly subversive."

"Yeah, well my definition is way better than Webster's. Sub-verse-ive: adj.-the act of undermining (subverting) the dominant paradigm but with a great sense of literary style."

"Do not you think it will just anger a certain type of human?"

"Well, then I must be doing something right if enough people are getting pissed off. Don't you perceive that the sleeper has awakened? We have remained silent for far too long. Silence is no longer golden. That's what I love about my country. Just as bad guys have freedom of speech, so do I. I am free to express my opinions and ideas, even if they do contravene current popular thought. I can be opinionated even as a vampire. We have rights, too."

He glances down again at the manuscript sheet.

"But, Shira. All those Yiddish words and what is this here...German? How will your readers even understand what you are trying to convey?"

I refuse to be swayed by his attempt to vitiate my argument.

"Galen, get with the times. We are in the 21ˢᵗ century. Take a look around you the next time you are in a public place full of humans. Not a single one is not connected at *all* times, by a very short umbilical, to their particular piece of technocrap of choice 24-7-365. With an effortless thumb tap, the universe via the appropriate search engine is literally clutched in the palm of their hands. Hashem forbid they walk into an actual library and open up an actual dictionary in (gasp!) book form. Now, all they have to do is open that palm."

He is still not convinced that this venture is a good idea. He purses his lips ever so delicately (which I actually find quite endearing) and furrows his brow as he places the paper back onto the stack.

"But why Jews, Shira?"

"Just look at it this way, Galen. And I know you'll appreciate its pithy quality. In a nutshell: because Jews are sexy, too."

Footnote to 2017 AD, Tel Aviv

Well, that's enough about the four of us. How we met as individuals and formed a collective is the stuff of legend in our society. We all did great things in the past and hope to continue to be among the fighters in the future. Most of us keep silent about our exploits, though. I wouldn't want to share the details of my colleagues' work without their permission. See Galen, I do have some common sense and the utmost respect for your privacy. But since Vietor and I share a history, albeit a rather brief moment in time, he has ever so graciously green-lit a snapshot of our first encounter.

But you know, three can keep a secret if two are dead (thanks, Ben). Although, since we are already dead, how does that work?

THEY TRIED TO DESTROY US,
WE WON, LET'S EAT!

2017 AD
Tel Aviv

The Festival of Lights. Another shining example which illuminates our illustrious history and shows how we can kick ass if we put our minds to it.

Ah, the Maccabean revolt. Just goes to show you that "nobody steps on a church in my town." Well, actually a temple. *The* Temple. See, there was this ruler of the Seleucid Empire in 175 BC. If you are lost already you can:

1-get out your Apocrypha, see 1 Maccabees, or

2-if you are still totally confused, you can Google it.

Jiminy Crickets! Don't they teach Jewish history in public schools?

After Alexander the Great's death, his vast empire was broken up and divided among three of his generals. The Ptolemies eventually acquired Egypt, Judea came under the control of the Seleucid Greeks, and in Asia Minor, the Kingdom of Pergamon was in power.

Anyway, there was a movement to 'Just Say No' to the process of Hellenization-thanks ever so much Alexander. This ruler, Antiochus IV, was a complete dictator and you might say very anti-Jewish on religious matters. Basically, he was a corrupt politician with an "I've got the power now and let's make wide-sweeping changes and I don't care if I completely subvert the dominant paradigm that actually works for the majority of the populace" kind of guy. There was conflict, corruption, assassination, and rioting in the streets over the appointment of various and sundry High Priests. Antiochus desecrated the Temple, attacked Jerusalem, and took women and children captive. Then he began a policy of forcing Jews to adopt Hellenistic practices. He tried (emphasis on the tried) to accomplish this by banning all forms of Jewish religious customs and according to Galen, putting up those "damned Greek idols" in the Temple. Some modern day scholars see the impetus for the revolt and ensuing fracas as a civil war between traditional and reform aspects of Judaism. Other academics are proponents of the idea that the initial rebellion and resulting turmoil, while religious initially, gradually shifted into a war of nationalism and a quest for liberation. Even the authors of the First and Second Books of the Maccabees are not in harmony. We got the job done; who cares why.

One family in particular decided enough was enough and took Antiochus to task. Mattathias initiated the revolt by refusing to worship Greek gods and his son Judah finished it by hammering the Seleucid dynasty with guerilla warfare. Victory! They nabbed the Temple back from those heathens and gave it a good scrubbing down with a ritual cleansing.

The festival of Hanukkah is a celebration of the rededication of the Temple. After the victory, the only uncorrupted oil to be found for the Menorah was one day's worth in a small jug. The miracle of the oil was that it lasted eight days! That's why we burn the candles for eight nights.

For the uninformed no, Hanukkah is not a religious holiday. Neither is it the Jewish complement to Christmas (duh!) although they usually both happen in December. The most wonderful part is that we get eight days to celebrate, enjoy great food, even greater company, and receive gifts (ha-ha, we get Hanukkah Gelt and you don't) and you only get one day.

So you see, when a Gentile asks you why there is always so much food at every Jewish celebration you can give them an informed answer: we are just so dad-blasted happy to be alive, what better way to celebrate our victory than with a feast (because you never know when the next famine will hit).

Essentially, Hanukkah celebrates a military victory (read kicking butt) to save our Temple. Just imagine how powerful you would feel, fighting to save your house of worship from the heathens, the sun glinting upon your blade as you raise your arm, brandishing your weapon high above your head. What a spectacle to witness the dust, the battle cries, the crunch of gravel under your sandal as you leap forward out into the fray, conquering the enemy and carrying the day (thanks, Pippin).

Ah, would that I could have stood alongside Judah Maccabee, wielding a sword. Wait, I did do that.

5 December, 2010 AD
Westport

"But Ma, it's for little kids...."

My mother and I are going at it hammer and tongs as usual. She is trying to persuade me that I need to go to the Hanukkah celebration at our local shopping mall again this year. I'm trying to convince her that I don't. Don't get me wrong, it's a lovely ceremony. All the synagogues from the tri-county area are represented and there is an abundance of food and fun: latkes-yum, games, crafts, musical performances, and it never fails to draw a large crowd of both Jews and Gentiles alike. There is always plenty of room as the pavilion is open to the night sky: it is this great half-moon shaped, airy space with a fountain and decorated with mosaic tiles. The dénouement is the lighting of the gigantic steel Menorah (electric bulbs-thank you very much).

The only reason I hesitate to go tonight is that I've gone every year throughout my entire life. At first it was incredibly fun, running around the pavilion, meeting my friends from Hebrew school, singing in the youth choir, stuffing my face full of latkes, and generally acting like a kid and being crazy. The older I got, the crafts didn't hold so much sway for me, but I still was happy to meet with my girlfriends and talk about the more important issues of the day: boys, clothes, boys, music, and...boys.

As an adult, it was fun for a while to watch my cousins' children delight in those moments for the first time. I was right there at the craft table with them, helping them to make a paper dreidel, putting colored sand on the peel and stick Menorah card, and heel-to-toe alongside them as we tried to see how many latkes we could snag before they were all gone.

I began to notice however, that my mother's attitude towards this event changed the older I became. It was no longer just a place to experience with my friends and relatives but rather a venue for husband-hunting. Now it became an annual ordeal of showing Shira off to her best advantage because of all the 'fresh meat' on display there from all of the other synagogues. It sounds harsh I know, but my mother became increasingly concerned as the years went by and I was not even close to being engaged. I kept telling her that I wasn't worried, she shouldn't worry. Absolutely the wrong thing to say to your Jewish mother. Jewish mothers are genetically pre-programmed to worry; it's in their DNA; it is something over which they have no control.

"Mom, do I really have to go tonight?"

"Shira, of course you do. We go every year."

Precisely my point.

"That's just it, Ma. It's the same every year, the same people, the same schmoozing with the other congregations, the same everything."

"Now, Shira."

Here we go.

"You know how important it is to all of the family that you attend. All of your cousins will be there with their children."

Another dig.

"Your father and I couldn't possibly attend this event without you. What would everyone say? They'd ask if you were sick or something. Then I'd have to make some excuse for you and...well, you wouldn't want me to lie for you now, would you?"

Oy! I hate it when she uses that tactic!

"Of course I don't want you to lie for me, Mom. But it's kinda boring now and I feel like I'm too old for it."

Uproar.

"Too old for Hanukkah?? Too old to be seen with your parents? Or too embarrassed? Well, which is it young lady?"

I sense defeat looming in the distance, smothered with resignation and garnished with big gobs of guilt. My mother adds the finishing embellishment and I'm sunk.

"Shira, honey. I just want you to be happy. I'm looking out for you and trying to help you. You know that Debbie always appreciates your willingness to get the youth choir rounded up behind the stage and ready to sing."

I can tell from the expression on her face that she is holding back a pertinent piece of information and...here it comes.

"Besides, I happened to hear that Rabbi's cousin, Moshe is visiting from Jerusalem and is looking forward to meeting you. But of course, if you'd rather not go this year, I suppose I could think of *something* to say to Rabbi."

My dad just gives me that look that says 'let it go' and chimes in with his usual:

"Make your mother happy, Shira."

I know when I'm licked and decide it's better to just leave the room before I say something I may regret. I'm still pretty miffed, however and stomp up the stairs to my room to show it.

Needless to say, here we all are at the pavilion, thirty minutes too early as usual. Naturally, without delay I was introduced to the aforementioned Moshe, who seems rather shy and introverted upon first inspection. Not at all like Avram. Avram had presence; you couldn't take your eyes off of him. Wow, I haven't thought of him for a while. Not since Friday night Shabbat after we met in the parking lot. Not since he left me standing during the L'cha Dodi at synagogue two months ago.

WHAT'S PHYSICS GOT TO DO WITH IT?

2017 AD
Tel Aviv

There is a certain point where all science fiction is credible, where future technology presented is absolutely plausible. Just look at the Star Trek Original Series flip-up communicators...now we have cell phones. Every senior officer on The Next Generation had a desktop computer...even us NCOs can get a laptop these days. All rather quotidian.

But then you come to the point in the presentation where what is described or acted upon crosses the line of the possible to the improbable (remembering that nothing is impossible). There is that exponential jump that is made and bang! You have to suspend your disbelief. But you do it because the acting is superb, the sets/costumes/special effects are nonpareil, and the concept is attractive and enticing, luring you into the world. The suspension of disbelief is paramount to any well-written and researched science fiction. That's why we like it. But what it does do is attempt to stick a finger in G-d's eye. This is where the physicists enter the picture.

Just like Westport exists if you are not there, so too does the past exist, even if you are not there. The fabric of the universe is malleable, like some gigantic cosmic blanket you can shake out, causing it to ripple with waves. There are a multitude of possible outcomes, based solely upon your observations.

But what if all that were unnecessary? What if one doesn't need all those patterns of ones and zeros to be involved in the process? There's nothing the matter. There's nothing exotic about it. What if Hashem Himself had the mother of all wormholes, divinely shortening the distance from Point A to Point B and it was readily available to those who never felt it necessary to suspend their disbelief? What if you didn't have to involve the science of physics at all? What if a change that was actually bigger than science were effected? You know, like that great bumper sticker: 'Big Bang Theory? Yeah, G-d spoke and BANG! It happened.' I don't have to suspend my disbelief for that. He changeth the times and the seasons. G-d needs neither particle nor device. No machinery is necessary, no binary code is required to get the program up and running to achieve His will. There is only One.

SHABBAT

1 October, 2010 AD
Westport

The music is penetrating my soul. The thrumming of the guitar and the voices raised together are pulling me stronger than ever before. I feel very light, as if there is no weight to my body. I am floating and the only thing keeping me anchored to this spot and to this moment is the grip of Avram's hand upon mine. We are sitting next to each other in synagogue, right next to my parents who have not failed to notice where he has placed his hand.

I'm still woozy after my spill in the parking lot and I'm finding it hard to keep my focus. I didn't even know services had started until well after they had begun. I keep hearing a buzzing sound and I think how rude, someone's cell phone is on vibrate and they should really turn it over to silent right now. My hand is burning; I must have scraped it pretty bad when I fell or whatever Avram put on it to clean away the dirt was really strong. He is watching me intently during services, probably to make sure I don't keel over.

With a start, I hear we are at the L'cha Dodi already, the welcoming of the Shabbat Bride into the synagogue. This has always been one of my favorite moments during services. I always feel closer to G-d and am overcome by my emotions when I hear the words and the melody of that song. It is a blessing to know that the love He has for us is akin to the love a husband has for his beloved bride. What could be more beautiful, more lasting, or more joyous?

As we stand, Rabbi asks Avram to open the synagogue doors to welcome her in. Avram turns to look at me. He is smiling as he reaches out to take my left hand. He turns it over and as his lips touch my palm, his eyes move up to meet mine. His gaze does not waver during his kiss. While still gripping my hand, he leans forward to whisper in my ear.

"Come back to me, little one."

I feel my face go hot with embarrassment and I am sure everyone in the room is staring at me, has heard what he has just said and all the tongues will surely be wagging in the Oneg room. As he makes his way through the row of chairs, my parents are looking at me. My mother's face seems ready to burst wide open in a huge grin and my dad just looks kind of sheepish. For some odd reason, I don't know where to look. Mercifully, we all turn to face the double doors and I see him standing there, his hand still on the doorknob. He never takes his eyes off of me. It's as if he is trying to claim me or capture a moment in time, a snapshot. During the entire song, I find that I am locked in his glance; I cannot look away. I see him smile, one last time before we turn around to face the Bimah once more. As we all sit down for the rest of the services, I realize that he is taking an awfully long time to return to his seat. I look over my shoulder but he is neither at the door nor walking towards the row where my parents and I are seated. My eyes do a quick scan of the entire room and I cannot find him anywhere. Where would he go? Services are not even over yet. He did mention earlier in the parking lot that he could not stay for very long but why would he leave right in the middle of worship, without even saying goodbye? For all his charm, this does not make a good impression on me. I know very little about him, even what he does for a living or when he may return. I'm now angry at myself for not listening to my mother when she asked me all those questions in the car on the drive home last night. Well, maybe he will call me tomorrow.

5 December, 2010 AD
Westport

My mind snaps back from the memory of that Friday night Shabbat two months ago as I see that the Hanukkah celebration has begun. Rabbi is on the mike up on stage, welcoming the other congregations to the event. As he introduces the last Rabbi, that's my cue to round up the youth choir and get them backstage. It takes longer than I anticipate because most of the kids are running around pell-mell in the pavilion. I do find a large bunch of them needless to say, stuffing their mouths full of latkes at the back table where the warming trays are.

"Oy, kids! Hurry up and swallow, you have to sing in a few minutes."

I hear a barely discernable chorus of "Okay, Shira" mumbled through mouthfuls of potato pancakes.

"Let's go, let's go. Follow me."

I feel like the Pied Piper leading my charges towards the backstage area. A few straggle-tags see us making our way there and join the group. I see Debbie, the choir leader back there already, counting heads.

"Oh, Shira. There you are. Thanks so much for rounding everybody up. Help me count, will you?"

We both come up with the same number and I get everyone lined up for their entrance. Debbie gives me the thumbs-up sign and I head back to my seat where my parents are already waiting for me.

"Oh, they all look so adorable. Don't they, Shira?"

She turns to my dad who has his nose glued to the evening paper.

"Just think Ezra, someday your grandchildren will be up there on stage singing."

Ouch! My dad knows way better than to respond to this barb so she turns again to me.

"Have you heard anything from that Avram fellow? I wonder why he just sort of fell off the map. And such a nice boy, too."

I find that it's better not to say anything when she gets this way, so I clamp my mouth tightly shut and pretend not to listen. She means well, but sometimes her delivery lacks subtlety. And timing.

The children begin their song and I am instantly pulled back to my days in the youth choir. I've always loved to sing but keep my current choral arrangements limited to the eerie acoustics of the downstairs bathroom. Nevertheless, I find myself mouthing the words. It's always been my favorite, sung to the tune of that funky disco hit, 'Shake Your Groove Thing' performed by Peaches and Herb.

Spin it, Spin it
Spin your dreidel, spin your dreidel,
yeah, yeah.
Show ya how to twirl it now.

Let's show the world we can spin,
Any chance to make–it–dance.
Hashem He gives us the chance,
We can twirl, throughout the world.

When we spin, we hear the Call,
Spinning motion keeps us standing tall.
Twirl it fast, ne–ver make it fall,
We're spinning dreidels, having us a ball, y'all.

Nun, Gimmel, Hay, and Shin.
When we spin we're truly in,
The spirit of Hanukkah.
Twisting, turning, we keep yearning.
On fire for our faith, we spin more
And that's for sure.

Spin it high or spin it low,
We twirl our dreidel where it oughta go.
Hear that hum, ne-ver stop,
Twirling fast, spinning like a top.

There's nothing more that I'd like to do,
than give a dreidel a spin with you.
Keep spinning, let's keep spinning.

Antiochus wants to win,
He don't know the trouble he's in.
He wants to mess with the Jews,
With Hashem's power, we know we can't lose.

The Maccabees came along,
Judah said, Seleucid law so wrong.
Hammering out in the streets,
Victory never tasted so sweet
(because those Greeks we really did defeat)

Ol' Judah did save the day,
Crushed them all, all the way.
Now there's only one thing to say,
We are Jews and we are here to stay.

I remember the first time the mike was placed in front of me at the Bimah one Friday Shabbat during Hanukkah for the traditional dreidel song. Each child was given a turn and when it came to me, my mind went completely blank.

"Uh...."

Nothing. Then inspiration hit.

"I had a little dreidel, I made it out of mush. But then I slipped upon it, and fell right on my tush."

Everyone started laughing. I must have been six or seven and even the thought of it makes me chuckle. I'm sitting here now, so many years later with my parents and sort of lost in reminiscing about the past, my childhood of carefree days.

The choir continues their set with another Hanukkah favorite, 'Eight Days of Oil' and all of the over-sixty-somethings sing along because they know that Beatles melody so well from the olden days.

Eight Days of Oil,
We burned.
Eight days of Oil,
And there was just enough to make it last.

Oh, we are the Jews,
Trying to get along.
Along came the Seleucids,
And told us we were wrong.

They did scold me, they did chide me.
I ain't got nothing but trouble,
Eight Days of Oy!

Oh, we are the Jews,
Fighting for our lives.
Against Hellenistic ways,
Praying to survive.

They did fight me, they did take me.
They did fight me, they'll never break me.
I ain't got nothing but pagan,
Eight Days of Oy!

Oh, we are the Jews,
Keeping our faith alive.
With the power of the Lord behind me,
I know I will survive.

Hashem, we praise Him.
We got the power of the Lord behind us
With those Eight Days of Oil.

Amidst the cheers and clapping, the Rabbi steps up to the mike. It's time for the Shema and we all rise from our chairs. The pavilion is filled with at least two hundred people and as the first notes make their way upward through the night air, I am thinking how beautiful it will be to hear every one of them joined together in song as one voice, one people.

But I think I hear someone calling my name softly, just a whisper in my ear and then my reverie is interrupted. At first it's just this faint but slightly annoying sound filtering into my brain, sort of like a fly buzzing somewhere in the vicinity but I don't know where. Then I get angry because I realize that someone's cell phone is repeatedly humming, disturbing the moment for everyone. The noise is very close to me and I am trying to locate the person who has forgotten to turn it over to silent. Just answer it you idiot or turn it off. I keep thinking it's somewhere near so I turn around and see Aunt Jackie and Uncle Ira in the row behind me, singing.

"Aunt Jackie, I think your phone is vibrating."

"It can't be, honey. I forgot mine at home."

She turns to her husband and hisses in a loud whisper:

"Ira, for Pete's sake, turn off your phone!"

Ira hurriedly fishes it from his jacket pocket, but even I can see that it's turned off.

Where the heck is it coming from? I turn back to face the stage too quickly, lose my footing, and grab the back of the chair in front of me. I take a few halting steps, trying to regain my balance. Suddenly, I am very nauseous and I feel the first pangs of a headache. It can't be low blood sugar; I just had a half-dozen latkes. The buzzing of that phone is getting louder as I try to take a deep breath. Big mistake. I feel worse now. I've got to sit down but I can't seem to find my chair. Oh, crap. I'm going to fall. At least my chair is somewhere; I won't miss it by much. Just sit down, Shira. No one will notice. Just relax your knees and sit down. Wait, where is it? I should be seated by now. Did someone move it? It's not there and I have that sickening sense from the all too rapid descent in an elevator, my stomach lurching as I go down. Everything starts to tilt and go cattywonk at an uncomfortable angle in front of me. Something is happening as I start to fall onto the tiled floor of the pavilion. The blood is pounding so loudly in my ears that I no longer hear the voices of the people singing around me. And now there's not just that droning sound, but rather something so much louder and infinitely more distracting that I am slowly losing focus of my surroundings. It's like static, radio static slowly penetrating my consciousness as if someone is fiddling with the tuner and can't quite connect to a strong station signal. Who's fiddling with the radio knob, I wonder? Then I think, what an absurd thing to say. Who brings a radio to the mall? Wait, who even has a radio anymore?

The static ceases abruptly and is replaced with a strong, distinct voice which comes crashing into my eardrums, jolting me into awareness. It's as if suddenly, the fiddler found a clear, audible station but I cannot tell what I am listening to. It sounds like an old-style, old-time radio broadcast reporting the news. But it's scratchy like an old phonograph recording when the needle on the vinyl hasn't quite picked up the grooves of the music yet. The reporter keeps going on about the past, like a recap of the year for a New Year's celebration. But this is really weird because this marathon of events is not of this past year but, wait...what is he saying? Why is he talking about the assassination of Yitzhak Rabin? Now, it's the Six Day War? The rebirth of the new nation of Israel? World War? Every story is racing by me, a great blur of sound bites, each one treading upon the heels of its forerunner but older than the previous one.

"It's 9 o'clock in Central Europe, the news is next on AFN."

Why am I hearing the Armed Forces Network? Then the radio announcer elegantly switches to an introduction and I am totally out of my element:

"Ladies and Gentlemen, this is the BBC wireless and I am pleased to be playing for you the latest popular song to come out of the United States performed by the Andrews Sisters."

The last thing I hear before I black out is jaunty swing music, the rich resonance of Bing, and the tight harmony of three female voices..."Lay that pistol down babe, lay that pistol down. Pistol-packing mama...."

MOUNTAIN MEMORIES

29 September, 1943 AD
Gilleleje

"Ouch!"

I land with a thud. A very painful thud on my rump. I try to break my fall with my hands onto what I discover feels like rough cobblestones and not the smooth mosaic tile of the pavilion. My eyes are clenched tightly shut, a sense of vertigo is still upon me and I feel nauseated beyond belief. I don't want to open my eyes because I'm sure everyone standing near me has turned around to stare at Shira the klutz.

"Mom?"

No answer.

I don't hear singing anymore. I don't hear any voices at all, for that matter. But I am relieved the din of that damn cell phone or radio or whatever it was, the discord of that moment, is over. I must be hallucinating however, I think to myself because something doesn't smell right. I smell water, saltwater, like that first tang of the ocean air that hits you when you get out of your car for a day at the beach. But before I see anything, before I can even begin to think about opening my eyes, what I do hear is far more disconcerting: an exclamation I don't fully recognize and the crunch of gravel as it turns under a boot.

I'm still on the ground. I slowly open my eyes to see a man sprinting across the road towards me in the evening moonlight. He's beautiful. I have to remind myself to breathe. A torrent of words is streaming from his mouth. Wait, is that Yiddish I'm hearing? He is standing in front of me, not out of breath in the slightest and all I can do is stare blankly up at him for a few seconds to try to collect my wits, gather my bearings. By now, I can see that I am completely alone in a dark street. The air is crisp and it's freezing cold. I'm no longer at the pavilion with the press of warm bodies all around me but in a very different location. Now I am afraid.

He keeps talking to me in this vaguely familiar language as he kneels down. Great. I only know a few choice expressions in Yiddish (thanks to Uncle Murray) but those are mostly ones that would make my mother blush and yours cross herself. But this is rapid-fire and way over my head. I think he is asking me if I am hurt, if he can help me. I try to salvage a little high school German, hoping he might understand.

"Ich kann ein bisschen Deutsch sprechen."

He starts and then grasps my hand to pull me to my feet. At the first touch of his hand to mine, his attitude does an about-face and he is no longer solicitous but rather abrupt. His hand is like ice, shockingly cold as it makes contact with mine. I start to shiver. I don't know why but it feels as if it's at least twenty degrees colder and I am only dressed in very light clothing. The man carelessly shrugs off his coat and drapes it over my shoulders.

"Komm, Makele. Nicht auf der Strasse. Hier gibt es keine Sicherheit."

I've never been as thankful for my mother's pushiness as I was at that moment. Here I was completely disoriented, wondering what was going on, what happened to the pavilion, the crowd, the lights, the singing, everything. And all I can think about is how incredibly grateful I am for my mother making me take German in high school. This stranger was telling me to come with him, that there was no safety out on the street. I was too bewildered to protest. He had pulled me to my feet rather brusquely and way too fast for my comfort level. An instant wave of exhaustion and dizziness hits me like jet lag and I am totally jarred by this sudden movement. My head feels thick and I'm achy all over with a whopping headache. I'm thinking I must have cracked my head pretty hard on the way down because nothing looks familiar and it still doesn't smell right. I find myself standing in a dark street, a small neighborhood of homes actually, completely unlike the cookie-cutter tract homes in my neighborhood. Each one unique. Very European, in fact. Painted in the moonlight in Ring's hand, casting an impression on my mind, soft and slightly out of focus. If this is a dream, it certainly is a very pretty one, I tell myself.

He guides me decisively and with a firm grip as I am still wobbly on my feet across the road to a small house behind a much larger building with wrought-iron gates. Just before we enter the doorway, he reaches out to touch something on the right side of the door jamb. As he brings his fingers to his lips, our eyes meet. An overwhelming sense of relief washes over me at his gesture.

The room we enter is small, dimly lit by candles and furnished sparingly. The windows are all covered by heavy, dark curtains which let in little moonlight. At first glance, it seems like just one open space but as my eyes adjust to the low light, I begin to notice my surroundings. A kitchen is to my left with a very small oak table and matching chairs and beyond that a potbelly cast-iron stove with a burnished copper kettle resting upon it. Against the far wall, placed at a perpendicular angle is another piece of oak furniture, I guess you would call it a sideboard with an upper cupboard space. At the back of the kitchen, there is a closed door that probably leads to a bedroom. All of these I see filtered through a flickering firelight as images dance upon the walls, as I try to feel my way in this strange place. The man steers me towards a large and very worn leather armchair in front of the stone fireplace.

The fire is burning low, but I am grateful for the soft chair he places me into and for the scanty amount of warmth the glowing embers give. I am comforted by this small kindness but what I truly want is something to calm my nerves and quell my rising apprehension at my present situation. I really need a drink.

"Ich hätte gern etwas zum trinken."

He turns and walks towards the wooden table in the kitchen. He lifts a cloth which is covering a stoneware pitcher and I hear splashing in a cup.

"Nein, danke. Nicht Wasser. Etwas stärker, wenn Sie es haben."

He jerks his head up quickly to look at me, a frown forming on his face. From my perspective, he must consider this an odd request because he doesn't move. But I really need it so I try again.

"Bitte."

Apparently, this does the trick. Although he sighs heavily, he produces a bottle from the sideboard cupboard. As he leans forward to hand me the glass he has filled, I catch the scent of red wine and I look up into his eyes. The firelight is captured in them. It was too dark in the street to discern anything but the vaguest outline of his face and I was way too disoriented to focus much anyway. But now I can see his features fully. It hits me all at once: the grace with which he moves, the pallor in his cheeks, the vivid blue eyes. All are much too marked to be mistaken.

"Avram."

He stands up abruptly, clearly startled and immediately wary.

"Wieso kennen Sie mich?"

"Avram, it's me Shira."

He is visibly troubled by my switch to English. His words come out haltingly at first, as if he seldom speaks the language.

"Forgive me, I do not know you. I know of no one by that name."

"Look Avram, what is going on? Of course you know me. We met at Simchat Torah at the synagogue in Westport. I remember the day very well. It was the 30th. Of September."

"You are mistaken. Today is September 29th."

"Avram, I have not seen you for two months."

"That cannot be."

His stubbornness is beginning to rattle me and I have to admit, now that my head is beginning to clear a bit, I'm getting pissed off. I change to another tack.

"What did you call me in the street just now? Is that Yiddish?"

Avram inhales swiftly.

"Do you not know?"

"Would I be asking you if I did?"

He hesitates, discomfort plainly making a show upon his features. He makes a few false starts and then speaks.

"Makele. It is German. It means tainted or stained."

"What the hell does that mean? Who are you really? What are you doing here? Where am I anyway? The last thing I remember was standing with my parents at the Hanukkah celebration at the pavilion and we were starting to sing the Shema. I heard this weird humming sound and I became dizzy and felt sick. Then I had this eerie sensation like I was falling and suddenly I'm on my backside and you are helping me to stand up in some dark street. The last time I saw you at Friday night Shabbat, you left me at the synagogue wondering where the hell you went. You didn't even say goodbye. I thought we had made some sort of connection, that you liked me and wanted to see me again."

Slowly, the look of utter puzzlement on his face changes to an awareness, like an awakening. I see a slow realization coming into his eyes as if he is uncovering something he sincerely did not know. He takes a step towards me and I cannot believe the words that come out of his mouth.

"I believe I understand now. We did make a connection, Shira. More than you can possibly imagine."

"What are you talking about? You totally led me on and then blew me off without a word."

"Shira, you must believe me when I tell you I do not know you, that I truly have never met you before. But...I have brought you back, nonetheless.

My words come tumbling out all in one gigantic, hysterical rush.

"I don't understand what is going on, Avram. This is completely insane. How is this even possible? You expect me to believe you are immortal and that you turned me into some kind of freak which now allows me to travel to the past but you don't even know who I am because it's 1943 and we haven't met in 2010 yet?"

This outburst is my most incoherent to date and well, by this point I don't care. Avram had just spent almost an hour repeating himself and being greeted by my blank stares, very angry and confused words, and continuous requests for something stronger than the wine he kept forcing upon me. His explanation of events that he surmised to be true about how I arrived here could not possibly be true. The manifold paradoxes that were so obvious to me, were screaming at me from all sides and making my head ache were not even fazing him. It was his story and he was sticking to it. Great, and now he is looking at me in an almost condescending way which gets me fuming all over again. The last thing I need right now is to be patronized.

"Shira, it will take some time for you to become acclimatized to your environment. It always will."

"What do you mean, it always will? This is *not* going to happen to me again! Is it?"

I feel like I'm in some horrid dream from which I cannot wake. If this is true and I am really sitting here and something has happened to me, how could he be responsible? Then logic kicks in (finally).

"Avram, wait just a minute...that can't be right. If you say we've never met, that you have absolutely no idea who I am, how come you called me... what is that word again?"

"Makele."

"Okay, Ma-ke-le, whatever. You said that in the street. If we haven't met, how did you know to call me that, that something had happened to me that changed me? How did you know that I was... Makele?"

The word sounds odd and so completely foreign on my tongue.

"It is rather complicated."

"You owe me an explanation, Avram. I'm sure if you just start at the beginning, I can follow you."

"Shira, when you first appeared in the street, I thought you were just someone from the village. I turned the corner on my way home and there you were, in a huddle in the middle of the road. I thought perhaps you had fallen. But when you did not respond to me and I knelt down beside you, I could tell that something was wrong, that there was a difference. And then, when I grasped your hand I felt it and I knew for certain."

"What did you know?"

"That you were not entirely human."

With the absurdity of that last comment, I was done. Completely done. The utter lunacy of what he had been saying all along finally hits me. I can't help myself, but I burst out laughing.

"Okay, Avram. We're finished here. Where's the hidden camera? I'm being pranked, right? Very funny, guys. I bet TJ and Jess are behind this. Okay, girls! Come on out from wherever you are hiding. The game is over."

I rise out of the chair and walk over to the door beyond the kitchen, thinking that's the only logical place my friends could be hiding. I quickly throw the door open, trying to catch them unawares. I fumble for the light switch and the room is suddenly brightly lit and I blink and hold my hand to my eyes against the glare.

"A-ha! Oh."

There is no one there. All that is staring back at me is a bedroom, also minimally furnished. An oaken armoire is to my immediate left with a matching ornately carved wooden board at the head of the twin bed facing me. The nightstand follows the same pattern with a basin and pitcher sitting atop it. At the far left of the room is a tall wooden closet with double doors. Across the bed is a finely embroidered coverlet in pale hues. These are all that greet me in the bedroom. I peek under the bed but there are no giggling girlfriends hiding beneath it.

I turn away and walk slowly back into the main room to find Avram standing by the fire, his hand upon the stonework mantle. His face is very calm and very serious.

"I don't get it. Where are they?"

"There is no one here but us, Shira."

"Okay, this isn't funny anymore."

"I assure you this is no game. There is no going back to being merely human ever again."

"Whatever you say, Avram. Look, I don't know what's going on but I think I just need to call my parents. They must be worried sick about me."

I'm fishing in my skirt pocket for my cell phone but I can tell right away by the absence of the tell-tale lump of it that it is not there.

"Shit, I lost my phone. Can I borrow your cell?"

I look up to find his eyes wide with shock and he is actually blushing.

"What's your problem, Avram?"

"Shira, you must not swear."

"Are you kidding me? Can I just have your phone? I need to let my parents know that I am okay."

"You do not seem to comprehend. They will not be there."

"What are you talking about?"

I walk over to where I had been sitting and start looking on the floor to see if my phone has fallen underneath the chair by the fireplace.

"Huh? What do you mean, they will not be there?"

"They will not have been born yet."

I snap my head up. Now I am very angry.

"Look, I really need to talk to my mom right now."

Avram shrugs.

"I have no telephone here but you may use the one in the synagogue."

He nods his head in the direction of the building we passed on the way into his home.

"That's the synagogue?"

"It is."

I am suddenly and completely disturbed out of all proportion by this new information.

"Wait, you're the Rabbi?"

"No, Shira. I am only the caretaker here. I maintain the synagogue and see to the grounds and in exchange Rabbi has allowed me to live in this house."

"So, that's your job, Avram. You work for the Rabbi?"

"In a manner of speaking, yes I do work for him. But what I do here right now is just a small part of how I live my life. My true occupation is complicated, on a much larger scale, and vastly more important."

"My mother told me when we were introduced that you lived and worked in Israel. Now, I've never been to Israel but I'm pretty sure that I'm not there right now, am I?"

I am remembering the chill in the night air, the salty tang on the breeze, and the picturesque homes in the street.

"No, we are in Gilleleje."

Thanks. That really helps. I totally know where I am now, thank you very much. I am completely blank.

"Avram, this whole situation is hard enough and my headache isn't getting any better and I really don't like mysteries. Please don't make me guess where I am."

"My apologies. I was not trying to be mysterious. You are on Sjaelland, the largest island of Denmark."

"What? How is that even possible? How can I physically be in another country when not much more than an hour ago I was standing in the pavilion in Westport?"

"In my experience, I have learned that it is better not to question the Lord's doing in these matters. He has His reasons for placing you here in this time and place."

I am bewildered by his remark. Why is he bringing G-d into the mix?

"What does Hashem have to do with any of this? What do you mean?"

"He is why you are here, Shira. He is the reason you have come back to me. For I believe that you have indeed travelled back to fulfill His promise. He has kept His word."

"Whose promise? What promise?"

"G-d gave me His word to send someone, a helpmate. I was anticipating your arrival."

"You were expecting me? How could you be if you said you don't even know who I am? You seriously believe that Hashem made this promise to you and that I'm it? That He took me out of my time, essentially kidnapped...no, time-napped me and brought me back to this time and place so I could help you with your job?"

"Yes."

"How do you know?"

"He told me."

I'm starting to feel like I need to slowly back away from him, make no sudden movements and just get the hell out of here. Okay, I took a ton of Psych courses at university but no way did anything I ever read in any textbook or hear my professor expound upon in a lecture equip me for being face-to-face with someone who actually believes he has conversations with G-d. How could anything prepare me for this moment? It obviously shows in my body language as I try to inch towards the door. Avram swiftly walks toward me and blocks my way.

"Shira, you must calm down, have patience, and try to understand. Please come sit with me by the fire. All will be revealed in time. I did not know you were coming on *this* night. I have never known when you were to come or that it even would be *you*. I could only pray that you would someday be here with me, as G-d foretold. I have been waiting so very long for you, been searching through time for you. Praying to G-d. Tonight my prayers have been answered."

"Now I am really muddled. You said you were expecting me but not tonight? Well, how long have you been waiting?"

"A very long time. There have been too many days to count."

"How long is that? Could you be more specific, please?"

"Very well. If you must know, I have been waiting for you ever since Shavuot."

"Since the spring? You have been waiting for me for over four months?"

"You misunderstand. It is neither the Shavuot of the year you come from nor of the year to which you have now come."

"Well okay, *which* Shavuot are we talking about then?"

"*The* Shavuot, the Giving of the Law."

"Avram, I don't follow you. What do you mean *the* Shavuot? Shavuot is every year."

"No, Shira. There is only one true Shavuot. Each successive one only commemorates the anniversary of Moses bringing the Commandments down the mountain to our people. I have waited for you ever since then, from that night when I was there."

"Where?"

"At the foot of the mountain."

"What are you talking about? What mountain?"

"The mountain referred to as Mt. Sinai where I turned away from the covenant with G-d."

"This is ludicrous, Avram. You can't have been there. Even if I believed everything else that has happened this evening, what you are saying is physically impossible. You are seriously telling me that you were present when Moses brought down the Ten Commandments? You were actually there? That would make you, what...3,000 years old?"

I can barely do the math at this point I am so upset and exhausted.

"I am."

"I don't believe you."

"That is entirely irrelevant. It matters little what you believe. Whether you trust what I am saying or not, the truth of the matter is that you are here now. I believe you have arrived for a greater purpose than we yet comprehend."

"Well, I'll give you that. I'm certainly somewhere, that's for sure. I guess some 'when' is more accurate. But Avram, you need to believe me when I tell you that I am having an extremely difficult time wrapping my head around any of what you are saying."

I catch his baffled expression over that last phrase so I try to be more plain.

"Perhaps if you start at the very beginning and tell me how this happened, I can put the puzzle pieces together in a way that works for me."

"It will take some time."

"Well, you apparently have that in abundance and I have no way at the moment of going anywhere anyway. So please, Avram. I do want to know what is going on. If I am supposed to be here and help you, I need you to help me understand."

His smile is compassionate and almost grateful, but it is tinged with sadness as well.

"I will try, Shira. But the memory of those distant days is very painful to me. I do not often think on them, for if I do, a heavy weariness descends upon me and I find it difficult to focus on my work."

"Wait, Avram. All along you have been talking about your work. What exactly are you, I mean we, supposed to be doing?"

"G-d has placed us here so that we may help."

"Who are we to help?"

"Shira, we are Jews. By our very nature, the one that G-d has given us, we have an obligation to help. We are here to assist those of our brethren who are in need, at this time and in this place."

"Avram, I know what Tzedakah is, but what does that...."

Slowly, odd bits and pieces of that puzzle are starting to move on the board, slipping into the correct position, clicking into place. As the picture starts to form before me in my mind, I can scarcely comprehend the magnitude of what he has been saying.

"Oh G-d, Avram! I am here in Denmark...are you telling me that, wait... we are in the middle of...the war! But the war is...."

"Shira, you must stop at once!"

"I know how to help you! Now everything makes sense, don't you see? I can tell you what will happen, what we will need to do, when it will end."

"No."

"What?"

"You must not reveal the future to me or to anyone else you encounter here in Gilleleje or any other time to when you will be brought back. You must never do or say anything to alter the timeline or the natural course of events. Under no circumstances should you give yourself away."

"You're kidding me, right? Are you seriously telling me that this is going to happen to me again?"

"You have no choice. You have been tainted, Shira. You are forever stained. You will always be connected to the past and ultimately linked to me."

"Avram, how did I really get here?"

"I will tell you, Shira. I will tell you everything."

"I was not always as I am now, Shira. The man you see before you is vastly different from the man I was so many years ago. I was mortal once, so very human. Flawed. Full of pride. I was not unlike the rest of my family. For many generations, we had been living in Egypt and prospered under Egyptian rule. When it came to the standard of living allowed us, we had nothing about which to complain. For as long as my ancestors could remember, we had served under Pharaoh as his royal artisans, living in the royal city. My family's special art was the crafting of gold. Housed in the servant's quarters, we were well cared for and never endured hardships of any kind as the Egyptians were fascinated with this precious metal. We were kept obscenely busy designing the most ornate of jewelry that they were fond of wearing on all occasions. My father found especial favor during the reign of Seti I when I was a young child and not even an apprentice yet.

I can still recall accompanying my father from the royal servant's household into Pharaoh's presence like it was yesterday. Bowing low before the living god, my father would offer up an intricately designed necklace or a tray of precious gems to be worked into rings to adorn him. I was a wiggly boy and found it difficult to keep my eyes on the polished floor and was constantly trying to sneak a peek at the young boys who stood upon the dais at his side. They were just as lavishly bejeweled as the King, but seemed fidgety like me, itching to be out-of-doors. I knew their names, of course. Who did not know the young princes, the heirs to the kingdom? Ramses and Moses were sons of the living god and no one of my station was permitted contact with them. Officially, I could only snatch a glimpse of them from an odd angle while my nose was plastered to the floor or when there was a procession through the streets with all of the pomp and splendor afforded the great ruler of Egypt. I would never formally be permitted to play with either of them. Nevertheless, precocious boys of any station can find ways to circumvent conventional rules of decorum. Moreover, we did. We excelled at that."

"I remember the first time we caught each other staring out into the lush gardens when we shouldn't have been, during a serious moment in the court. My father had just presented Pharaoh's sister with an ornately carved circlet of gold for her upper arm. I was getting bored with all of the ceremonial protocol and just wanted to get out of this stuffy room. Almost of its own volition, my eyes wandered to the reflecting pool just outside the court."

"How cool and refreshing the water looks I thought, compared to the stifling throne room with the censers spitting forth incense fumes which stung my eyes so terribly. How relaxing it would be to lie upon a soft skin under the shade of the acacia tree, escape the pervasive dust and oppressive heat, dangle my feet in the water, a tray of half-eaten figs and a handful of dates close at hand; I need make no effort to reach them."

"Through sleepy eyes I observe the geese dozing, barely moving, floating languorously upon the water. Every few seconds, to see the smooth back of a glistening fish rise just enough to break the surface of the water with the curve of its back was all I needed to stay my lovely vision."

"What a relief to have no duty more pressing than to be making plans for a glorious adventure to be had upon awakening. To remain in the midst of the daydream to see where it led was luxurious. There I am grasping the bow, feeling the tension, finding my mark, learning just when to release the arrow. Now my fingers are gripped tightly upon my javelin. I am poised for the throw upon a high outcropping of rock and below me is the old, curved tusked boar snuffling in the undergrowth, unaware that I am strong and mean to kill him. The next moment my dagger is raised high, dripping with the blood of the slain leopard whose throat I have just cut, alone in the desert. Immediately the clang of my sword jolts me into focus. I dodge the mace and thrust home. The enemy of my King lies at my feet. I leap into my chariot, snap the reins and race homewards, victorious."

"All these thoughts came to me drowsily as I stared at the lotus blossoms resting placidly upon the water. It was in the midst of this boyhood reverie that I saw Moses. We had both had our attention fixed upon the shimmering pool outside and turned to face each other at precisely the same moment, catching each other with our eyes strayed from the proceedings. I am sure I blushed crimson and immediately cracked my nose on the polished floor in my haste to return my gaze to its proper station. But in the instant before I was looking down, I saw it: an impish grin, not unlike my own. I felt it a very good beginning and he must have as well. It was to become the high point of my early days. Many times throughout my childhood and youth, Moses himself would descend from upon high down into the royal servant's quarters to seek me out. Although I was becoming more skilled in my craft, I was still an assistant to my father. But little by little, I began to serve Moses myself as an artist in my own right, crafting especially beautiful items for him. He could never just show up without a reason; our times together had to be couched in some sort of formal occasion: the inspection of a recent acquisition of gold or gems, to check the status of a certain piece of handiwork, or the repair of some item. Moses was never unaccompanied; his royal guard was ever-present. But we often found ways to communicate and could even go for walks, ostensibly to conduct business or discuss a work in progress. Sometimes he would show up unexpectedly, unannounced, for no apparent reason. It mattered little; we would always find something about which to speak. At times, he would find me in my father's workshop, my head bent over, completely engrossed in my work and utterly oblivious to my surroundings."

'And what do you craft for me today, Master Goldsmith?'

"I do not even look up at the interruption, my hand swiftly reaching for a tool to hurl at the impertinent servant who has dared interrupt me. Just before the small hammer leaves my fingertips, I raise my eyes. Instead of a penitent servant apologizing, I find Moses leaning in the doorway, smirking."

"I jump up, my tools spilling to the ground, clanking as they fall and land in a heap at my feet. In the next instant I am beside them, prostrating myself before him. We are friends, but I know my place."

'My lord, I did not hear your guard announce you.'

'I doubt you would have heard a lion roar in your ear the way you were focusing on your work. Do you know you frown when you are concentrating?'

'No, my lord. I did not realize.'

'Indeed, you do. Come, Master Goldsmith. I believe we are both in need of a diversion. Shall we continue our game?'

"Moses was quite skilled at both Senet and Mehen, games I had heard of but had never played. But it was the game of Hounds and Jackals that became our favorite. He styled himself my teacher and many an evening had seen us consumed with these games of skill and chance. There were more times than I can count that we had been jolted from the intensity of our play by the sound of the royal guardsman's voice, calling to him that the hour was late. I cherished those interludes; they became as a sanctuary for the both of us and broke up the monotony of my days."

"It was on such an evening, like so many others throughout the years, that I was working late and Moses came upon me in my workshop. I had learned to expect him at any hour of the day or night, to listen for his guard, and I tried to make a point of not letting him find me at my labors. It had become a competition between us to see who would catch the other first. But this night, all that changed. Our youthful pleasures were at an end. Tonight his coming was so abrupt and found me so utterly unprepared, that when I rose from my table at his footsteps, I remained standing. I stood there, stock-still for some moments, aghast at his appearance. Disheveled and distracted, he had burst through my door. We stared at each other, neither of us speaking, he out of breath and I holding mine. I started at my own insolence, lowered my eyes and began to make my way to the floor in obeisance. Then he spoke my name and I hesitated. I lifted my eyes to see his arm reaching out to me to halt my downward movement and I was completely astounded by the emotion in his face."

'My friend.'

'Your servant, my lord.'

'Do not speak of such things now, Avram.'

"He turned away from me and lowered himself into a chair and I did not know where to look or what to do. I had never seen my friend and master so disturbed. His was always the face of assurance and confidence. I could not read him tonight and I was afraid."

'My lord, have I done something to displease you?'

'Avram, you could never displease me. Your friendship has been the greatest in my life and I will never forget you.'

'Forget me, my lord? I do not understand. Have I offended my King? Has he forbidden you from visiting me? Forgive me my lord, if I have caused you any discomfort. I have no wish to be the source of enmity between either of you. If it is the desire of my master, I will leave the city and kindle no further unpleasantness.'

'My friend, it is I who must leave the city.'

'Leave? You cannot leave.'

"Moses raised his eyes to mine and then he smiled. It was a deep, weary smile that made me blush when I perceived what words I had just spoken."

'Oh, forgive me my lord. I spoke out of place.'

"My eyes were rooted to my feet as I berated myself for speaking so brazenly."

'Do not fear, Avram. You need not be so formal with me now. After what I have done today, I no longer warrant the respect of any man, servant or god.'

'You frighten me, my lord. Moses. You must let me help you. Whatever you need of me my friend, it is yours.'

'You have been a comfort to me all these years, Avram. That is payment enough. You owe me nothing further.'

'But will you not tell me my lord, what has happened to distress you so?'

'I will confide in you my friend; I owe you that at least.'

"I see the hesitation in his face and I am about to speak, to try to comfort him but before I can find the words to help him, he rushes forth."

'I have done that which is unspeakable. I have killed a man.'

'My lord!'

'Yes, you are shocked. But no more than I. I have transgressed against the law, against my King, and I will pay the ultimate price.'

'But my lord, I am at a loss. What has happened?'

'I have taken the life of a man who would have taken another's, that is all that need be said. It matters little now to the King my reasons. He has decreed my death.'

'Oh, my lord!'

"I am at his feet, clutching at his hand, my face upon his knee."

'You cannot die!'

"Through my tears, my mind is racing. I will hide him, I will defend him, and I will fight to my last breath so that he may live. I feel the warmth and the weight of his hand upon my head for just a moment, one small moment of my life, and then he rises to his feet pushing me gently away from him. I am on the floor, devastated by his words and unable to move in my despair. I look up to find him leaning at the door with his back to me, his arms outstretched above him upon either side, his head bowed down."

'Avram, do not weep for me. I am no longer the noble man you once thought me. Forgive me.'

"At these words, I am mobilized into action. I jump up quickly and come to him. I place my hand upon his shoulder, something I have never done, never dared to do, but now I am resolved."

'My lord, you need not ask my forgiveness. You owe me nothing. I am only a servant. I am nothing. But I will serve you until the end. Listen to me now, my friend. Let me find a way to help you.'

'There is nothing to be done for it, Avram. I must away and tonight. Now. I must flee all that I have ever known. I do not know what will happen to me or if I will ever return. It may be that we shall never meet again.'

'Take me with you, my lord.'

'Would that were possible my friend, but it cannot be.'

'Let me serve you, my lord. Do not punish me so with your absence.'

'You are kind, Avram. It is your kindness that has sustained me all these years and that which I will keep with me for all the years to come.'

"He turned to look at me, one last time. He smiled and then was gone from the room; his very presence had filled it and now it was devoid of all trace of him. I stepped out into the night air."

'My lord, Moses!'

"I saw only his retreating figure in the moonlight, sprinting across the distance, leaving me alone in the doorway. I never spoke to him again."

"My family never understood my relationship with Moses and frankly were in awe of the attention I had received. Although I knew my place, I felt a kinship with him that I could not explain. Though we were as different as chalk and cheese, outward appearances were deceiving. After many centuries of association, one could not tell us apart from the Egyptians we served. We adopted their ways, style of dress and manner of ornamentation, though less ostentatious as befitting our station. Clothed in the like garments of our masters, painted and bejeweled ourselves, we even adopted their gods and served their false idols."

"But we were not Egyptian. We were from the house of Abraham. For all our paint and mannerisms, we stood apart in the eyes of our masters. Although we lived high above the standards of other servants and never wanted for anything since we were readily accepted for our skills, we were still servants to our Pharaoh. Indeed, we did live well above the lifestyles of our fellow Hebrews. For this we were shunned by our kin and segregated by our masters, caught between two worlds, each foot set upon opposite banks of the same river."

"Throughout the years of my adulthood, I continued in my apprenticeship, perfecting the craft of the goldsmiths of my forefathers. When my father deemed the time to be right, I married a woman from the servant household and we had a son. We continued to serve under the rulers of Egypt, almost completely isolated from our brethren. We seldom heard from the slave quarters anything but idle gossip. I never knew and was not even interested in the plight of my kin. I had been born and raised in the household of the royal servants, forever set apart and having no connection. By the time we started hearing talk from those quarters, it was almost too late. It was just rumor at first. My family and I ignored them initially. We thought them of little consequence and not to be taken seriously. They just seemed like stories to us, warning tales told to children at bedtime to keep them safe."

"But they persisted and grew in the telling. The Redeemer will come they said, to lead us out of captivity. Little did I comprehend that the one I had known my entire life since my early childhood and had served so faithfully was to become my destroyer."

He paused at this statement and looked at me with such sadness in his eyes that I could not help but interrupt him.

"Avram, when did...."

But he held up his hand, drew a deep breath and continued with his story.

"It was the Exodus, Shira. My family was among the multitudes that Moses led out of Egypt. All during the time of the plagues, we endured the suffering along with the rest of the Egyptians. I had my opportunity to obey and follow the word of G-d. He was more than generous. He gave me more than one chance. He gave me nine. But it was the last one, the tenth plague when my world came to an end, the final one that destroyed me utterly. I had lost forever the only chance I had ever had to lead a normal life. My wife had implored me."

'Oh, husband! Do you not see what is happening? We must do as Moses says.'

'Do *you* not see? I have been betrayed by my friend.'

'But there is still time. We can find redemption.'

'I need look no farther for redemption than the throne room of my living god. I have lived so long under the grace of his benevolence, I owe him my fealty for all that he has provided for me. I cannot, I will not betray my King and face his alienation.'

"I had refused to put lamb's blood upon my door. And then it came. The Hand of G-d came in the night and I was undone."

"My son, my first born...oh, my child! He died in my arms. He whom I held most dear. Forever lost to me by the hand of Moses who called upon his G-d to annihilate the faithless. But my pain did not end there, Shira. Not only for the loss of my son did I weep and curse the name of Moses. My elder brother, Mordecai, was also taken from me."

"I was disconsolate, devastated and filled with a fury like I had never known. My wife was silent in her grief but ultimately more forgiving. I could not even look at her. I told her I could never forgive. She said this was the payment G-d had exacted for our transgression of defying Him for so many generations and denying our true faith. She tried in vain to console me."

'Avram, we have sinned against the one true G-d and we have paid the price.'

'He is not my god!'

"I screamed at her in my grief and horror. My parents tried to intervene. My father could not allay my greatest fear."

'Avram, you must understand, we are Hebrews. We have always been G-d's Chosen people but we turned away from Him and the religion of our ancestors to profit from our deeds and dealings with the Egyptians.'

'What are you talking about? It matters little what those people believed. We are Egyptian, have always been. I grew up worshipping the gods of Egypt. You yourself taught me to bow low before Pharaoh, the living god.'

"We had worked, lived, and behaved liked them. I could not fathom being anything else. My mother went on to explain that for many generations we had kept our identity a secret. We needed to survive, to find a way to fit in and the only way was to blend into Egyptian culture. My family's craft was the gateway into society and prosperity. The handiwork and expertise in goldcraft of my predecessors had caught the eye of the great Egyptian kings of the past. Ever since, our family had been employed by the royal household. We were assimilated into the culture and religious practices of our employers. But we were Hebrew, originally from the house of Abraham. All of this was never discussed as in the same way it had been denied to Moses."

"I spent those last, horrible days in Egypt drinking myself into a stupor to try to assuage my agony. But I would neither forget nor forgive. When my family came to me and said they were leaving the city, I could not believe they would abandon our way of life."

'How can you possibly follow the murderer of our son and my brother?'

"My wife tried to explain."

'Avram, the Lord has made a distinction between Egypt and Israel; there is nothing for us here now. Egypt is lost and Pharaoh will not call for us. We have been abandoned ourselves and our lives can never be as they once were.'

"I was dumbfounded. Everything I knew about the gods and our duty to them was being shattered in an instant like clay jars falling upon the stone. My parents wanted redemption from the betrayal of their forefathers against the one true G-d. I could bear it no longer and wailed in my anguish."

'There are no gods!'

"My wife implored me to go with them."

'We must try to find our way back to Him, Avram. There is nothing left for us here. We are His Chosen and we must follow.'

"I refused to go."

'Oh, my husband! Do not forever be separated from my side. Do not abandon me to suffer alone in my grief.'

"Her voice pleaded with me and in her eyes I saw the devastation of a woman who has lost the most precious gift any god could give her. We argued back and forth for many hours. In the end, I relented under the gaze of those sorrowful eyes and her tear-stained cheeks."

'My love, I will go with you. But do not ask me to believe.'

"We travelled with the great, mixed multitudes taking much of our wealth with us in gold and precious gemstones. All around me I observed my brethren and the meagerness with which they were accustomed. For the first time, I saw real poverty and it disgusted me beyond description. Among the throngs of people, I kept myself hidden. I did not wish to see him. I could not have brought myself to look upon his face. If I had encountered him, I believe I would have killed him. I need not have feared for surrounding me was an enormous horde and we were just one of many nations who left Egypt."

"But I was nothing like my fellow travellers. Clothed in the garments of the royal servant's household, my kinsmen only saw what anyone would see: a finely-garbed Egyptian. To them, I must have seemed a prince. A prince among beggars. They shied away from me at first, noticing my jewels and my painted eyes; I had vainly brought kohl in an alabaster jar for a journey into the desert! The way I carried myself was too distinct to be mistaken for anyone other than a member of the royal household, even a servant and they were right. What could I possibly have in common with this tribe of outcasts? We were incongruous in every way possible."

"It took many days and nights to shed my stubbornness. But little by little, I began to cast off many of my Egyptian habits and heathen ways. The desert has a way of making you decide. You must decide what to retain and what to discard. But it is not just what you are physically carrying that becomes a burden. The burden of ideas can weigh you down even more than a heavy load upon your back. Living in such close proximity to the Hebrews made it impossible not to be influenced. Even something as simple and basic as food became an issue. Our supply from Pharaoh's house had long since run out and I had to steel myself to eat that which I was unaccustomed."

"My wife was more flexible and welcomed the changes to our ways. I believe for her it was a distraction. I would not be distracted and my stubbornness, my insistence on my pagan ways was a barrier to all things, including finding my way back to G-d. I did not begin to know Him until it was almost too late."

"We journeyed for a long time in the wilderness, coming at last to the foot of the mountain. It was the place that was to become a flashpoint between the old customs and the new life, the locus of my destiny, where I died and was reborn."

"When Moses left us and was gone for so long, the crowd began to grumble. Though they believed he had forsaken us, I did not care. I felt vindicated in my distrust of him. All around me, the people were falling away from the word and the way of G-d. Our defiance was our undoing. When the cry went up for the gold for the calf, I was at the forefront of the smithies, the first to cast the golden earrings I had pulled from my wife's ears onto the fire. It was I who helped Aaron hammer out the molten metal once it had cooled. Then the wine began to flow in an endless, consuming river, bathing us all in its sweet intoxication. We shed our clothing, our inhibitions, even our sanity and danced naked around the altar Aaron had built, reveling in our new god, idolaters all. Most assuredly, we had corrupted ourselves. I committed unspeakable horrors at the foot of that mountain. My parents and wife remained in our tent throughout the orgy of madness that consumed us. It was then that we heard it: Joshua's cry. We looked up at the sound of a voice descending from a cleft in the mountain and were thunderstruck at the sight we beheld. Moses had returned. His wroth was unparalleled as he cast the tablets upon the rock. He threw the calf onto the fire and from the ashes of gold that were mixed with water, we were forced to drink of it. But when he commanded the faithful to him and asked the sons of Levi to take up their swords, for indeed they had left Egypt armed, I looked up at him and knew that I would not survive. I saw the flash of moonlight upon the metal and I ran. I was afraid for my very soul. Little did I realize that I had far more to fear than the sword. G-d's vengeance was all around me. I heard the screams of the mob as they fell before the blades. Those screams haunt me to this day. It was then that I felt Him, Shira. I felt His presence and I knew it was the end. I was in fear, so I hid."

"Wait, you ran away from G-d?"

"I was full of pride and ignorant enough to believe He could not find me. He is everywhere, all-powerful, omnipotent. There was literally no place I could go. He is all things, Shira. I weep for all that He is."

"What happened?"

"He found me in the wilderness and cursed me. He saw me for what I truly was: a sinner, vainglorious, disobedient to His will, His law. In my shame and regret, I begged for His forgiveness."

"G-d found you and...spoke to you, you actually heard His voice?"

"I did."

A torrent of questions was racing through my head. I managed, all in a jumbled rush: what did He say, what did He look like, what did you say?"

Drawing a deep breath, Avram continued. The look upon his face both frightened and yet held me captive.

"Shira, it was simultaneously the most terrifying and yet unbelievably exhilarating moment of my life. I heard a humming sound like the buzzing of honeybees but the air was quite still. The whitest light shone all about me though it was the deepest part of the night. A voice thundered in my ears yet spoke with the caress of a butterfly's wings. At that moment, I did not know myself; I lost all sense of who I was, all proportion. Time no longer existed for me."

"In my mind, I heard His disappointment and anger for disobeying His will. He gave me a vision of the fiery abyss–a world without Him. I cried out. I wept for the destiny of the Fallen. I cannot share with you that revelation, Shira. It would thoroughly destroy me."

"He then showed me a world of such unspeakable beauty, unparalleled contentment, and so wondrous a vision of paradise beyond the scope of all imagination that I lost myself within it. But then He spoke of a purpose.

'I will give you a gift, Avram. A gift that will enable you to serve Me utterly and without fail. But you must choose now and your decision is irrevocable.'

"What choice could I make? I saw my life for what it had been. Nothing. Irrelevant and lacking purpose. Merely human, without G-d. That insight into the abyss so terrified me, I am ashamed to admit that my first instinct, my decision was made more out of fear and a sense of self-preservation than for love of Him. But I have come to G-d since then and I understand that it is not about me at all but rather Him. I was given a choice. There was redemption. I chose to walk with G-d."

"But how did G-d want you to serve him, Avram? What did He do to you?"

"Oh, Shira. He touched me with this great light, I was bathed in it. I swam in the beauty of that light. But the peace and the joy of that moment could not last. It was then that I felt the Hand of G-d reach in and tug at my very being. It was like a great pressure, an enormous weight pressing upon my body. Then I felt the release of that weight from my chest, like the breath of life was being pulled from my lungs. As if the spark of every cell in my body was dimming, losing its life force. The light began to recede and I felt an emptiness. My perception was fading and the landscape began to change, becoming grey, lacking all color and vibrancy. All the sound and the light of the universe, the beauty of the physical world has been lost to me, ever since that moment in the desert. I cried out for Him."

'Do not leave me my Lord, stay with me.'

'I will never leave you, Avram.'

"Those were the last words I heard and then the light was gone and I was alone in the wilderness. Changed, profoundly changed. I fell to the ground, weeping for my loss."

"Avram...what did you lose?"

"My soul, Shira."

My disbelief must have shown on my face because Avram held up his hand to halt my questions, took a deep breath, and patiently continued with his tale.

"The Torah is not just a story or a book of ideals. It is the chronicle of a people. All of it really happened, every event is true. When G-d found me in the desert and took from me my only possession, all that remained was immortality. He gave me a purpose, but at a price. Oh, Shira. Such a price!"

"Then through my tears, I heard another voice. I thought at first that my Lord had returned but I was mistaken. It was the voice of many men, calling out my name, searching for me in the darkness. Before I ever saw them, I smelled them. Their presence came to me upon the wind. It was their human scent and I realized it was discernible from all else that was floating upon the evening breeze. When my family found me, disheveled and inconsolable, on all fours upon the ground, it was then I felt it: a desire that I had never known and it was rapidly overpowering my will. At that moment, I did not yet know what I had become but I comprehended that I was no longer human. I saw I would forever be distanced, standing outside the whole of mankind. The men were panic-stricken, exclaiming loudly over all that had transpired and then to discover that I had been lost amidst the tumult and the dust and the blood of the massacre was more than they could bear. It was my father's deep voice I heard at last, piercing my senses, cutting across the din."

'Oh, my son! You are saved. We thought you had fallen before the sword.'

"He had brought a wineskin and was pressing it upon me to revive myself. The instant the heady fluid touched my lips, I spat it out. I knew I could not tolerate it. I began to tremble as if a flush of fever had come over me and I was suddenly filled with a fury I could not explain. I did not know why, but I felt I had to get away from them or I would not be able to control myself. I had to think, I needed a quiet place to try and sort out all that had happened. And all around me was the press of humanity and they would not be still. They were asking questions, yelling, shoving each other, crying to G-d for guidance. I pleaded with them to let me in peace for a moment but they were urging me back to the camp, pushing me along with them, disregarding my wishes."

"They were all so very near to me, Shira. And then I heard it. Like drumbeats in the stillness, I was aware of the push and the pull of their hearts. It was like a soft coaxing call, entreating, whispering to me as would a lover in the darkest part of the night. My father put his arm around my shoulder. It was more than I could bear."

'Father...please, you must away!'

'Avram. My child. What is wrong? You are safe now.'

"This wholly unfamiliar and disconcerting need was quickly consuming me, overtaking my will. I found I could endure the proximity of these people no longer. I pushed my father's arm roughly from my shoulder. I did not even look back as I ran, leaving them standing there at the far edge of the camp, calling to me in the darkness."

"I had never run so fast or so far and before I knew it, I must have been miles from the foot of the mountain. No one was near; somehow I could tell that I was alone. I flung myself down on the ground and raised my eyes to the starry sky. Oh, Hashem! What have you done to me? As I lay there in the darkness, in the solitude of the night, I heard it. I heard it all. My senses became attuned to all manner of noises as if they were no farther from me than my own hand. I was aware of the scurrying of the jerboa across the sand, the fennec in her den nursing her kits, and the shrill cry of the night birds overhead. All seemed as near to me as you are now. I lay there in the seeming quiet of the desert, listening to the sounds of the world around me. But slowly, ever so slowly, I felt my senses become attuned to something else, something within myself. I felt the fever return. No, not a fever. It was the desire, the hunger. Before I could even define my movement, I was up and sprinting across the rocky plain. I did not even know if I was running from this passion or running towards it."

Avram turned away from me at this. Everything I thought I knew about the will of G-d, the nature of good and evil, the universe and my place in it just came crashing down around my ears.

"G-d took your soul? How is it that you are still alive? How do you continue to exist?"

"The body houses the soul and it in turn nourishes that in which it dwells. When He took from me, He left that house empty and so I must provide for it in the only way left me. Without this essence, how does one sustain that house? I have no soul, Shira and there is but one way to feed for such a one as I am. It is the ultimate blood sacrifice."

"Are you saying what I think you are saying? Do you honestly expect me to believe that there are actually vampires in the world? That G-d Himself would create creatures who survive on human blood?"

"He is omnipotent, Shira. I have witnessed the might of His power first hand on many occasions."

"Avram, this makes no sense at all."

"Logically, it makes perfect sense for the Lord to have made us. We are unlike any other creatures ever created. Something so incredibly differentiated as we could not have occurred by chance or random change. We did not evolve."

"I still don't understand why."

"Indeed, I did not at first either. But I believe I was chosen to witness and participate in His designs. He did surely create us as a mechanism for good, to facilitate and effect change in the world. His plan for us is infinite and without end. You can see that we are sitting here in front of the fire and that should be evidence enough of all that He can do."

"That proves absolutely nothing. This might still be one great hallucination on my part."

"The fact that I exist right here and can relate to you the events at the foot of the mountain should be enough demonstration for anyone. I am as Hashem created me, a creature of linear time able to travel forward as any other creature, whether they be human or animal."

"So, you are saying we did not meet at synagogue. That I imagined it all?"

"That is the future. I do not exist there. I exist here. I am old, Shira. But I am not the eldest. I have encountered throughout the centuries many of my kind who are far more ancient than I. In reality, this has very little to do with just me. I am one of many who serve and we will all spend eternity, as if in purgatory, atoning for our sins. We have always been. We will always be."

"Great, there are more of you and you have always existed? How far do you go back?"

"We are very old, Shira and we are not alone. Every culture since the advent of civilization can claim a blood mythology. Ancient peoples created fables and tales to explain what they did not grasp when they came upon those of our kind."

"But that is just what those stories are, a myth."

"There is a basis in truth for all myth. Let me show you something that will help you. Come with me."

Avram rose from his seat and I followed him into the kitchen. He placed his left hand upon the top edge of the sideboard panel closest to the wall and looked directly at me.

"Shira, what I am about to reveal to you, you must never reveal. It is of the utmost value and if it ever fell into the wrong hands it would not only be my downfall but the destruction of a vast network of others who also serve. You must promise to me that you will never discuss it outside these four walls."

"I promise you, Avram."

"Thank you."

He then slid his hand about one-third of the way down the smooth surface of the wood. With his right hand, he reached around to the recessed section of the cupboard where several teacups were hanging from hooks, rocking back and forth with the movement. I heard a click as if a catch were released and the panel popped open ever so slightly.

"Cool trick. I don't suppose the piece came from the manufacturer like that."

He smiled at this.

"Indeed, it did not. Along my travels I have learned many skills. Carpentry is just one I possess."

Avram reached into the hidden section and removed a rolled up piece of fabric, very dark in color and weightier than it appeared. He carried it over to the kitchen table and with a swift motion, unfurled the cloth and laid it down, smoothing it gently with his fingertips. At first glance, all I could see was a woven tapestry of intricate design. I was about to speak, but the firelight flickered over something in the weave, catching my eye. It was Avram's name in Hebrew, woven into the fabric. And then I saw it arranged before me, the entire composition as it truly was, not just as it appeared upon first inspection. It was no longer just a piece of spun cloth to my eyes. Hidden in the tapestry like a photo mosaic where, if you looked at it from a different angle an entirely new work is revealed, I saw something that took my breath away. It was a map. But it was unlike any map I had ever seen. It was not just a portrayal of continents, countries, and oceans but a sort of chronological family tree, a genealogy incorporating dates, names, and events.

"This is the Chronokiah, the map of my history."

I ran my hand along the timeline, seeing a great pageant of recorded history unfolding beneath my fingertips. Hundreds of years were displayed on this worn piece of cloth, like some gigantic textbook woven upon an even larger loom. Jewish events and historical figures from all over the world were unveiled before me.

"This is amazing, Avram. Wherever did you get this?"

"I created it."

"That's not possible. The first date goes back to the 15th century. There are dates here before Columbus."

"I have told you, Shira. We are all very old. This particular map details approximately the past 500 years alone and this is but one of many in my possession. But I am not the only keeper of the Chronokiah. There are many who are far older than I am who go much farther back than my experiences."

"All of those people listed here, who are they?"

"They are those who have served faithfully."

I am taken aback as I uncover Avram's name throughout the weave, popping up again and again as I run my fingers over the cloth. But his presence is not random or haphazard. Each time it appears, it is during a watershed moment in our history. The dates, the events, and the pictures playing in my mind all begin to blur in a kaleidoscopic image, each angle juxtaposed against the next one. Every thread is bound tightly to its neighbor, spliced within the fabric of the whole. I am beginning to lose focus and I place my hands upon the table to steady myself.

"Avram, I think I overdid it on the wine. All of this is too much to digest, especially on an empty stomach. Do you think I could have something to eat? Oh."

I stop as I perceive what I have just said. Idiot. There will be no food here. Before I can apologize for my gaffe, he answers.

"How inconsiderate of me. I do apologize. Of course, you must be hungry. When did you eat last?"

I look up quickly at him. He used almost exactly those same words in the synagogue parking lot just after I fell. I mean, he *will* use those words. But he doesn't realize, I mean remember. For him, it has not happened yet.

"Shira?"

"What? Oh, I had latkes at the pavilion. But it seems so long ago that I was there."

"No matter. I keep some food here for appearance sake as well as for the occasional visit from the Rabbi. Will bread and cheese do? I have an apple I believe, as well."

He starts rummaging in the top cupboard.

"Somewhere, ah yes, here we are."

He begins to set out a tray for me at the sideboard.

"Avram, should I put this away?"

My hand is upon the map and I begin to roll it up gently.

"If you would be so kind, Shira. It would be well for you to know how to retrieve it if necessary."

I place it in the hidden space of the sideboard and close the panel. I fiddle with the catch a few times next to the teacups to get a feel for it as Avram slices bread and cheese for me.

I make my way back to the table and am about to sit down when I notice that the fire has burned very low. There is a stack of wood next to the hearth.

"Shira, please do be seated. I will serve you."

"I was just going to put more wood on the fire."

"Thank you."

As if another thought occurs to him, he continues.

"Are you cold? How careless of me."

"No, I'm not cold. I would just feel more comfortable with a little more light, if you don't mind."

"I do not mind, Shira."

He smiles and places the tray upon the table.

As I am tossing a log onto the glowing coals and the sparks fly up, I wonder how long I have been here. It seems I have lost all track of time. I look along the mantle and then scan the walls but there are no clocks at all anywhere.

"Shira, you may be seated."

"Thanks."

Avram joins me at the table and as I sit down, the aroma of fresh-baked bread hits my senses. I can feel just how hungry I really am. Bread, cheese and apples have never appeared as welcome as at this moment and I am grateful for even this meager fare. For a few moments, all I can do is savor the chewy bread, pungent cheese, and crisp tartness of the fruit.

"Avram, how long have I been here? What time is it?"

"It is still well before midnight, I believe."

"No wonder I am hungry. I hadn't had much of a lunch today and I think I ate those latkes around six o'clock."

Then I see that I can't have been here more than a couple of hours at most.

"Avram, when you found me in the street, it was very late in the evening, wasn't it?"

"Yes, it was well after dark when I first saw you."

"Well, what were you doing out so late at night?"

"I was on my way home."

"From where? What had you been doing?"

"I had some business to attend to after my duties at synagogue."

"What business?"

I could tell that he was becoming increasingly distressed with this line of questioning. Why is he not being direct with me? The more questions I ask the more withdrawn and evasive he becomes.

"It is exceedingly personal."

"Avram, you are asking a lot of me to trust you that this whole evening is not just some delirium on my part or a grand prank being played on me. Can't you have a little more faith in me and tell me where you were? Why are you so uncomfortable?"

"Shira, you know what I am, how I survive. Do I have to be explicit and spell it out for you?"

His shyness and reserve with me are really getting on my nerves. I reach for another piece of fruit but something occurs to me and I stop, the slice of apple halfway to my lips. And then came the dawn.

"Wait, Avram. Are you telling me you were on your way home from the...kill?"

I found it difficult to even say the word.

"Indeed I was, Shira. You need to know that I deeply regret that we met under such, how shall I put it? Such brutal circumstances? I had hoped that our first encounter would not have touched the reality of my existence quite so soon. But yes, I had just fed. And killed."

"Avram, it is a sin to kill."

"It is a sin to *murder*, Shira. I kill because I must feed. My survival is paramount to continue my work."

"Your entire existence is a paradox. You save and you destroy. How can you live with yourself with the knowledge that, although you are extending lives, entire generations, it is at the expense of death to others?"

"Being alive, if I could call it that, is a gift from G-d. He could have destroyed me utterly at the foot of the mountain. On the contrary, He employed me for a purpose much bigger than just my existence."

"Have you no sympathy for your victims?"

"My dear girl, I am not as unfeeling as you would suppose me. It is a great and terrible thing to take a life. When you hear the penultimate beat of a human's heart, the melancholy of that death remains with you forever."

"It sounds like a curse."

"No, Shira. It is a blessing to do good work in His name. What purpose could be greater and more fulfilling?"

Under his breath and just above a whisper, I could have sworn I heard:

"Be worth more of a reward?"

All evening, the entire time Avram had been speaking, it was as if a movie was playing in my head showing me all the actors, the sets, practical effects, the CG of these events. Scenes displayed themselves out before me like some fantastically deranged deMille film. But these episodes were the stuff that was happening just off-camera, out of the shot, on the sidelines. I was witnessing the takes that were never actually being captured on celluloid, not even ending up on the cutting-room floor, but occurring nonetheless. Some brazen extra with aspirations for a screenwriting or associate producer credit was acting out his own little drama out of view. Hoping beyond hope that it might catch the eye of the 1st A.D. and he would rocket to infamy in the biz because of course, the director will see what a true genius you *really* are and hire you with an obscene salary on the spot. It couldn't possibly be real. No, it was impossible that this soft-spoken man seated across from me was present at Shavuot. He was just telling me a story, right?

With a deep sigh, Avram broke my absurd little reverie of trying to translate his tale into something that made sense to me. I was obviously overwhelmed and it plainly showed on my face.

"Well, little one. G-d has placed you here in this time for a reason and throughout my travels I have found that we cannot make time, we can only spend it. We must discover His purpose for you being here, must we not?"

I saw a familiar smile that lit up his entire face, that sort of goofy grin that I beheld when he hoisted up the Torah in his arms and stopped in front of me at synagogue. Wait...that hasn't happened yet. He still has no idea who I am, that we have met. Before. Not yet.

Oy, I really want a real drink. Where's the Patrón when you need it?

It is very late now when Avram gets up to minister to the fire. The evening has been an adventure in itself and I am feeling all that has been said like a great weight upon my shoulders.

"Avram, what happens next?"

"Do you not think it would be best to sleep now? You must be exhausted from all that has happened."

"Yes, I am. But I feel like I should be doing something. I'm obviously not here for a vacation."

"No, that is true, but...."

"But what? Is there something else you're not telling me about why I am here now? Avram, please."

"As a matter of fact, there is something I have not mentioned for fear it would overwhelm you."

"I don't think that's at all possible."

"I did receive some information this morning that is relevant to my work here but it is too soon to act. You have only just arrived."

"Don't worry about me. What is the information?"

"Shira, you must understand...."

"Avram, if I believe everything you have told me so far, it's possible that I may be involved in a dangerous situation. I may have to put my life on the line for someone I don't know, that I may never see again. I need to know what is going on."

"Very well, Shira. I will tell you. The Danish Underground has obtained some critical intelligence from an unlikely source. Our morning Rosh Hashanah services were canceled and we received warning that there will be a massive round-up and deportation of Danish Jews at 10 pm on October 1st."

"Oh my G-d, Avram. Today's date is the 29th! This is why I am here? I read about this, we have to...."

"Shira, you must remember you cannot...."

"I know, I know. But what are we to do?"

I feel a rising apprehension and a knot in my stomach, remembering all that I have ever read about the rescue of the Danish Jews in 1943. I cannot believe I am here and will actually be witnessing something which only exists for me on paper.

"You must remain calm. All will be well. I have been making preparations with my contacts all day and arrangements are under way. Calls are being made giving warning to as many as we can. I myself will be hiding a family and see to their transport across the strait to Sweden."

"An entire family? How can we manage that? Aren't there patrols everywhere?"

"The majority of the SS stationed here tend to look the other way when it comes to us. Denmark has become the bread and butter for the Germans. They rely on our production of meat and dairy to sustain them. But yes, no matter how the next days transpire, we will have to keep a close watch on their activities. We must be quick and silent. Many

Danish families have offered to support us in our endeavors. Actually, the family I am to help will be split up between other members of the Underground until we can safely see them to the harbor and aboard a vessel, a local cargo ship. It will be less conspicuous that way."

"Who are we to transport?"

"A young girl, about ten years old, I believe."

"What is her name?"

"I know only the father. I was planning on meeting with them this evening and bringing the girl here to stay overnight. But I had this little interruption."

"Is it too late to go there now?"

"No. We all will be working around the clock and as timely as we are able. Already many locals have volunteered to house and help transport families. Do you wish to come with me?"

"Avram, there is no way I'm staying here by myself!"

"Very well. But...you are improperly dressed for the weather. We must find you something warmer and...more appropriate."

He casts his eyes to my bare legs and I catch his face going red as he notices the hem of my skirt which is well above the knee.

"Avram, are you looking at my legs?"

"Certainly not! But you must change into something less conspicuous. Your attire is completely incongruous with the locale and the time period.

You look like...well, if you were to be seen in those clothes at this time of night, people would think that you were a...."

"Just precisely *what* are you intimating about the manner in which I am dressed?"

"Nothing! I did not mean to insinuate, that is I...."

"Okay, okay, I get it! But where am I supposed to find something more... concealing and appropriate at this hour? I'm sure there aren't any shops open now and it's not like we can just pop out and do a Wal-mart run."

"Wall what?"

"Oh, never mind. What do *you* have in mind?"

"We receive donations of clothing at the synagogue. I am sure we will be able to find something to cover you up."

I decide at this point it is wiser to hold my tongue at his puritanical remark than to stand there debating the intricacies of modern fashion. As we leave his home, the chill night air instantly clears whatever residual haziness I had from my over consumption of his wine. My thin layer of clothing, perfect for a balmy night in Westport, offers little protection. Quickly we make our way through the garden that separates Avram's home and the synagogue. The distance is short but I am still shivering as we enter the hush of the dark building. Avram turns on a small table lamp just inside the door and leads me towards the rear of the building. I stop short in the middle of the room because my first glimpse of the interior takes my breath away. The polished wood of the Bimah, the moonlight glinting upon the Menorah, and the very scent of the place all tell me that I'm no longer at home. I've never been to Europe, never set foot in a European synagogue. This one is intimate, but beautiful in its old-world charm. I just stand there, breathing in the atmosphere of the place.

"Shira, please come here."

"Yes, I'm coming."

Avram motions for me to enter a very small back office; there is barely room enough for a desk and chair. Then I let out a laugh as I notice the telephone on one corner of the desk, the one Avram mentioned I could use when I wanted to call my mother. It's actually one of those old-fashioned candlestick-type phones from the 1920s. You know, the kind you hold with two hands: one hand holds the earpiece and with the other you raise the slender base to your lips to speak into the mouthpiece. No wonder Avram looked perplexed when I was fishing in my pocket for my misplaced cell phone.

"Here is the box of donated clothing. But I do not believe we have anything in your size. You will have to make do with what is here, unless you are handy with a needle and thread."

"How would you know what size I am?"

He gives me the once-over. Twice. Like he's appraising cattle at a stock sale. I know my cheeks are starting to blaze but I keep my mouth shut.

"I have met many women in my life, Shira. I have become a good judge of a great many things."

I have no idea how to respond to this so I busy myself with rummaging through the box. The selection is spare, but I do find a black wool coat, dark green pleated trousers and a cream cable-knit sweater that is rather moth-eaten but will serve.

"We have nothing here for your feet, I am afraid. Perhaps the family may be able to lend you some shoes."

He looks down at my thin, little ballet flats and laughs.

"Well, they do go with what I'm wearing now, Avram."

"This is something for which you will have to be prepared, Shira. You will not know the time period in advance each time you travel."

"Avram, I can't even think about anything else at this moment. Where can I change?"

"I will leave you here. When you are done, I will be waiting for you."

He turns to go out but stops at the door and looks back at me. I think he is going to speak but he only smiles and then shuts the door behind him. I just stand there for a minute in this tiny room, unable to move, holding these clothes that belonged to someone I will never meet. What am I doing here? How am I ever going to get home? I don't even have any money on me. Oh man, my parents must be crazy with worry. With a start, I hear Avram's voice. At first, I think he is calling for me so I hurriedly change out of my skirt. I'm not sure what to do with it so I end up just shoving it under the pile of clothes at the bottom of the box. I don't think anyone in 1943 is going to pick a skirt that short anyway. I sit in the desk chair and slip my legs into the trousers. The waistband is way too big. I search through the desk drawers but have no luck finding a safety pin. I had not been able to find another shirt in the box so I just throw on the sweater over my blouse, grab the coat and leave the office. I'm clutching the trousers at the waist, trying not to trip over the hem.

"Avram, I'm swimming in these pants. Do you have...?"

I stop suddenly as I realize Avram had not been calling to me, but rather to someone far greater. He is standing near the Bimah, one hand upon it, the other covering his eyes. His head is bent and he is speaking the words I know so well. From across the distance of that small synagogue, I say the prayers along with him. We finish together and our eyes meet.

"I am ready, Avram."

"Then let us begin."

As we walk out into the street, I lose my footing on the uneven cobblestones and trip over the cuff of the pants. Avram quickly removes his belt and hands it to me. I don't know why, but I'm actually embarrassed as I slide it through the belt loops, standing there in the unlit road of this little village. We continue walking and he explains how we are to proceed.

"The daughter will stay with us tonight and we will rendezvous with the parents at the harbor during the next evening."

"Why would you split them up? How could they bear to be separated?"

"It is highly likely that the patrols will be doing a house by house search. The girl can be kept better hidden in my home."

"Your little place? How could anyone hide there?"

"You will see when we return. Ah, here we are."

We have come upon a quaint home, nestled within a beautiful garden overlooking the cobblestone street. Avram softly taps upon the door which is opened swiftly by a very young man, backlit from the glow within.

"Guten Abend, François."

"Ach, Gott sei Dank, Avram. Bitte, kommen Sie herein. Aber, wer ist das?"

"Meine Freundin, sie heisst Shira."

Avram pauses to let me pass as François extends his hand to me.

"Ich freue mich Sie kennenzulernen, Shira."

"Oh, nice to meet you too."

"Englander?"

He gives Avram a quizzical eye.

"Nein, aber es wird besser als wir Englisch sprechen."

François turns to me and makes a face.

"Mein Englisch is not so gut."

"That's okay. My German is probably about the same."

He ushers us through the hall entryway into the kitchen and introduces us to his wife Camille, who is seated at the table. The nook is a classic European style, L-shaped and surrounded by bench seats with embroidered cushions. It is the kind of place that is cozy and inviting with floral chintz curtains and in springtime would have freshly-cut wildflowers in a glass jar gracing the checkered cloth covering the table. The kind of kitchen that beckons you to have nothing more urgent on your agenda than coffee and cake and a good friend with whom to spend the afternoon. But the mood in the room is far from cheerful. Camille's face is full of anxiety and her eyes are red from recent crying. François invites us to sit.

"My wife, she has no English, so I will speak."

"You need not worry, my friend. Everything has been arranged. My colleagues will escort you to the docks tomorrow night. We will meet you both there and see you all safely onto a boat. Your daughter should stay with us until that time."

"But Avram, my wife is not wishing to separate from her."

"François, you must reassure her that it will only be for a short time and it is safer if you are not together."

"But can we all not go now?"

"The strait is too rough tonight. A crossing at this time is not advisable."

François turns to his wife and explains the situation. I don't catch all of the words but her look of desperation is more than I can bear, so I turn away. I do not need to see her face to know her reaction. I can hear it in her voice. Even though her words in reply come fast and are not discernible in her dialect, they are full of emotion. Avram turns to me.

"Shira, François will take you upstairs. Could you help him get a suitcase ready for his daughter? Have her bring only what she can carry. I need to speak with Camille."

"Of course, Avram."

I hear the two of them converse rapidly in German, one voice pleading, the other reassuring, as François leads me out of the kitchen. The steps creak noisily as we head up the narrow, curving stairwell to the upstairs floor. We reach the top of the landing, but he stops with his hand on the doorknob and turns to me before he opens the door.

"You must know that for your kindness I am grateful."

I am too choked up to reply at this and I don't even know the proper, formal response in German anyway, so I just smile. We enter a very small bedroom, dimly lit by moonlight filtering in through the lace curtains at the window. I have to duck my head a little as the ceiling is slanted at a steep angle; the bedroom is situated under the slope of the roof.

It is the middle of the night and I guess I expected the girl to be sound asleep, completely unaware of the impending danger. But no, there she is wide awake and sitting up in bed, clutching a sleepy, purring cat.

"Papi!"

"Was machst Du, Kind? Du sollst schlafen sein."

"Das kann Ich nicht. Aber wer ist das, Papi?"

"Sie heisst Shira. Shira, may I present my daughter, Gertrude."

While François was speaking, I had automatically been extending my hand to shake hers, but then I stop abruptly before I can help myself. It is a mere fraction of a second that I pause, but it is just enough for her to look up into my eyes. As I grasp her warm fingers in a handshake, she greets me in her small child's voice and I hear it: that same melody and cadence that I remember hearing oh, it seems ages ago.

"Ich freue mich Sie kennenzulernen."

"Hallo, Gertie."

Her face lights up as I use her nickname. It's all I can think to say. I am struck almost speechless by what is unfolding before me. I just stand there not moving, trying to figure out how all of this is even possible.

François senses my hesitation.

"Shira, you are alright?"

"Yes, of course. What can I do to help?"

"Already my wife has a case packed but...you could help her to dress, perhaps?"

"Natürlich."

I remain there for a few seconds in the middle of the room after he has shut the door behind him, trying to think of how not to give myself away. The German I learned in school is nothing like what is actually spoken, not to mention the fact that foreign language textbooks never delve into the intricacies of regional dialects anyway. There are too many for that. But I have nothing to fear. Gertie comes to my rescue. She smiles and launches into a great mishmash of Danish and German, all streaming together in one great river of words, the flow of which less than one-third I understand. I think it has something to do with the cat that lies contentedly on her lap but I didn't quite catch its name.

"Wie heisst es?"

"Sie heisst Schatzi. Sie kommt mit, gell?"

"Nay Gertie, das geht leider nicht."

"Aber warum nicht?"

There's no way I can translate what needs to be said. I don't think she should be told anyway, so I try to distract her.

"Du brauchst dich jetzt anziehen, Gertie. Es gibt wenige Zeit. Draussen ist es kalt. Hast Du Hosen? Du brauchst auch einen Pulli."

"Ich hab' alles hier. Mein Mantel ist da unten. Aber wohin gehen wir?"

"Du kommst mit mir und meinen Freund. Du bleibst bei uns, aber nicht lange."

"Aber Mutti und Papi kommen, oder?"

At this point, I'm lost again for the right words. She's going to have to ask her parents or I'll just make a mess of things.

"Du kannst mit deinen Vater sprechen, gell? Jetzt brauchst Du dich anziehen, okay?"

"Okay, das kann Ich."

Schatzi mews discontentedly as Gertie throws the quilt off and jumps out of bed. I help her out of her nightgown. I don't know exactly how long she will be with us or how much she will be able to carry, so I help her to put on as many layers as comfortably possible. All the while, she is cooing endearments to her Schatzi, saying how much she will miss her and I am thinking this child has no idea what is going on. This is not just some overnight stay at a friend's house and she'll be back tomorrow. I know that she will not see her cat again for almost two years. I must speak to Avram about this. We can't just let the cat fend for itself out on the street.

Gertie is now bundled up and I grab a small leather valise that is by the door. We are at the top of the landing when she turns and runs back into her room. I thought it was for one last hug for Schatzi but she comes back out clutching something small in her hands.

"Alles okay, Gertie?"

"Ja, gut."

She holds out her hand to reveal a small doll made entirely of cloth with yarn hair and black button eyes.

Avram, François and Camille are all waiting by the front door. Camille's eyes are full of tears and she is holding a small coat. Avram takes a step forward.

"Shira, let us wait outside for a few moments."

I am relieved I do not have to witness their goodbyes. We stand out on the front stoop and I rub my hands together. It is so cold, I can see my breath as I speak.

"Avram, do you know who that is?"

"To whom are you referring?"

He is only half listening, his eyes making a quick scan of the dark street, every sense attuned to the sounds of the night.

"The little girl, it's Gertie."

"Yes, I know her name."

"But we know her already, from before. I met her. You spoke to her in synagogue."

"Shira, you must stop referring to the future. It does not exist for me and this line of discussion will only serve to confuse the present by alluding to it."

"But...."

My reply is cut short by the sound of the front door opening through which I catch a glimpse of only the back of Camille as she runs up the stairs. François and Avram shake hands and before I can take a step forward, Gertie comes to me. She grasps my hand in hers and we turn to leave quite possibly the only home she has ever known.

We arrive back at Avram's house without incident. Gertie had become tired from the walk and he ended up carrying her about half the distance. As we reach the front door, I manage to stop myself before entering and I reach and touch the Mezuzah. When I press my fingers to my lips, it's Avram who smiles at me this time and I hold the door open for him. He carries Gertie into the back bedroom and gently lays her upon his bed.

"Avram, how will you ever keep her hidden if we are discovered?"

"Do you see this closet? It has a false wall behind it. Let me show you."

The closet in his room is not a modern, recessed one at all but rather a structure built apart from the wall. He opens the twin doors and I see raw, wooden shelves piled high with clothing and linens. He swiftly removes a stack of dark, woolen blankets from the lowermost shelf and I place them at the foot of the bed. Gertie is still sound asleep and stirs only a little as I unfold one to cover her.

Avram removes the bottom shelf and slides the plank of the back wall of the closet to the right, revealing a small, brick-lined space. It is just large enough to crawl into on all fours. It could possibly hold two people but it would be a tight, cramped fit.

"Avram, did you build this?"

"I had some help from a friend."

"I get the impression you've done this before?"

"My home is well-known to the Underground and has been a temporary way station, a safe haven if you will, for quite some time."

"How long?"

"I have been assisting families to flee Denmark since the Nazis invaded and took control in 1940."

"Three years? How many have you helped to escape?"

"A great many people have passed through my doors, Shira. But the number is not important. If I only succeeded in helping one person to find freedom, then I have found favor in the eyes of the Lord and have served Him well."

Every time I think I have this man pegged, he amazes me with something new. He hands me some linens and I crawl into the space to make a bed up for Gertie. There is a small mattress inside, barely big enough for a child. I don't know how anyone could stay in here for very long, the space is absolutely claustrophobia-inducing. I pop my head out and find Avram cradling Gertie in his arms. As he passes her to me she only murmurs softly in her sleep. She rolls over still clutching her cloth doll as I lay her on the mattress. Once outside, with the panel shut and all the shelves and linens replaced, I flop down on the bed.

"Avram, what happens if Gertie wakes in the night? Won't she be afraid in a strange place?"

"I had her parents tell her about the cupboard before we left the house."

"Didn't she think it strange or seem frightened?"

"Her father said it was part of a great and secret adventure they were having and that she must remember to be very quiet and very obedient."

"I can't imagine being a child and having to endure hardships of this kind. Not knowing when you will see your parents again or having to think how you will just survive. To live in a constant state of fear and apprehension. It makes me think of my generation and how spoiled we all are. It makes me feel very old and very tired."

"But of course, you must be exhausted. You are still mostly human and in all of the preparations it did not occur to me that you would require sleep."

"I wish you would stop referring to me like that. I still feel totally like myself."

Wait, that wasn't entirely true. If I thought about it, I could pick out things that were different. Little things, changes that were hardly noticeable to others but were whacking me upside the head daily and had been occurring for a couple of months. I no longer needed my glasses, I always felt like I could hear people talking about me, and my body was no longer a panoply of multi-colored bruises from my lack of coordination. You could even say I was graceful. But it wasn't just how I physically felt that smacked of a change. The world around me *looked* different as well. Colors seemed more intense, sounds were sharper and like a cat, I could pick up even the most minimal light and see what was around me very well, even on a moonless, dark night. But there were still some very human qualities I retained. I had hunger for food and right now, I was incredibly sleepy.

"My apologies. Yes, you should sleep now. You are welcome to my bed."

"I don't want to put you out."

"It is no trouble. I seldom sleep but I can rest in the front room."

"Are you sure?"

"Do not worry, Shira. I will be perfectly comfortable. But I am afraid I can only offer you this."

He goes to the armoire and removes a large, cotton flannel shirt. Dark blue, well-worn and very soft to the touch. Total boyfriend shirt. It's the kind of shirt your boyfriend lends you for snuggling up together the next morning. The morning after the night before. Whoa. Slow down, Shira. One step at a time.

"Avram, is there a place where I can wash up?"

"I will bring you some water for the basin."

He removes the pitcher from the stand and takes his leave. I guess there is no point in asking for a hot shower, which I really need and would be most welcome right now. There's not even a bathtub. Why would there be? It's not like he'll ever need to freshen up after a hard day. I bring the shirt to my nose out of habit and realize the only smell

I perceive is the scent of cedar which must be from the inside of the armoire. His knock at the bedroom door makes me jump.

"May I enter? I have brought the water."

He places the heavy porcelain pitcher in the basin and hands me a cloth from the drawer of the stand.

"Is there anything else you require?"

"No, I'm sure I will be fine."

"Then I will say good night, until tomorrow."

I sit there on the bed almost too tired to sleep. After I undress, I drape my clothes over the back of the chair next to the washstand. The soft flannel is a comfort as I slip the shirt over my head. I wet the end of the small towel with the warm water and lie down on the bed and try to wipe the day from my face. And what a day it has been. Scenes are flashing before me, disordered, out of sequence, revealing neither rhyme nor reason. The last thing I remember is hearing Avram stoking the fire in the other room and the scent of cedar from my nightshirt all around me.

30 September, 1943 AD
Gilleleje

I think I must have fallen asleep as soon as my head hit the pillow because before I know it, daylight is hitting me in the face. I had heard Gertie call out for her mama once in the night but I must have slept on after that. I hear voices and quickly get dressed. I'm still only half awake as I make my way into the kitchen.

"Avram, oh. What time is it? I didn't know it was so late."

Both he and Gertie are seated at the table. Her appetite is apparent by the way in which she is wholly engrossed in her meal of bread, cheese, and milk.

"It is not late, Shira. You were sleeping so soundly and you looked so at peace that I did not want to disturb you. But I am glad you have risen. Today we should busy ourselves. We have no time to waste. I must use the telephone in the synagogue and call as many people as I can to spread the word to evacuate. This means that I will be unable to care for Gertie today. Perhaps you could help with her?"

"Of course, that's no problem. But there must be something else I can do to help with all of the preparations."

"Unfortunately, you both need to remain housebound today. There will most certainly be patrols on the street and you will not be safe if you venture outside the house. As you have arrived unexpectedly, naturally you have no papers and there has been no time to secure identification for you. But more importantly, a house-to-house search may be initiated very soon. It would be prudent for you and Gertie to practice getting into the hidden cupboard as soon as possible. If I am required to leave the premises today, you both should stay hidden. If the house is searched, I would not be able to protect you."

"I understand. But when are we to take Gertie to meet her parents at the dock?"

"We will not make an attempt until late this evening. My colleagues and I have been watching the Danish police and keeping an eye on the German activities. We have organized our efforts according to a specific schedule of their patrol rounds and will be escorting people in small numbers at intervals. It must be a well-timed act while seeming to be entirely random in appearance."

"How can this all be happening so fast and right under their noses?"

"It is by word-of-mouth and by telephone. If it were not for that most ingenious of devices, Mr. Bell's great invention, I believe we could not accomplish so much in so little time."

Boy, I think to myself, is he in for a surprise in about sixty years if he thinks an archaic candlestick-type telephone is the ultimate in modern technology. There is no way he could fathom at this point the speed of texting and social networking. If I want, I can connect to the entire planet at the tap of a button. And here he is, going to spend the bulk of the day dialing a rotary phone, number by number, painstakingly repeating the exact same message to hundreds of people, spreading the word throughout the community. The future is going to knock him for a loop. But it is the present that now stares me in the face.

Gertie had been eating silently during our exchange but was now finished. She probably had followed very little of what we were saying.

"Also, was machen wir heute, Shira?"

Yes, what are we going to do today aside from hiding, worrying, and stressing about how I was ever going to get back home? That sounds like loads of fun, especially for a ten-year-old. I had no idea how to fill the day and no words in German to explain to her the situation. I shoot Avram a helpless glance. Thankfully, he comes to my rescue and launches into a completely unintelligible babble of German, Danish and whatever local dialect is spoken in this community. Most of the colloquial expressions go right over my head but I can piece together the gist of the conversation. Avram is planning on making calls all day and will be away in the town for a short time, coordinating the efforts of many other Danes who are willing to risk their lives to hide their neighbors. Gertie and I will stay here. At this piece of information, she looks crestfallen. I'm guessing she was thinking this was going to be like a little vacation filled with sight-seeing and novel activities. How am I going to keep this child entertained until nightfall in this little house? I had noticed earlier that there were a few books on the mantle but it is unlikely that any of them are for children. I guess I'll have to use my wits but it's not easy to be witty in a foreign tongue, especially since I've been away from the language for so long. I have barely spoken any German since high school. Avram has finished speaking to Gertie and prepares to leave.

"Shira, although I will be very close this morning, you must stay on the alert. Under no circumstances should you answer the door or wander outside."

I know he will just be at the synagogue right next door, but I still get a surge of anxiety as he makes his farewells before opening the door. Then the door closes and I am left standing in this little room, with a little girl's face staring up expectantly at me, and little to no idea how to proceed. But I had little to fear for Gertie was all action. She jumped up promptly and began clearing the table, chatting away amiably as if she hadn't a care in the world. I was trying to keep up with the flood of her words but she subject-hopped with such speed and dexterity that I resigned myself to mostly smile and nod. The main subjects as well as I could discern were her cat Schatzi, her best friend Gisele, how much she loved mathematics (that's my girl!) and something about some boy named Bengt who persisted in remorselessly teasing her and she couldn't figure out why. I asked her if perhaps it might be possible that Bengt pestered her because he actually liked her a little bit. The look on her face was a classic triple take: shock, confusion and refusal to believe such an absurdity, then a slow, sneaky smile. It's something we girls learn early. A boy ignores you, he's intrigued. He pulls your hair, he really likes you. He pushes you off the swing, he's mad for you! Gertie, armed with this new found revelation, talks almost exclusively about boys from this point onwards. We finish up in the kitchen and head towards the bedroom. She makes a beeline for the bed, straightening up and flapping the blankets on one side as I get the other. I ask her if she thinks we should make up her bed as well when without warning, we are stunned into immediate silence. We hear a loud banging and angry voices at the front door. Without a word, we look at each other for a full second. She then holds out her hand, I grab it from across the bed and we run to the cupboard. After she has crawled in, I follow and close the closet doors. Scooching my back end into the space, I put up the shelf, top it with a folded blanket and slide the panel shut. It has taken no more than ten seconds but we have only just made it. I hear the front door being forced open and the shouts in German of several men. I look over in this confined space that we are in to see Gertie clutching her doll, eyes clenched tightly shut, barely breathing. We are sitting right next to each other and I want to put my arms around her to reassure her but I fear I will make a noise. So I just sit there trying not to breathe, thinking that my pounding heart surely sounds like cannon fire. I notice the vague outline of Gertie's suitcase in the darkness but I don't remember putting it in here. Avram must have hidden it earlier this morning. I hear footsteps and conversation I don't follow. The sounds of the rapid opening of drawers and furniture being shifted across the wooden floor of the main room are all that penetrate my understanding in the blackness of this little space. The noises come closer and before I can even take my next breath, the squeak of the closet doors freezes all thought of breathing at all.

Someone has opened the closet and is rummaging through the shelves. I can't move. Now it is real, now we are actually in danger and I am paralyzed. Gertie slowly reaches over and silently grips my fingers. I don't understand how this is happening. How can it be that we are in danger of discovery? It is absolutely not possible because I know how this story ends. I experienced the outcome. I have met this girl in the future so I know she survives. But what if this is not the only possible conclusion? What if something goes wrong just at this moment and the future I know, the one I have already lived, ceases to exist and the slate is wiped clean starting with this one simple act of opening a closet door? The future altered, *my* future erased in one swift movement and an entirely new history created for me because of this one small gesture, this blink of an eye. My mind is racing, my heart is thumping and it is all I can do to just keep it together and be still. The seconds tick away but time seems to be frozen. But the moments do drag on, as if shuffling their feet, weighted and leaden, slowing almost to a standstill. After what seems like hours, I hear the closet doors close and the voices and the steps receding. Gertie finally opens her eyes and we look at each other for a long time in that little room. Then we hear the front door slam shut and I exhale the longest breath I have ever held. Gertie wants to get out at once but I stop her with my hand and a warning.

"Warte, noch nicht."

I whisper that we need to wait until we are sure they have left the synagogue premises. In my fright of the past few minutes, I had completely forgotten that Avram was there working, making his calls, alerting the very people being searched for in his home. Will they have taken him in for questioning? Arrested him? I am more scared now to think that I will really be stranded if Avram does not return. I am just reaching for the panel when I hear the front door open and shut very quickly. They have returned. My stomach is in knots and I am certain that this is that possible outcome that will change everything. This new destiny will wink out my life as I know it, forcing me into an alternate universe from which I can never return. The footsteps are closer; the closet doors are opening. I can't help it but I am breathing hard when I hear my name whispered urgently.

"Shira!"

"Oh, Avram!"

I gulp over his name. I hear the jerk of the doors and linens landing in a lump. The panel slides open and I see his worried face break into a grin of relief. Gertie scrambles out first and I extend my hand. I fall into Avram's outstretched arms and we just sit there on the floor for a few moments. In my relief of seeing his face again, I find that I am momentarily at a loss for words. I can only smile but it does not matter.

"Oh, my Shira-la! You are safe. I was in such a fear that you and Gertie would be found."

"What happened? Before I knew it they were at the front door and we were bolting for the closet."

"They came to the synagogue first."

"How is it that you were not taken?"

"They asked only for my papers, which are forged. According to the government, I am a Danish citizen. A Gentile, no less."

"But didn't they think it odd for you to be working as a caretaker for the synagogue? Surely they suspected you were Jewish."

"I told them I was an atheist."

"Oh, that's rich."

"It did not prevent them from searching the synagogue and ransacking the office. When they were headed for my house, I knew I must not move for fear of giving you away. They left a guard posted at the back door so all I could do was pretend not to care and to straighten up the mess they made. Oh, Shira! Those were the hardest five minutes I have ever had to endure, waiting for them to leave, thinking that you might be apprehended."

"Five minutes? That's it? It felt like forever in that little space."

"You are safe now. It is unlikely they will search here again."

"When I thought I might not see you again, I was so very afraid. How will I ever get through this day?"

"You have no choice. Each day follows the next and all we can do is try to do our best to be strong for each of them."

Then we both turn as we hear Gertie's little sob. There she was, just sitting on the bed, quietly crying to herself as Avram and I had been speaking. I quickly forget my own fears and gather her up in my arms. I'm not sure what to say, but Avram fills in the gap with words to soothe her. For a few moments, she and I just sit on the bed, holding each other for comfort. As we rest there, I come to believe that this whole situation is really no longer about me but about this girl. I don't belong here; this is not even my time. I am out of my time. This is Gertie's time and it is all about her survival. I am merely a minor character and I do not mind. Then Avram breaks the silence.

"Shira, I hate to leave you now after such a frightening experience but I must go into the town to confer with my contacts and see to travelling supplies. I suppose we will also be needing more food for you and

Gertie. I am afraid I do not keep much here in the way of stores as I seldom have visitors for very long. I will see what I may find but I cannot promise much. Is there anything in particular you would like?"

Yeah, I'd kill for a cheeseburger, fries and a pop. A triple-size hot fudge sundae with nuts. And whip cream. And two maraschino cherries. No, three. Or maybe just a good, strong belt of tequila, hold the salt and lime. But I think any of those requests will make little sense to him.

"Whatever you can find will be fine, I'm not fussy. Hungry, but not fussy. But won't people think it strange if you are loading up on supplies?"

"If I stop at a few different places, I believe it will not be noticed. Is there nothing you wish to have?"

"I'm in serious need of some serious coffee."

"Ah, coffee is not so easy to find."

"I suppose tea is out of the question?"

"We shall see. Gertie, was willst Du essen?"

"Schokolade!"

Naturally, the kid wants chocolate. I don't blame her. A big hunk of dark and bittersweet sounds great right now with some of that red wine Avram keeps stashed in the sideboard.

"Vielleicht. Shira, I will leave you now. But I will return as soon as I may."

Gertie and I sit there on the bed, listening to Avram leave. The front door clicks shut and we are once more alone in the house.

"Well. Here we are, Gertie. Again."

"Wie, bitte?"

"Oh, never mind. Nichts."

I have to do something to keep us busy or I'll just stew. I have never been able to sit and do nothing. I tend to dwell on the minutiae and overanalyze my problems to the nth degree. Without a doubt, my troubles right now are inconceivable compared to my life back home. Wait a minute. What did Avram say? Next time? What if this is my real life from now on? What if I can never go back? Or at the very least, can never return to my regular life such as it had been.

Gertie shifts on the bed, bumping me out of my funk with a soft elbow to the ribs.

"Hupp-ala, Kind. Pass auf!"

"Shira, es gibt hier nichts zu tun. Ich will nach Hause gehen."

"Das weiss Ich. Also, was tun wir denn jetzt?"

"Keine Ahnung."

I ask Gertie to show me what is in her valise. She brightens at this and excitedly retrieves it from the cupboard. She shows me a new dress her mother had made for her. It's a classic 1940s-style with a Peter Pan collar and smocked front. After we rummage a bit through her clothing, repacking and securing her belongings, she asks for a story. I've no idea if Avram has any appropriate books in his house so we head to the fireplace mantle. As I run my fingers over the spines, I'm shocked to discover the eclectic array of subjects on display. Of course, they are all in German: philosophy, medicine, engineering, chemistry, law. All are way too technical for me, the lingo being completely outside my area of linguistic expertise and terribly dry for a young girl. My finger stops at Bram Stoker's Dracula and I think no, that's way more information than she needs to know right now. A-ha! This looks promising. A Danish cookbook, complete with pictures. Gertie says it will do and carries it under her arm back to the bedroom. Neither of us need to decide if that's the best place to be. We know it by now. We plop ourselves down on the bed and Gertie becomes my tour guide through the wonderful world of Danish cooking. All I ever wanted to know and some things I'd rather not were contained in that tome. I now understand the quickest way to off and skin a rabbit (yuck) and decapitate a chicken (double-yuck). But by far our favorite chapter was the desserts. Whatever Aebleskiver is, it sure sounds delicious. The recipes certainly were a distraction from our present situation but they didn't help our empty bellies much. Every time we turned the next page, our mouths started watering all over again. But Avram came to our rescue; his timing was impeccable. We can't have been perusing the book for more than an hour when I heard him return. He called my name as he opened the door, probably to reassure me.

What a feast he had brought back! The table was laden with a great, round loaf of fresh-baked, very dark bread, a small wheel of cheese, and wonder of all wonders, a brown glass bottle of beer! There were even two small ceramic crocks of what turned out to be fruit preserves and butter.

"It looks like you have enough food for an army; there is more than enough for us."

"I was able to get to the Metzgerei as well."

He hands me a small, square packet neatly wrapped in tan butcher paper. As I unwrap it, the aroma hits me. I am looking at what feels like almost a pound of freshly-sliced meat.

"However did you manage to get your hands on this?"

"I have connections in the town."

His smirk is unmistakable.

"Are you telling me this is black market beef?"

"Well, if you put it that way, yes. I did acquire it through an alternative channel. There are supply runners all throughout Denmark. It has been a necessity ever since we became the market basket for meat and dairy for the occupying forces of Germany."

All the while Avram had been speaking, Gertie had been excitedly setting out the food, gathering plates and cutlery, squeaking with delight when she uncovered a small bar of chocolate. She wasn't interested at all where the food came from; she was just in a hurry to get to the eating of it. While I start slicing the loaf, I hear Avram crack open the bottle. As he hands me a glass, the aroma of that dark and heady beer makes me lick my lips in anticipation. That first frothy sip, bubbly at the outset, then hoppy at the aftertaste is a panacea, a cheery welcome of familiarity. I swallow and savor this moment.

"Oh, man. That is exactly what I needed. How did you know?"

"I thought you seemed tired of my wine."

"Not tired. Just wishing for something with a little more of a kick to it."

"I am happy then that I ran into my friend. He is a connoisseur though he does not partake himself."

"A connoisseur? You mean a smuggler."

"Perhaps."

"How can he be a collector of beer and not even sample it? That's sacrilege."

"Ah, well. Who can say? It seems he used to be a frequent imbiber of all things alcoholic but now he no longer has a taste for it."

"He doesn't know what he's missing, this is really good."

I take a deep pull which boosts my appetite.

We enjoyed a rather noisy dinner. Of course, I could have gone for a second bottle but was happy to at least have had the one. I'm sure it was difficult enough procuring it. Besides, I'll probably need a clear head for our trip over the water.

"Avram, how long will it take to cross to Sweden?"

"It will take some hours depending on our speed and how many craft are upon the water. But we should retire early this evening since we must leave shortly after darkness falls. You and Gertie will need to get some sleep before we depart."

"We will be ready. I have gone through Gertie's case. Her parents have packed surprisingly little for her. And well, I'm wearing just about everything I own at this point."

"I told her parents that the less carried the better. They will be well cared for in Sweden. Many Swedes have offered asylum to the Danish

Jews here. But, perhaps we should clean up and get some rest before the journey."

Gertie had finished eating long ago and had sat quietly while we spoke. She did not even notice that Avram had not shared in any of the food. He rises and begins to clear the table while I hustle Gertie off to her cupboard hideaway. Once she is settled, I turn to leave the room but Avram's bed looks so inviting. Just for a minute. Twenty at most. I shut my eyes for only a few seconds; the beer I had guzzled at dinner paved my way into easy drowsiness. I thought I had barely closed my eyes for a few moments when I awake with a start to find Avram sitting in the chair next to the bed.

"Oh! You startled me, Avram. How long have I been asleep?"

"Not long. The sky is just beginning to deepen. It will be dark soon. Gertie is still asleep, we have time."

"Time for what?"

"Talk."

"Oh, I see."

"Shira."

"Yes, Avram?"

"I...you must know that what we are about to do will be dangerous."

"Yes, I know, but...."

"Please, let me finish. Even if we are able to make it through the village to the harbor without being accosted, the patrols may still stop us once we are upon the water."

"Avram, I know what the dangers are. I had a taste of them this morning."

"No, you do not realize the actual peril in which you find yourself. You are mostly...ah, I remember. You do not like that phrase. Let me put it another way. You are not strong like I am, not impervious to...that is, if we are fired upon I will do my utmost to protect you and Gertie. But I need to ask you if you are certain. Do you believe in your heart that you will be able to make this crossing? If you decide that you cannot, you must know that there is no shame if you remain here at my home until I return."

"Avram, I can't imagine that the help G-d promised you was someone to just sit on the sidelines and baby-sit. I think I'm supposed to be a bit more involved than that."

"The choice is still yours to make, Shira. I cannot coerce you into anything against your will."

"Don't worry. And don't think I'm not afraid either. I think pure adrenaline and the fact that I'm still not really sure if this is only a dream are the only things keeping me from having a meltdown."

"So...you will journey with me?"

"I will."

"I am glad."

We are walking quickly but as quietly as we can, making our way towards the dock. We are weaving in and out of people's backyards, through a gate, behind houses, trying to keep to the shadows, remain hidden, stay silent.

We are up against the wall of a house, on a narrow road between two homes when Avram stops suddenly. It is deadly quiet to my ears but he tells us to halt nonetheless. Then I hear them, the unmistakable sound of footsteps on stone as they draw near to where the three of us are standing in the darkness. Avram hisses over his shoulder.

"Shira, get back! Get Gertie out of here!"

A whirlwind of movement, too brief and blurred for a strictly human's eye is very discernible to me. It all happens so fast yet I can pick out every single scene. Before my eyes, a slow-motion choreography is playing itself out. First, a shadow upon the wall, looming larger as someone is advancing. Then the cry of "Halt" breaks the stillness followed by the vision of the soldier. I see the uniform to begin with but that sight is immediately overpowered by that first glimpse of his weapon, a Mauser. The gleam from the moonlight reflected upon the gun metal transfixes me for a moment, so much so that I find I am rooted to that sight and Avram has to push me roughly behind him. In a moment that is barely the blink of an eye, he is no longer at my side but face-to-face with the soldier. Avram's hand is too fast for him. He was trying to unshoulder his weapon and lift it to a firing position, but it clatters to the ground before he can even raise the alarm and shout to his comrades. Then Avram's hands are upon him.

We are in the alley. Gertie is standing behind me, clutching my hand tightly, her grip so hard that I feel my fingers start to tingle; the circulation is being cut off. But I am too terrified by the sight of Avram and what he is doing to the soldier who discovered us to remove my hand. I cannot move. I keep thinking that I should be horrified by what I see and yet

I am mesmerized, being lured forward. I can't take my eyes off of the sight of these two men locked together as if in an intimate embrace: one striving to maintain life, the other seeking to destroy that life. The man is strong. His face is full of confusion and fear but he makes no sound. He never cries out, even in pain. He cannot understand the inhuman power of a grip so forceful. I can see him fighting to free himself, his hands and arms flailing, beating against the body of his enemy. But he is no match for Avram. The struggle continues and Avram is forced to pull him around so that the soldier's back is to me. The man is weakening, becoming slack in his arms. The end is coming fast but Avram still has his mouth upon this man's neck as he looks up at me. I am jolted out of this reverie of impending death by the sight of that gaze. Black eyes that seem not to see are lifted to look upon me. For the very first time, I am terribly frightened. All at once, the reality of what he is hits me like a wave and I feel a sudden rush of adrenaline cascade through my body. My first instinct is to flee, to run away. I call out to him but no sound comes. My mouth is dry and I try a second time.

"Avram."

He does not respond. I am wary of being too loud, of attracting more attention. I try to remove my hand from Gertie's. I wonder why she won't let go and then I look down and see that she has her eyes tightly shut. My fingers are stiff from her grasp and I take a step forward. As my heel makes contact with the stone, Avram jerks back, blinking. Without thinking, I am rushing towards the soldier to try to catch him, to break his fall with my body. I am at Avram's feet, cradling the man in my arms when I look up as I hear him speak.

"You need not bother. He is dead."

Our attempt to make it to the cargo ship has failed. We have returned back to Avram's home and are now sitting in front of the fire. I have put Gertie to bed in the hidden closet, making it up for her with extra blankets. I tried to comfort her as I tucked her in. She saw nothing of what transpired in the alley since she was behind me during the struggle. She only wanted to know when she will see her parents again.

In the alley I had watched as Avram, with no seeming concern or respect, deftly remove every article of value from the soldier's body. The last item he took was his gun, which had been kicked across the stones to the alley wall in the struggle. As he had knelt down to retrieve it, it seemed he had forgotten that Gertie and I were even there.

Now, back here in Avram's living room, I wonder just how we are going to make this all work.

"Avram, what will happen when the soldier's body is found?"

"It will not be found. My colleagues will see to that."

"What do you mean? How on earth are they going to dispose of it without getting caught?"

"Shira, it is best if certain aspects of how we operate are not discussed. It will all be taken care of, the details of which are rather indelicate in mixed company."

"I see. You are saying it's better not to know. Well, maybe you are right. But do you suppose Gertie's parents made it to the boat? Shouldn't we contact them?"

"Shira, our main concern is to get Gertie to the harbor. Last night I spoke privately to François. We discussed the possibility of failure. Irrespective of whether they made it across the strait or not, we must make another effort with Gertie. I know of someone, a friend who might be of use to us. Yes, I have need of Vietor now."

We have left Gertie asleep in the hiding place behind the closet wall and are on our way through the village to where Vietor lives. All during our walk I have been dying to ask a question.

"Who is this friend of yours...this Vietor?"

"He is a member of the Danish Resistance. I have known him for many years."

"Is he like you?"

"No, Vietor is still human."

"Still? Does he know what you are?"

"No, he does not and he must never consider that I am anything other than what I appear to be. Vietor believes I work only as a caretaker for the synagogue and occasionally help out with underground activities. You must never betray me to him, Shira. If he ever found out, it would be my undoing and fatal for him."

"What are you saying?"

"I could not permit him to live knowing what I am."

"But you told me he was your friend, Avram. I don't believe you. How could you hurt him?"

"I will permit nothing and no one to interfere with my work."

"Even me? What if I betray you?"

Avram stops short.

"You will not."

"What if it were an accident?"

"There will be no accident. Ah, here we are."

We have now come to a small, stone cottage outside the village, full of rugged character with an overgrown, unkempt garden. However, the picturesque scene I see before me is completely juxtaposed by the music I hear coming from inside the house. Before Avram can knock at the front door, it is opened by a very tall man who greets us in what I think is some Scandinavian language, possibly Norwegian. They all sound the same to me. Avram greets him back and I realize that he must be conversant in many different languages to be able to work and travel as he does.

Vietor welcomes us inside as Avram introduces me, shifting over to English. Vietor's speech is heavily laden with guttural sounds and his grammar leaves something to be desired but I can make out what he is saying.

"I am please to meet you, Shira. You would like to sit?"

We are at the kitchen table which is littered with tools and rags and some piece of equipment that looks like it has recently been disassembled, but I can't make out what it would be if it were right way up again. The entire room is a jumble of dirty dishes and piles of heaped clothing and newspapers. Then I see an object that is completely out of place in this obvious bachelor's house. Sitting atop a small cabinet is an old-fashioned Victor phonograph with the large, iconic fluted horn curved over the record still spinning upon the turntable. That explains the music.

"I heard music when I came up to the door. I thought you had a radio playing, Vietor."

"No, the phonograph only. At one time I am having a radio, but the Nazis confiscate them when they are taking control of this country."

The look on his face at first is harsh but then he notices my smile.

"It sounded so familiar to me. May I look?"

"Yes, of course."

I walk over and read the label on the record. I was right. It's Carmen Miranda's 'South American Way.' I love that song, it's so 1940s in that Bing Crosby/Bob Hope road trip kind of way.

"Oh, I haven't heard this for ages."

"What are you meaning? This song is just new."

Avram shoots me a warning look and interrupts with something to distract him. It takes me a second to get what I just said. I almost blew it by referencing my time period. This is going to be harder than I thought. Maybe it would be better if I don't speak at all.

"Shira, Vietor and I have some important matters to discuss. You do not mind if we speak Norwegian for a while? It will be easier for him if we do."

"Not at all, Avram."

The men switch back to Vietor's native tongue and I am completely lost and utterly at a disadvantage. But this gives me the opportunity and time to take a better look at Vietor. He is tall, much taller than Avram and built like an alpine skier: long, lean, and muscular. He could be right out of the pages of some glossy, Swedish travel brochure with his Nordic blond hair, ice-blue eyes, well-chiseled jawline and an inviting smile that says:

"Come explore the scenic wonders of our wintry tundra by day and the relaxing waters of my hot tub by night."

Avram had told me more about him on our walk over to his place. Vietor was about thirty years old and captain of his own small cargo ship and normally did the Aberdeen to Stavanger run. But now, he would be helping to transport a very different cargo aboard his vessel, the Svane. The men continue to talk but I hear that it is now in English.

"Avram, you know I am having no love lost on the government of Norway for what they do to the Jews there."

"I understand your feelings, Vietor. I appreciate any help you can give us."

"It will not be easy, but across the strait the journey will not be too long. The Svane is yours, Avram. She will get us there."

"Tusen takk, Vietor."

Before I can stop myself, I interrupt.

"Am I getting you both correctly? The Germans must at least suspect by now after all of the activity that has been going on in the past 24 hours. They will be on high alert. How are we to get past the patrols and the harbor police?"

It's Vietor who answers me.

"We must make the effort."

"But it seems hopeless to think that we can make a difference."

"Your faith should keep you strong, Shira. There is no room for doubt. G-d is the ultimate pilot, but He does want you to step up, put your hand upon the tiller and navigate as well."

"Well-spoken, Vietor."

"Takk, Avram. All is settled then. But I am not seeing why this girl is here?"

"Shira will assist us in our endeavors."

Vietor throws a glance my way that any girl would recognize: a wolf leering at a lamb, licking his chops. He's still grinning through his teeth when he turns back to Avram. I half expect him to wink.

"That is all very well and good. But what skills is this girl having that could possibly be of any use to us? She is looking like she has never done anything but kept house."

Whoa, buddy. Slow down. You are going to hurt yourself. I interject before Avram can speak.

"I'm a member of the NRA."

Vietor's expression immediately registers shock followed by skepticism but he gets up and removes a leather satchel from a cupboard. He raises an eyebrow as he reaches in and removes a firearm. I hold out my hand and am taken aback by what ends up in it. No way I say to myself, it can't be, it's not possible that this is a...and then I finally blurt out:

"Is this a Liberator? This can't be an original 'gun to get a gun.' Can it? The Woolworth gun? Where did you get this? Was it air-dropped?

Wow! Vintage are few and far between. Really hard to come by these days. You know, they just started reproducing them but originals are unbelievably expensive, way out of my budget for sure."

I blather on while I examine this small, simple gun that looks like a toy and initially cost about two dollars. Its purpose was ingenious: use it to obtain a bigger, better gun by dropping the owner of said bigger, better gun. I check the chamber, look to see how many bullets are stored in the grip, and try to get a feel for the weight of it in my hand. As I stand there admiring it, I realize that the room has gone deadly quiet. I look up to see the men staring at me open-mouthed, utter disbelief showing on their faces.

"What? Don't girls play with guns in 1943?"

Vietor smirks.

"Not any girls I know."

"Well Vietor, you really should get out more."

"Our little Shira is full of surprises, is she not Vietor?"

Avram holds out his hand and I place the gun in his palm. He turns and hands it to Vietor who sets it back into the satchel and then looks at me and smiles.

"It seems we must learn to expect the unexpected."

You have no idea.

"Avram, please don't talk about me as if I'm not here. I am here. For a reason. If I am supposed to be a part of how this whole scenario plays out, then treat me like a major player, not some minor leaguer sitting on the bench. Deal?"

Avram and Vietor look at each other, obviously unsettled by the directness of my speech. Then they both grin. Broadly. Avram gives me a wink.

"Deal."

We hurry back through the chill night air to Avram's house and wake Gertie. The plan is not to wait another day and night but to leave at once. We cannot afford to push our luck and wait for another nightfall.

She is sleepy and fidgets as I try to get her into her sweater and jacket. I am very nervous this time as we wend our way through the village. On high alert, listening to every sound, scouting for the slightest movement, we hurry through the streets. We come to the dock by another route and are waylaid by no one this time. Before we turn the last corner to the open sea, I smell and hear it: that salty tang to the air and the slap of the water against the seawall. I don't know what I was expecting, but one could hardly call it a harbor. More like a small inlet, a finger-like projection denting into the landscape. One minute we are passing through yards and then we turn the corner and we are there. The pier is very small and fishing nets and their attached floats are draped over every possible surface. We walk past wooden barrels rotting where they sit, their iron rings rusty with age and the corrosive effects of saltwater.

There are few boats tied up and Avram quickly leads us to the Svane. I take one look at our transport and feel like I'm in some sci-fi movie: it's a total rust-bucket and there is no way I am going to leave the safety of dry land and put one foot onto that tin can of unseaworthiness. I don't know much about seafaring but it seems to me to be a complete disaster. Avram had told me it was a standard 36-foot fishing trawler. Whatever I was anticipating when I heard we were going for a boat ride, it certainly isn't this ungainly contraption which is rising and falling with the motion of the water. It almost puts me off ever eating fish again. It is a veritable smorgasbord of senses in its ugliness: the constant squeak of the rubber tires secured to the starboard side against the slimy stone of the retaining wall, grimy, coiled ropes everywhere, the rusty, weathered cabin with nets draped over the top reaching down the sides to the deck, not to mention the horrid diesel fumes mixed with the rank perfume of rotting fish.

We make it down the seawall steps which are slick with moss when I spot Vietor, just stepping out from inside the cabin. I almost laugh out loud. He looks like something straight out of a fish stick commercial: navy pea coat, off-white, hand-knit Aran turtleneck sweater, and black fisherman's cap frayed at the edges. All that is missing is the hooded, yellow raincoat. Wait, there it is in the cabin, draped over the wheel. He greets us briefly as we come aboard. I can tell something is up from his expression. He and Avram confer for a moment as I get Gertie settled.

"Avram, what is it?"

"There is some slight trouble with the engine. But we will not be delayed for long. Perhaps it would be best if you and Gertie went down now into the hold."

"The hold?"

I don't like that idea at all. I look over at the wooden trap door and there is no way I am crawling into that small space from whence the pungent stench of overripe fish is emanating.

"I can't go in there."

"It will be necessary for the crossing."

"No, you don't understand. It's a small, confined space. I won't last five minutes in there."

"Shira, there is no alternative."

"There has to be. What about the quarters under the cabin?"

"You will not be as protected there."

"Avram, I'm sorry. But I can't go into the hold."

"Very well. You and Gertie may go below now. I need to assist Vietor with the repairs."

Gertie and I step into the room below the cabin. It is as neat as a pin, the complete opposite of Vietor's home. We sit there on a rumpled pile of filthy canvas without speaking. Huddled there together in the darkness for what seems a very long time, we eventually hear the droning whump, whump, whump of the motor as it rhythmically starts up. I stick my head out of the doorway to see Avram back on the stone pier, uncoiling the mooring line. He releases it, throwing the line onto the deck with a slap, the rise and fall of the Svane inching itself and us from the seawall. We are slowly pulling away but he remains there, scanning the darkness for any sign of patrols. As he turns to face the retreating boat, I gauge the distance to be way too far for him to make the jump. He can't be leaving us. Why is he still standing there?

"Avram, hurry!"

At almost the last minute he leaps forward, landing noiselessly on deck. I breathe a sigh of relief. We are under way and Avram motions for Gertie and I to come topside as he makes room for us on a small bench seat.

"Avram, why did you wait so long on the pier? I was afraid you were not coming."

"I had to be sure that the patrols would not delay us."

"How did you make that jump? I was sure it was too far."

"You need not have feared. We have passed the most difficult point in our journey. But you must realize that if the harbor patrol plans to board, you and Gertie must go down into the hold."

"It smells wretched."

"There is no room for squeamishness. I must go into the cabin and help Vietor keep a lookout. If I call to you sharply, you must go below."

"I will, Avram."

All about me people are on the water in boats of all shapes and sizes. There are even small dinghies bouncing along with just a few passengers bundled in blankets, huddled together for warmth. Vietor's trawler is a leviathan amongst all of the craft making their way across the strait.

I've never done well on the water. I go as green as the sea just thinking about ocean travel. For some reason, I guess I'm too distracted by what is going on around me. I totally forget to be queasy. Perhaps it's the hypnotic noise of the water, slapping the sides of our little ship which seems to be lulling me and I forget my trepidation.

Avram is up at the wheel with Vietor helping guide him through the sea of refugees all around us. Everyone has kept their running lights off and we periodically hear a few bumps as smaller vessels collide with each other. Gertie is cuddled next to me, shivering and gripping her doll. She has been chatting to me the entire time, expressing fear and worry over her parents as well as her cat.

"Wo sind Mutti und Papi?"

"Sie warten auf uns in Schweden. Wir sind fast dorthin."

The boat is rocking continuously. I'm trying to keep Gertie distracted when I look down after a particularly bad jolt to see her doll lying in a puddle on the deck. In the same instant that I reach down to retrieve it wondering why it's lying there and not in her hands, I hear a yelp and then a splash.

I do not even give myself time to think: one moment I am sitting on the bench and the next my feet are no longer on the Svane but behind me as I dive head first into the choppy water. I can only vaguely recall rising up, throwing off my coat and hearing the buttons pop and clatter on the deck. In that split second, as my fingertips break the surface of the waves, before my body breaches and neatly knifes the churning water, I hear Avram shout my name and I think, Mensch! That water is going to be so cold.

It must be the adrenaline warming me because I do not feel at all the jarring shock that should be taking my breath away as the water touches my skin. I feel only the wet of the ocean as I open my eyes, right myself and look up towards the moonlight making a play upon the water above me. My clothes are becoming heavier with every stroke as I slowly make my way to the surface. I am thinking it will take me forever to get there and I will be too late to find her. And then I am there, gasping for air, choking on the spray and scanning the surface for Gertie. The water is black, the waves roil all about me, and the noise of the swells drowns out all other sound. And yet I see and hear: the slap of an arm as it strikes the surface and the strangled cry of "Hilfe!" Then I see her being dragged down about twenty feet away from me. My arms have a mind of their own as I slice the water towards her. I am only a few feet away when I hear Avram swimming up behind me.

"Shira!"

"She's here, Avram!"

I am clutching Gertie around her ribs with her back against my chest, keeping her head above the water as I start to make my way back to the boat. She is choking, crying for her mother.

"Mutti, Mutti!"

"Ich bin hier, Gertie!"

Avram is pulling us both back toward the Svane which is heading in our direction. I hear Vietor shouting in Norwegian as I push Gertie to the side and he hoists her up. Avram and I are clinging to the ladder, rocking along with the boat as it is tossed about in the waves. The look on his face startles me as I grip the lowermost rung and start to climb and then I am back on board.

Vietor has removed Gertie's jacket and wrapped her in a blanket. She is shivering and sobbing. Avram retrieves my coat from the deck floor as I pull my drenched, very heavy sweater over my head. I tell him I am not cold as I take it and drape it over Gertie's shoulders and scoop her into my arms. Avram is standing over us both and I cannot believe the expression on his face. He is actually frowning.

"Shira, what were you thinking?"

"I wasn't."

"That is obvious."

"Avram, I don't know what happened. One minute I am next to Gertie and the next she is overboard and I am in the water."

Vietor has returned to the wheel but then looks over his shoulder.

"How did you reach her so quickly? Uff da, I've never seen anyone swim so fast."

"Vietor, it was a gut reaction. I can barely dog-paddle. Your guess is as good as mine."

Avram is silent during this exchange. But I sense he knows the answer.

I cradle Gertie in my arms for the rest of the voyage over the Øresund strait. Her teeth are chattering and her little body is vibrating from the cold. I keep up a steady stream of words to try to comfort her in her distress but in the stress of our present situation, my German completely fails me. All my words are lost on her and she doesn't understand a single thing I say, but it doesn't matter to her. The tone of my voice is enough. She nestles closer into my arms with her doll clutched tightly in both her hands. It was the first thing she retrieved when she was back on deck. I grip her tightly to keep her warm. As we sit there, rocking with the rhythm of the swells, I find I'm having trouble fathoming the enormity of what has just happened and the implications of what we are doing. Am I really on this little boat riding the choppy waves, soaking wet, holding a ten-year-old girl that I just pulled from the icy water? Does she become the woman I will meet in 2010? Wait, we have already met and she remembered me. Oy, now my head is beginning to hurt. I was never very good at all that sci-fi time-travel nonsense and here I am smack dab, right in the middle of the mother of all paradoxes, staggering in its consequences. This is just too much to wrap my head around. And then I look down at my feet. My bare feet. My shoeless feet that keep losing traction on the slippery boat deck. It takes me a full second to realize that I no longer have my shoes. I lost them the moment I dove into the frigid waters of the strait. For some reason, the sight of my naked feet pale in the moonlight against the background of the dark night strikes me as hysterically funny. I can't help myself, I start to chuckle. Gertie looks up, curious as to why I am suddenly laughing and I nod my head towards my feet. I wiggle my toes and she looks back at me and smiles. Then it's all over and neither of us can help ourselves; we both start giggling like schoolgirls.

Vietor shouts out that we are nearing land. We see many other small vessels coming into the harbor and I wonder how we are ever going to find Gertie's family amidst the crowds searching for their loved ones.

"Avram, look at all those people. Where are we supposed to meet her parents?"

"Shira, do not worry. We shall find them. I will know where they are once we disembark."

Vietor cuts the engine just before we bump against the seawall. The rubber tires hanging against the side of the Svane squeak in a familiar way against the algae-covered stones. Avram ties off the mooring line and Gertie and I make our way across the deck and then onto the pier steps leading upwards. We both find we still have our sea legs and stumble a bit on the top step. The dock is full of people, bumping against us as we try to jostle our way through. They are talking loudly, crying, and gesticulating around us as other craft make port. Avram scoops Gertie up in his arms as I push forward ahead of him, trying to press my way through the crush. I am sidestepping husbands looking for wives, mothers looking for children, and panic-stricken children looking for any familiar face as my bare feet come in contact with the rough wood of the pier. Then I hear someone calling Gertie's name. It's Camille and François. I hear them before I see them. I can tell where they are amidst the throng. And there they are. I see them running towards us from across the street.

As Avram places Gertie into her father's arms, Camille breaks down and rushes into mine.

"Danke, danke."

Even though the rest of her words are choked with sobs, I've no need for a translator to understand what she is saying at this moment. Her emotions are clear.

Avram and François are speaking in low tones and then I hear my name. It's Gertie who reaches out to me, fumbling to get her hand out from under the blanket in which she is bundled. The look in her eyes needs no deciphering and despite myself, I feel a lump in my throat as I grasp her small, cold hand in mine.

"Alles ist okay, Gertie."

She squeezes my hand and pulls me close so she can whisper in my ear. She asks me again not to forget about her Schatzi. I promise her I will not.

"Versprech Ich dir, Gertie. Hab' keine Angst."

No more words come, for either of us. I give her one last hug and then turn towards Avram.

"Shira, we must leave now."

He has finished speaking with François and grasps my elbow to guide me back to where Victor is waiting for us aboard the Svane, her diesel engine idling in the water. As I stand on the top seawall step, I turn one last time to wave goodbye. But the crowd is thick and it is too dark to make out their individual figures. And then I set foot once again on the slippery deck, my fingers clutching the small cloth doll that Gertie had pressed into my hands when she whispered in my ear.

The trip back over the strait is less eventful physically. But it's all I can do to keep it together. Avram sits beside me and puts his arm around me. That does it and I let go, crying on his shoulder, and leaning into him for the duration of the ride back. We do not meet any harbor patrol ships, the water seems calmer than I remember, and before I know it Victor is killing the engine and we slowly bump the seawall. I do not let go of Avram once until we are again back on the slippery stone steps of the pier in Gilleleje.

Victor has just finished tying up the mooring line and I turn to make my farewell to him. As he hands me my wet sweater, I proffer my hand but I don't really know what else to say other than thank you. He grips my hand in a strong handshake, pulls me close and leans forward to whisper in my ear:

"Bis zum nächsten Mal, Shira."

I'm not really sure how to respond so I just smile and turn to leave the pier with Avram. They had made their farewells while still aboard. The night is still and dark and cold as we slowly walk back to Avram's house. There are no lights at all emanating from the homes we walk past, as if every villager is aware intuitively of the need for silence. The stones are cold on my bare feet and I feel every rough curve of them as I gingerly make my way. Avram has not let go of my hand since we left the pier. Once, he brought it to his lips and then held it pressed against his cheek, but said nothing. Something is nagging me about Vietor and I break the silence.

"Avram, why did Vietor say that to me just now? What did he mean, until next time?"

"Vietor is the ultimate male optimist. He does not know how long you will be here in Gilleleje."

"What is he optimistic about?"

"He is a flirt, Shira. Can you not see? He is well-known in the village as a bit of a ladies' man. For all his nobility of action, he is rather a scoundrel."

"You mean after all that has transpired this evening, he's hoping we might hook up?"

"Hook up?"

"Never mind. I get what you mean. I just can't believe he's thinking of that now."

"Vietor thinks of little else."

We have arrived back at the house and stop at the entryway. This time our fingertips meet at the Mezuzah and we hold them there just for a moment, regaining our strength together, praising G-d for our safe return.

Once we enter, Avram immediately stokes the fire. I stand there in my dripping trousers, barefoot, holding Gertie's doll in one hand. In my other hand, I am still clutching the sopping wet knit sweater. It is becoming heavier with each passing moment and yet I can't seem to put it down. I remain standing trying to warm myself but I think I am too numb with shock to be cold anyway. Avram leaves the room and returns with the dark blue flannel shirt, another pair of trousers, and a towel.

"Shira, you must get out of those wet clothes. You are still vulnerable to illness."

"I...."

"Give me your sweater."

"Avram, I lost my shoes."

"I know. All will be well. But you must change your clothing."

He reaches down for the sweater still gripped in my hand. It's all I can do to let it go. He begins to slide the wool coat off of my shoulders and I shiver involuntarily.

"Shira, you are cold."

"I am tired, Avram."

"I know. I will leave you here in front of the fire to change."

I watch as he retreats to the bedroom. I stand there for just a moment, trying to figure out what to do next. I fumble with the belt buckle and then the trousers drop in a wet heap at my feet. I quickly remove my blouse and step into the dry pants and pull on the soft shirt. The small comfort of this familiar item hits me all of the sudden. I am completely exhausted and utterly overwhelmed by the gravity of what I have just witnessed and participated in. No...what I have made happen. Avram comes back into the room and I see that he has also changed out of his wet things. He picks up my clothing from the floor.

"I will hang these outside."

I am trying to dry my hair with the towel but it seems pointless and I don't have the energy anyway. When Avram returns, he lights a candle at the kitchen table and in this small, dark room all I can do is sit on the floor in front of the fire and stare at the flames. I am incapable of processing anything beyond that light.

"Shira, you need to drink something. Let me get you some wine."

I watch as he fills a glass, looks over at me, and then brings the entire bottle over to the fireplace. He hands me the glass and sits down next to me on the hearth rug. I down the first without even tasting it but sip the second more slowly. I don't even know how to begin but if I don't say something, anything, I may just end up bursting into tears.

"Avram, those people tonight. They really existed, I mean exist? I'm here right now and there really will be 7,500 Jews transported to Sweden in 1943 in just a few weeks, right before the Nazis were going to capture and deport them to the death camps. I didn't hallucinate these past two days, did I? I actually was there helping one girl to find her family? That was really Gertie?"

"You saved her life, Shira. You were an instrument of G-d tonight, a woman of valor."

"But how could this have happened? Why does G-d allow so much evil in the world?"

"To keep the fighters from being idle. We must not become indifferent or complacent to the good when we encounter it or let it pass us by without recognizing it. Evil exists so that we may have a purpose."

"That is too much of a burden. How can you bear it?"

Then the tears come and I feel a fool. Avram takes my hand in his and kisses it. Through my tears, I look up into his eyes.

"At some point, you will discover that good and evil do exist and with that realization, you must choose one or the other. I have no choice but to obey the will of G-d and abide by His laws. He has commanded me and I will not refuse. My penance is to spend an eternity atoning for my sin. But do you not see, Shira? G-d has made my task one that I have come to recognize I would gladly give my life for, if it were at all within the realm of possibility for me to die. You must understand now that this is a Holy War that I am waging. It is a war against all those who would oppress and persecute my people, those who would defy G-d and His law. You see, I am fighting to protect those whom He has chosen."

"But why did He choose me? I am no one, just one of many who lives their life like everyone else. Why have I been placed here? I am tired, so very tired."

I feel a lump in my throat, I choke and I cannot go on.

"Do not weep, little one. It is time to rest, it is over for now."

He starts to rise but I don't want him to leave my side. I pull him close in an innocent embrace and whisper:

"Please stay here with me a while, Avram."

I can tell he is not expecting my touch and is clearly startled by my request, but I cannot help myself as the tears begin to stain my cheeks again. I lean into him. At this moment, my emotions seem beyond my control. Everything I thought I knew about the world and about G-d has been turned upside down. The past hours spent in hesitation and fear have taken a toll on me both physically and emotionally. All of this is so completely outside the parameters of my experience that I find it difficult to concentrate. Avram puts his arm around me, attempting to give me comfort in my distress. Brushing the hair from my eyes, he leans close to me, breathing deeply. I do not realize that he is quietly and very quickly losing his self-control. Before he can help himself, he is drinking in the perfume of my hair.

"Avram, I am afraid."

"I know, little one. The first time it was difficult for me as well. You will soon adjust."

"I don't know if I can."

He draws back and his manner is suddenly cold, his voice surprisingly harsh.

"You will not survive very long if you do not."

I am taken aback by the sharpness of his words but he is the only warmth I have at this moment. He starts to rise once more but I do not let him go.

"Please, do not leave me now. I need you."

"Shira, we dare not."

His voice is deeper now.

"Avram, do not let me go."

I tighten my grip upon his arm.

"Very soon it will be too late, my Shira. You do not truly comprehend what it will mean if we do this."

"Will I become like you?"

"No, not like me. You will not be as I am until you prove your commitment to G-d."

Then he slowly, ever so gently moves in to rest his cheek against mine. His lips are very near and I close my eyes as he whispers softly to me:

"No. Not yet, Shira. But soon little one, very soon."

My eyes snap open with a start. A slideshow of images from my past is suddenly all around me, flashing briefly, jogging memories I didn't even know I had. Snapshots are rapidly materializing and just as swiftly dissolving from view.

"It's you, isn't it? You held me close and whispered in my ear all those years ago but in the future. It's always been you in my life. Is this what you meant?"

He draws back and looks into my eyes.

"No, you must wait to become like me. But if you desire me now my beloved, I...."

I do not let him finish as I lean forward and brush my lips lightly against his. He hesitates for a moment and then takes me in his arms. I feel the press of his lips upon my mouth. His kiss intensifies with each passing moment and I'm finding it difficult to breathe. I am still entwined in his embrace as he slowly leads my body to lie upon the floor. His grip is strong as he slides his hand and then his entire arm around my back, pulling me against him, closing the space between our bodies. I am beneath him, caught in the power of his grasp; I couldn't move even if that is what I wanted. But it is not what I want. At this very moment, I have never wanted anyone more. His hand is moving slowly, ever so slowly over my entire body, running over the soft flannel, as if he is savoring the feel of every curve, every intimate part. Soon, very soon, it will be too late for me to stop and yet we are both still fully clothed.

"Avram, I...."

"Shh...do not speak, my sweet."

With one hand, he begins to slowly unbutton my shirt. I see a brief flash in his eyes as the firelight is caught and reflected off of my Star of David.

"Your star is very beautiful Shira, as are you."

And then I feel it, that first touch of his hand upon my bare skin and I am shocked to my core. I cry out his name as I am consumed by the intensity of his touch.

"Do not fear, little one. I will not harm you."

He pulls me close and silences me with his mouth. In Avram's kiss, I behold the longing of so many years.

1 October, 1943 AD
Gilleleje

The next morning, the rich smell of coffee brewing filters into my consciousness, slowly waking me with its easy, delightful familiarity. For a moment, I don't know where I am. I half expect to hear my mother's voice from downstairs calling me to get a move on. But as I lie there wondering why she doesn't, I remember. I remember last night. I am stretched out on Avram's bed but I don't recall how I got here. It must be very early. The sky is just beginning to glow with the sunrise. I find Avram working in the kitchen, preparing a tray for me.

"Little one, you are up. I was going to bring this to you."

"Thank you. It smells delicious. But I thought coffee was difficult to find."

"I went out rather early this morning and was able to procure it from a friend."

"I guess in your line of work, it's all about who you know."

"That is aptly put. Shall we sit by the hearth?"

As I lower myself in front of the crackling fire that Avram has made this morning, my thoughts are drawn again to what happened here just a few short hours ago. I want to ask him so many things about his life, about what has happened, about what we have just done. I try to make a few starts as I slowly sip the very rich coffee he has served me. But I don't know where to begin. Then I think, maybe I should just wait for him to begin the discussion.

But we do not talk about what happened. It's as if it didn't happen. Avram is hard to read but I am thinking that perhaps he is just shy and reserved. I have to remind myself that he is from a most distant time and the frankness to which I am accustomed is completely alien to him and his world. The difficulty with which we have relating to the personal is not apparent in what we now find ourselves discussing. Well, discussing is probably too tame to describe what we are doing. Quibbling is more accurate. I am trying to ask him about all of those moments from my past. When I think on all of the events of my life that he has participated in, I have a hundred questions and I want answers. But Avram is firm.

"Shira, you must remember what you reference has not yet occurred. Please do not speak of things that for me, have not been."

"Okay, Avram. I won't ask you any more about the future. I mean, my future. I'm just having a hard time trying to figure out how all of this works."

I try to think of something we can discuss that doesn't run smack dab into another paradox. I think of Gertie and how she will spend the next few years of her life in Sweden.

"What will happen to Gertie's home? Will the Nazi soldiers confiscate it?"

"Not at all. I have made arrangements for an old acquaintance of mine to care for the house and the garden."

"That is a huge responsibility. What about all of the other people who have managed to escape? There must be thousands of homes throughout Denmark that are abandoned."

"Do not fear. The people of Denmark will rise to the occasion."

"Why would they do that? Why should they concern themselves with what may happen to these Jewish homes?"

"The Danes do not see their Jewish neighbors as separate. They consider them to be Danish first, all one people of Denmark. Indeed, they have become righteous in their efforts."

"It is amazing to think that they should care for people that have a different cultural and religious background. I can't imagine any group from my time that would do as much for their neighbors as what the Danish will be doing here right now."

I am thinking about what work this will entail over the course of the next two years. It seems insurmountable. Then I remember my promise to Gertie.

"What about Schatzi?"

"Who?"

"Schatzi. The cat. Gertie made me promise to look after her. I don't think she understood just how long she would be gone."

"It matters little how long she will be away. My friend will take care of all that is needed."

"Funny, Victor didn't seem to me to be the domestic, animal-lover type. His kitchen was a disaster, all cluttered up with gadgets and newspapers. He's a total bachelor."

"It will not be Victor."

"Who is it then?"

"As I said, he is an old friend, one whom I trust implicitly to do his job."

"Will I be able to meet him?"

"I think not. It will be best for all concerned if you have minimal contact with the locals."

"Why? Is it because he is like you that you don't want me to meet him?"

"My friend prefers anonymity. But that is not the reason you should keep your distance."

"Well, what is it then? What's the problem?"

"Shira, you put us all at risk by your presence here. We must try to blend in and well...."

Avram looks away, then over at the fire, then all in a rush he blurts out:

"What would the neighbors think if they caught sight of you leaving my house in the early hours of the morning?"

I can't believe it. Avram is actually channeling my mother!

"Oh, is that all? It's no big deal, Avram. They would just think your girlfriend spent the night."

Uproar.

"Shira!"

"Well...I did, didn't I? What's the matter with you?"

"Do you not understand? This is a very small and close-knit community. Tongues will most certainly wag because everyone here has known me for years, knows that I am not, that is, that we are not...you see I, uh...."

I can't help it but I crack a smile. I've never heard Avram so at a loss for words. The helpless, totally embarrassed expression on his face right now just makes me want to chuckle. Instead, I show pity on this poor, old-fashioned man and come to his rescue.

"You mean, because we are not married, Avram?"

Visible relief floods over his features.

"Yes, that is it. That is exactly what I meant to say."

"But what's the big deal? You are acting like it's taboo or something. It's no sin where I come from."

Then I perceive what I have just said. It *is* a sin.

"Shira, you forget where and most importantly, *when* you are. There are strict governances in this community regarding behavior. Licit or otherwise."

"Are you sure that's why you don't want me to meet this man? You had no problem introducing me to Vietor."

"That is wholly different. Vietor is human. He would not be a problem and...."

"A-ha! Now I get it. You don't want me to meet him because he is a vampire, that's why. But why should that matter? What difference would it make if I met another one now? I don't think I could be shocked or surprised by anything you could toss my way at this point. I am well beyond the realm of suspending my disbelief. What are you afraid of?"

Avram is staring at the fire again, obviously too uncomfortable to speak. After a few false starts, he finally forces something out that is totally unexpected.

"Because he may try to take you away from me, that is why!"

"Excuse me? What are you talking about? How could he take me away? You said we were connected, that I was forever linked to you after what happened to me in the synagogue parking lot. Which you don't actually remember because it hasn't actually happened yet."

"You are chained to me, Shira. You are. That is to say...you will be."

"I *will* be?"

"When you take the next step. Until you do, you are still vulnerable and at risk."

"At risk from whom?"

"Any vampire may claim you as his cohort."

"What? Are you kidding me? I can't believe you lied to me. You lied to me and another thing. I think you are jealous!"

"I would never deceive you, Shira! I...well, I did not reveal everything to you at first since I believed it would overwhelm you. You remember how long it took me to just convince you that you were in Denmark. I wanted to take it as slowly as possible. And...I am not jealous!"

"Avram, I think you are. Your body language is more revealing than any words you say. But you needn't worry about anyone taking me away from you. You were right all along. We are connected. You will see to that all those years in the future. I want you to believe that I don't resent what you have done to me. But...I don't know if I am strong enough to see this through."

I hesitate because what I next want to ask him of his experiences may soon very well be mine. I am not sure if I want to hear the answers to these questions that have been plaguing me in the scope of their enormity. I fear the answers. I am terrified by what he will say. I have too many questions and barely know how to ask them.

"Avram, how can you do it? To go through time, make a connection, establish an identity with humans and then lose them all to disease, accident, death, fate. How can you bear it?"

"My fidelity to G-d is my armor. There is nothing I cannot overcome through Him when my faith is unwavering."

"It would break my heart every time it happened. I would die having to witness death as much as you have. I could never recover."

"You forget, Shira. Although intense, vampiric emotions are not human emotions. I have had to battle even myself to overcome such weakness. If I felt every death I have observed or let every one I have brought about myself affect me, I would be distracted from my purpose. I cannot...no, I will not allow myself the luxury of indulging in a waste of time."

"How can you be so cold, so utterly callous?"

"Shira, feel my hand. There is no life in this flesh; my human blood has long since died. The only warmth I will ever have in this body is transitory and fleeting, for a few brief hours when I am flush from the kill. I was designed this way, intelligently and with immaculate forethought. Emotions would simply get in the way of my job."

"But when will your job be completed? You have worked for so long. How will you know when it will be over?"

"I do not know if my redemption will ever come. G-d may never appear before me again. But what I do know is that I must persevere. I shall continue my work in the hope that someday I may be forgiven for my transgressions against the Lord."

"But you've done so much good already, even just here in Denmark. I have witnessed the power of your conviction, your commitment to your people. Surely Hashem will forgive you. I can't believe He would condemn you for so long, to spend eternity in damnation. How could you possibly endure it any longer?"

He looks up at me with such tenderness in his eyes as he grasps both of my hands in his.

"He promised me a helpmate, Shira. One to ease my task. You have taken me out of my suffering and the purgatory of my existence more than you will ever know."

"Yes, I am here and I am glad of it. Avram, I am ready and willing to help you again."

He smiles at me in that same inviting way that has become familiar and comfortable, evoking a grin from me and an emotion that is involuntary. But what he speaks of after his smile causes me to lose mine immediately.

"You must know how deeply I appreciate your offer. But you cannot remain. We would need a plan to explain your presence here and to create a backstory for you and there is no time. Your true identity would soon be uncovered. Oh, I know it would be unintentional, a slip of the tongue and you might say something that would belie from when you were. I am established here. It has taken many years to forge a history, to build a background in preparation for these events. I am now compelled to move on alone, to continue my work. Sometime soon, I will hear the Call and I must respond."

"But you found me in the street for a reason and you called me Makele. Can't I stay with you?"

The look in his eyes tells me more than his next words.

"Would that it were possible and that it could be so, my love. You do not know what you are asking. If you become like me, you could never return home. Right now you are Makele, tainted and incomplete. Full of imperfection from being bitten. This allowed you to come back to me. I could have accomplished all that was necessary for your final transformation at our first meeting. But this sacrifice will ultimately be yours and yours alone. If you drink from me you will transform into that which is neither merely human nor wholly vampire, but a creature of both the light and the dark. You will be in limbo between two worlds, yet able to travel on your own. I will not need to call upon you ever again."

Before he even continued, I knew what came next from the pained expression on his face, his voice full of sorrow and regret.

"Shira, when you ultimately decide to make your first kill, to taste human blood, you will have taken an irrevocable step, one from which there is no returning. There is no grey area. When you become as I am, you must forsake the world that you have known and all you have ever loved and cross the threshold of immortality. You can never go back to the life you once knew. The love of your family, your friends, all will forever be lost to you as will your love for them. You must sacrifice to G-d with this ultimate loss. That is the blood price He exacts. It is the price that you must pay to become an immortal and thereby serve Him."

"But you must realize that an even greater love awaits you, Shira. As the consort of Hashem, you will gain such a love as you have never before experienced in your life. I have lived hundreds of lifetimes with this love and it has sustained me. We are His Chosen people and we are also vampires. We are both blessed and cursed."

"Yes, I have led many lives. But...I must confess to you, I do tire of my solitude. I am weary of this world, Shira. I believe that you have come back for more reasons than I can currently discern. Your presence here has been the impetus which has given me a renewed sense of purpose. You have become the catalyst that I have needed for so long and have brought the color back into my world. Just as Eve was presented to Adam, I believe I have found favor in G-d's eyes and He has given you to me. But, who can really know the mind of G-d and what He has in store for us?"

Avram pauses at this age-old question that has plagued mankind since time immemorial. He turns toward the fire and stares into it. Without taking his eyes from the flickering light, he speaks again. Barely above a whisper. Tentative. Hopeful.

"Perhaps you are willing to discover it with me, to share my burden?"

My eyes open wide as I hear what he is asking of me. This conversation has taken an abrupt turn and way too many thoughts and a jumble of emotions are racing through my mind. I cannot even begin to wrap my head around all that has transpired in the past few days. And now a bitter man, a sweet, soft-spoken immortal is asking me a question. *The* question. How could this even be happening? Wait. If I just wait a little while longer, I will wake up. I remain silent for a very long time and I can't even look at him.

"Shira."

I look up, directly into his eyes. He sees the hesitation in my face, the fear in my expression.

"You must decide if you are ready to commit to Him, unreservedly and with no regrets."

"I don't know if I can, I am so afraid."

"You need never fear again, Shira. In the might of His Grace you will find sanctuary. The power of the Lord will be with you."

"Will *you* be with me, Avram?"

"Beloved, I will never leave you."

"What must I do?"

"Do not fear, liebling. I will guide you."

Avram gets up and walks over to the kitchen table. As he lights two candles, he calls to me and I rise. The entire room is infused with the glow of the flames as he reaches out to me, taking my hands in his.

"These are the mechanisms by which you will achieve His Glory, Shira. Take my hands in yours now. These are *my* instruments. They work for G-d. You must draw your strength from my strength which comes from Him. Only then will you truly understand. Drink from me, Shira and you will see what you can achieve."

I hesitate. Can he really mean for me to do this? Am I actually even considering this? I am in fear, such a fear as I have never known and cannot even express. I am at a crossroad and...I am going to refuse him. I sense sorrow and passion as I raise his right hand to my lips to kiss his palm. Then the scent of him hits me. There is a shift in my perception but I do not know what is happening. I hear his sharp intake of breath before I press my lips to his open hand. I raise my eyes as I hold him there against my mouth and he is smiling down at me. His eyes are not fully open but rather heavy, half lidded, almost closed. With a sudden movement, his other hand reaches behind me, encircling my waist, drawing me closer to him. This gesture acts like a lash upon my skin, eliciting a deep response within me which I cannot deny. I close my eyes as I become alive to my desire for him. I kiss his palm again and the taste of him upon my tongue triggers what is needed. I know what I have to do now. No. What I want to do. But I am afraid. I hear his whisper like a Siren's call urging me on, entreating me further.

"Come to me, little one. Come to me now!"

His left hand slides up along my spine, between my shoulder blades, his fingers grip and press the back of my neck. My lips part. I find that I cannot resist. I want to consume him, his flesh, his blood. I am no longer human but some animal in a cage, straining to be released. I don't even know how that first drop of his blood, sweet and heady like wine, came upon my lips and then my tongue. Again, the crack of the lash upon my delicate flesh. Pain and pleasure in the same moment, combining to form an entirely new experience are coursing through my body. It is thoroughly destroying and reviving me all at once.

With that first taste of his immortal blood, my eyes snap open. I find him staring at me with eyes so black, his inhuman nature so vividly apparent for the first time, his manner so intent on what I am doing, that I am paralyzed in his arms. His lips part, he inhales deeply and with a strength far surpassing anything I have ever encountered, he pushes me roughly back towards the wall. His entire body is pressed tightly against mine; I am pinned and I don't care. I am no longer afraid. His blood is in my mouth and I swallow. I am wholly undone. It is utterly black. Then a great chasm opens up before me, full of light, blinding me. I hear His voice calling my name, reaching out to me like the Call of the Shofar.

The notes reverberate throughout my entire being as I claim more of Avram's blood. I do not know how I know but I recognize I can never reveal the nature of that Call. My betrayal will be my descent from Grace. This covenant is a great burden to shoulder alone and now I understand G-d's promise to him and his bittersweet sadness at his fate. Avram's blood is coursing through my veins, our eyes lock in an embrace of both death and life, and the rise and fall of our breathing is matched. He makes a noise in the back of his throat, but I am not listening.

Suddenly, against my will I am on the floor, knocked down forcefully, coming down hard, a crashing withdrawal. I look up at him as I hear a strange voice cry out. Plaintive. Feral. I realize it is my own as I drag the back of my hand across my mouth. Avram is gripping his palm, leaning against the wall. His head is thrown back, chest heaving, striving for breath, eyes black with desire as he lowers his gaze to stare down at me.

"Now you are no longer stained. There is no taint upon you, Shira. You have become half-caste; you are Mischling, my love. Now the real work begins...."

TRANSLATIONS

(for my gentle readers whose technocrap has low batteries)

Hebrew

Ahava-love

Ba'al Teshuvah-returned to G-d

Bat Mitzvah-Jewish tradition when a twelve-year-old girl gains the same rights as an adult (Aramaic and Hebrew)

Derekh Eretz-way of the land, decorum/correct conduct that should characterize a Jew at all times

Goyim-non-Jews

Hashem-used in casual conversation out of respect for G-d's name

Kashrut-set of Jewish dietary laws

Kosher-conforms to regulations of dietary laws/fit to be eaten

Matzah-cracker-like unleavened bread

Moshiach-anointed one, messiah

Oneg-food/desserts included as part of Friday night services

Rosh Hashanah-Jewish New Year

Shabbat/Shabbos-sabbath (Friday sundown to Saturday sundown)

Shalom-peace

Shema Yisrael, Adonai Eloheynu, Adonai Echad
Hear, O Israel: The Lord is our G-d, The Lord is One.

Shofar-ram's horn

Siddur-prayer book

Sukkot-Feast of Tabernacles

Tzedakah-charity, help

Yom Huledet Same'ach-Happy Birthday

Yiddish

Bubbe-Grandma

Bubele-sweetie

Chutzpah-nerve

Dreidel-spinning top played with during Hanukkah

Frum-devout/observant of the 613 Mitzvot (Jewish Commandments)

Futzing-fussing/messing with

Hamantaschen-three cornered shaped pastry mimicking Haman's ears

Kine-ahora-expression used to protect against the evil eye/don't jinx it

Kvetch-complain

Meshuggene-crazy woman

Nu-so

Oy!-oy!

Oy a broch!-damn it!/expresses disgust

Oy veh's mir-woe is me/does me pain

Rugelach-pastry

Schlep-to schlep, lug, an arduous journey

Schlub-clumsy person

Schmear-what you smear on a bagel (e.g. cream cheese)

Schmendrik-ineffectual nobody

Schmo-stupid person

Schmooze-to network in a social situation

Shiksa-non-Jewish woman

Shpilkes-nervous jitters

Treppverter-witty retort that comes to mind too late

Tuchus-backside

Zaftig-pleasingly plump

Zayde-Grandpa

German

Ach, du Schande!-for crying out loud!

Bissel-a little, also used in Yiddish

Bretzele-pretzel

Dreck-dirt/trash, also used in Yiddish

Gell?-isn't that so?/right?

Gelt-money (real or chocolate coins)

Hosen-pants

Kaffee Klatsch-coffee served with gossip

Katzenjammer-cat's wail/yammering

Liebling-sweetheart/my love (diminutive form)

Mensch-man/good person, or used to express frustration

Na endlich-ah, finally

Schmutz-dirt/a mess, also used in Yiddish

Spiel-literally game or play, used here as a lengthy speech intended to persuade, also used in Yiddish

French

Cause célèbre-famous cause/issue or incident causing widespread controversy

Certainement-certainly

Cherie-my sweet

Et voila'-ta-dah/there you go

Fracas-unpleasant situation/turmoil

La nuit, tous les chats sont gris-all cats are grey in the dark

Louche-rake (bad boy)

Mais oui-of course

Mille tonnerres!-Holy cow!

Mon petite-my little one

N'est-ce pas?-isn't that so?

Pardon, s'il vous plaît-excuse me, please

Petit four(s)-small cake(s)

Pour quoi pas?-why not?

Sans-without

Sapristi!-good heavens!

Latin

In vino veritas, in aqua sanitas, in sanguis vita
In wine there is truth, in water there is health, in blood there is life

Norwegian

Tusen takk-thousand thanks

Uff da!-oy!

Multi-Language Derivations

Bimah-elevated platform in synagogue from where the Torah is read-from the Greek and Arabic

GERMAN DIALOGUE

(when meanings are not explained in subsequent paragraph)

Ich kann ein bisschen Deutsch sprechen.
I speak a little German.

Ich hätte gern etwas zum trinken.
I would like something to drink.

Nein, danke. Nicht Wasser.
No, thank you. Not water.

Etwas stärker, wenn Sie es haben.
Something stronger, if you have it.

Bitte.
Please.

Wieso kennen Sie mich?
How do you know me?

Guten Abend.
Good evening.

Ach, Gott sei Dank.
Ah, thank G-d.

Bitte, kommen Sie herein.
Please, come in.

Aber wer ist das?
But who is this?

Meine Freundin. Sie heisst...
My friend. Her name is...

Ich freue mich Sie kennenzulernen...
I am pleased to meet you...

Englander?
English?/from England?

Nein, aber es wird besser als wir Englisch sprechen.
No, but it will be better if we speak English.

Mein Englisch...gut.
My English...good.

Papi!
Papa!/Daddy!

Was machst Du, Kind?
What are you doing, child?

Du sollst schlafen sein.
You should be sleeping.

Das kann Ich nicht.
I can't.

Natürlich.
Naturally/of course.

Wie heisst es?
What is its name?

Sie heisst Schatzi.
Her name is Schatzi.

Sie kommt mit, gell?
She's coming with, right?

Nay...das geht leider nicht.
No...I am afraid you cannot/unfortunately not.

Aber, warum nicht?
But, why not?

Du brauchst dich jetzt anziehen. Es gibt wenige Zeit. Draussen ist es
kalt. Hast Du Hosen? Du brauchst auch einen Pulli.
You must get dressed now. There is little time. It is cold outside. Do
you have pants? You also need a pullover/sweater.

Ich hab' alles hier. Mein Mantel ist da unten. Aber wohin gehen wir?
I have everything here. My coat is downstairs. But where are we going?

Du kommst mit mir und meinen Freund. Du bleibst bei uns, aber nicht
lange.
You are coming with me and my friend. You are staying with us, but not
for long.

Aber Mutti und Papi kommen, oder?
But Mommy and Daddy are coming, or?

Du kannst mit deinen Vater sprechen...
You can speak with your father...

Okay, das kann Ich.
Okay, I can do that.

Alles okay?
Everything okay?

Ja, gut.
Yes, good.

Warte, noch nicht.
Wait, not yet.

Was willst Du essen?
What would you like to eat?

Vielleicht.
Maybe.

Wie, bitte?
Excuse me?

Nichts.
Nothing.

Pass auf!
Watch out!

...es gibt hier nichts zu tun.
...there is nothing to do here.

Ich will nach Hause gehen.
I want to go home.

Das weiss Ich.
I know that/it.

Also, was tun wir denn jetzt?
So, what should we do now?

Keine Ahnung.
No idea.

Hilfe!
Help!

Wo sind Mutti und Papi?
Where are Mommy and Daddy?

Sie warten auf uns in Schweden. Wir sind fast dorthin.
They are waiting for us in Sweden. We are almost there.

Ich bin hier...
I am here...

Danke!
Thank you!

Versprech Ich dir...
I promise you...

Hab' keine Angst.
Do not be afraid.

ACKNOWLEDGEMENTS

I'd like to say that I had an extended support network of people during the course of my writing, outside that of my husband and children. But the truth of the matter is, I didn't. I didn't because I never told anyone I was writing. Not a soul. Not even my mother! Therefore, I can only say that there is one to whom I can truthfully give recognition for unwavering love, unswerving devotion, and a real kick in the pants when I needed it. I give thanks to G-d for all that He is and all that He has helped me to become.

ABOUT THE AUTHOR

Christine Brown is not ashamed to be proud to be from the Midwest where she really was a marching band geek who still reads the dictionary for fun. She lives in the middle of nowhere with her family, one zany Basenji and a barn-sour Appy. This is her first novel. You may visit her website at bloodandmatzah.com and her blog at blogandmatzah.com.

Made in the USA
Charleston, SC
05 December 2011